The Keeala Series

Crystal Clear

Kumari Gorman

By the same author

The Keeala Resort Series

Book 1 - The Last Resort

Book 2 - Village Secrets

Book 3 - The Road Home

The Keeala Resort Series

Crystal Clear

© Kumari Gorman 2014

National Library of Australia Cataloguing-in-Publication entry (pbk)

Author:	Gorman, Kumari, author.
Title:	Crystal Clear/ Kumari Gorman.
ISBN:	9780992388065 (paperback)
Series:	Gorman, Kumari. Keeala Resort Series
Subjects:	Resorts—Queensland--Fiction

Dewey Number: A823.4

Published with the assistance by www.inhousepublishing.com.au

The Keeala Series

Crystal Clear

Acknowledgements.

I would like to thank Ocean Reeve for his wonderful words of wisdom and his freely given support. He arrived at a time when I was about to give up. He guided me back on to the right track and I am very grateful that he inspired me to keep going. Thank you Ocean.

To my husband, John. Thank you so much. Thank you for your time, patience, advice and support.

Well, for some of your time and patience.

Well, perhaps tolerance is a better word.

Maybe I mean a bit of your time and occasional patience.

Definitely some tolerance and some occasional advice.

Whatever. You know what I mean.

Kumari Gorman

October 2014.

Chapter One

Di and Jim Watersen were accustomed to having their relaxation interrupted, but this was something new. As they sat on their balcony, they shared a chilled bottle of white wine and listened to the strains of a Mozart piano concerto. The sound of pounding feet, rapidly approaching on the driveway below, disturbed their peace. Their curiosity aroused, they jumped up and looked over the railing.

The managers of Keeala Resort knew there were plenty of fast walkers in the over 50's complex, but few runners. Whoever this was, sprinted in the direction of the front gate. Fallen leaves on the driveway scattered as a man ran past the residence in a blur of red and green. Jim strained to see the figure disappear around the bend toward the gate.

"Stop him, stop him," shouted one of two older men, who followed the runner with an ever increasing gap. "Call the police!" the other yelled, as the pair approached the manager's residence. They puffed and panted, and waved their arms at Jim as they swayed past.

Jim made his way down the stairs and out on to the driveway in pursuit of the intruder. He quickly caught up with the two older men. Jim saw them bent over, hands on hips, and struggling for breath. They tried to speak but could only gasp as they pointed toward the entrance gate. Jim did not wait. He took off and ran to the front gate. The two pursuers brought up the rear, as quickly as their creaking bodies would allow.

The entrance gates opened outwards by punching in a code on the gate, or by a vehicle tripping a switch in a sensor buried under the surface of the driveway. Jim stabbed at the buttons on the electronic keypad, and the gate started to open. He squeezed through to the street outside. He looked in all directions but could not spot the runner. The two residents caught up with Jim and stood beside him, still gasping for air. After a couple of minutes, it seemed obvious the runner had fled, so they came back through the gate and started back down the driveway.

"So, tell me," Jim said, "what happened?"

"Unbelievable," said one. "He just ... disappeared ... phew." He still had not completely recovered his breath. "I can't believe it."

"Yes, I can see he's gone, but why were you chasing him? Tell me what happened. Do we need the police?" Jim was getting frustrated.

"Yeah, yeah, sure. Call them, before he gets away."

"I suspect he's already done that," said Jim. "He may still be in the area though. What has he done?"

The younger of the two men spoke up. "Well, we were on our way to the clubhouse, for dinner, and we spotted this bloke climbing out of a window in a house, in one of those short streets off Main Parade. We shouted to him and he just took off. That's when we knew he was up to something, because he took off like a scalded cat, know what I mean? We were a bit stunned at first, then realised we were probably witnessing a robbery in progress. We could see he was too young to be a resident. We raced after him, so to speak. You know the rest."

"Was he carrying anything?" asked Jim, as he made his way to the phone.

"Didn't look like it, but maybe he had money on him, or something."

Jim called the police, all the time wondering if there had been a crime committed, or perhaps there was another explanation. After he explained the situation on the phone, Jim looked at his list to see who lived in that particular house. He put in a call to the owner but there was no answer.

"Look, gents, I'm slipping up to the unit to check if anyone's there. Can you wait for the police?"

The two elderly men walked back slowly to the front gate and waited outside. They chatted as they waited and went over the incident together. They speculated on what other possible explanations there could be, but came up with no satisfactory answer.

A police car squealed to a stop in front of them and the door flew open to release a young, energetic looking, female constable. "Where'd he go?" she shouted, as she bent down to tighten her bootlaces, like an athlete at the start of a race.

Jim arrived back at the same time and said, "These gentlemen saw someone, a young bloke, climb out a window of one of the houses and then head for the front gate. We weren't able to see which direction he took."

The constable put her head back into the car and spoke to the driver, who then parked and got out. They all moved over to the footpath and the constables introduced themselves. The men told their story. When they finished, the female officer suggested that she and her partner do a quick drive around the neighbourhood, and then they all meet back at the manager's office. Jim nodded and reminded the police constable of the gate code. The car did a noisy U-turn and headed back in the direction from which it had come.

The men suggested to Jim that they head off to the clubhouse.

"This is eating into our drinking time," said the older man. "You know where to find us if you need to speak to us again."

Jim met up with Di, who waited in the driveway and he explained what was happening.

She listened and then walked with him toward their house. "Do you think it was a burglary? It all sounds a bit strange to me," she said.

Jim shrugged and shook his head.

"I really don't know. There was no response when I knocked, so I used my master key to get in. I thought the residents might be in there injured, or worse, but there was no one there. Nothing seemed to be out of place."

"Well, if you don't need me, I'll go in and start our dinner."

"Sure, go ahead, I'll sort this out. I'll wait in the office for the police."

As Jim walked slowly toward the office, he sighed and shook his head, as he thought about the many exceptional incidents he and his wife had confronted since taking over the management of the resort. Keeala Resort had become the greatest challenge of their careers. It was the home of more than five hundred residents, all over fifty, and most of them were retired men and women. As joint managers, Jim and Di had survived almost two years of problems and disasters. They had hung on, despite having threatened to leave on countless occasions, but they remained to manage for another day. Their days were always busy with administration matters and general day-to-day management duties, and they were always on call for emergencies, day and night. One of the problems they had with living on the job was never having any time they could truly call their own, and as their residents aged, some could become very demanding. For Di and Jim, retirement was starting to look like an ever more attractive proposition. Jim reached his office and waited.

As Di stepped on to the path to her house, she glanced back toward the gate, where three industrial rubbish bins sat in a small, brick-sided alcove. *No,* she thought, then shook her head and walked on, wondering how long Jim would be, and if this could be another late night.

Chapter Two

Jason lifted his hand and tried to brush the garden waste from the back of his neck. After having easily outrun his pursuers, he had opened the lid of a green-waste bin near the gate, and swiftly pulled himself up chest high. He swung his legs over, but overbalanced. He toppled into the bin, almost head first, and only saved his head with his hands by the smallest margin. Now, his wrist hurt and he gingerly lifted it up to his eyes, straining in the semi-darkness to examine it. *Looks okay, but hurts like shit,* he thought, as he flexed his fingers and stretched his wrist in circles. He bent his hand back slowly. That was too much. He rubbed it all over and thought, *it may not be broken but it is bloody sore.* He stood and stretched for the lid handles, and ducked his head as he pulled the cover closed. In the pitch black inside the bin, he crouched, and tried to settle his backside into a sitting position, but let out a muffled, 'Shit', as the thorns from bougainvillea cuttings dug into his buttocks. He struggled to ensure he did not cause any movement of the bin as he re-adjusted his position.

"Bloody hell," he said, through clenched teeth. He sighed and tried to calm himself.

Just about everything that could go wrong, had gone wrong. That was how the young man started to think about his latest exploit. Despite his best-laid plans, Jason Ethridge, son and lifelong apprentice of Luke Ethridge, wondered what could go wrong next. His father was, by his own description, a highly respected, and soon-to-be-rich, local drug dealer. Luke answered only to Vinnie Markwell, who did not tolerate incompetence, especially if anyone in the organisation was stupid enough to be caught.

As Jason sat in the darkness, he contemplated his immediate future. He wondered what retribution Vinnie, one of Keeala Resort's newest residents, would visit upon him.

******

Vinnie was rising fifty-one, and had scraped in by a couple of weeks to fulfil the criteria for the minimum age limit. Well built, muscled, hairy-chested, and with a face that confirmed his pugilistic past, his strong legs supported a small paunch. He was only a casual user of the drugs he dealt in, and had not suffered the effects of long-term drug abuse like most of his acquaintances.

"This has got to be one of the best covers I've ever had. I had no idea of the benefits and opportunities old age can afford a person," he had said to girlfriend, Charlene, as they moved their furniture into the two-bedroom house off Main Parade, not far from the resort clubhouse.

Vinnie had looked for a new base for months, ever since his neighbours had complained to the council about the noise, the car bodies in his front yard, and the comings and goings at all hours of the day and night. He put the word out that he would be moving to a new, secret location, in another suburb. He had, in fact, only moved a couple of blocks away, to where he could easily afford to buy one of the best-positioned houses in the place.

Charlene had not needed much encouragement to move in with him. She idolised Vinnie; he was her hero. Charlene was a few months older than Vinnie, but unlike her man, she had always looked after herself, and was proud of her appearance. She pampered herself almost to the point of narcissism, and had once been very flattered when someone asked if her father often escorted her to social functions. Vinnie, whose arm was around her waist at the time, simply smiled as Charlene introduced him as, 'My very dear friend, Mr. Markwell'. Vinnie's pride in having such an attractive companion far outweighed the slight he might have felt.

Vinnie had spread the word around to his friends and associates that he would not tolerate visits from the usual riff-raff that had made him the centre of their universe. He wanted a new image, and an opportunity to clean up and expand his long-term drug business. Vinnie was not aware that the resort had recently harboured some very professional drug runners, all of whom were now incarcerated for an extended period. Whilst that had been common knowledge within the resort at the time, the resort owners had taken steps to ensure that the mainstream media had not seen fit to run a story on it.

******

The air in the bin was foul. Someone had dumped prawn shells into the garden-waste bin, despite repeated appeals from the managers for residents to deposit kitchen waste in the correct bin. Jason tried to shallow breathe, as he waited in the stinking hole. As he bided his time and waited for the cover of darkness, he thought through the events of the day.

It had begun as he had eyeballed his father across the breakfast table.

As usual, Luke's eyes were bloodshot and half-closed, and his face showed the permanent ravage of years of drug abuse. Most of Luke's teeth were gone. His head twitched, and his limbs jerked. His body craved the release of a fix. He hung his head over a bowl of cereal and slurped milk from the rim. The liquid ran from the corners of his mouth and spilled onto the tabletop. Luke stared at the mess and swiped it off the table with the side of his hand. He stood unsteadily, and walked out of the kitchen.

"Where're you goin'?" asked Jason.

"I'm goin' for a piss."

Five minutes later, Luke returned to the table. He picked up a spoon and began to eat. His hands were as steady as a rock.

Jason made no comment about the sudden transformation in his father's demeanour; he had seen it a thousand times before. He decided to keep the conversation businesslike. "So, where do we go to pick up our supply now?" he asked. "If we don't go to his house, I mean."

"We're settin' up here. I told you."

"No, you didn't," Jason snapped back.

Luke's hand flashed out and slapped his son on the mouth. "Don't speak to me like that, you little shit."

Jason slipped his chair back, and stood up in one quick, smooth motion. He gritted his teeth and clenched his fists, and struggled to hold in the words that would certainly have started a major brawl. He walked to the back door and was about to step out, when his father's words halted him.

"I want you here today to help move the equipment in. It's all goin' into your bedroom, so clear your stuff out – right now."

Luke lifted the bowl and swilled down the dregs of his breakfast. When he looked up, Jason had already turned and walked back to his room and slammed the door.

What followed was a noisy, hot, frustrating day of comings and goings, with three ute loads to unpack. Jason was the one with the technical expertise. He set up the laboratory. He had done it all before, but liked it less and less. He hoped he may break away from the business altogether.

As he waited in the bin, Jason sighed heavily, and began to wonder how he could ever free himself from the murky world in which he had been raised. His father had drug distribution convictions, starting with marijuana; later heroin, cocaine, and meth. Luke had been inside twice in Jason's nineteen years, and Jason knew Vinnie had also been locked up for drug offences. In his early teens, Jason had tried marijuana a couple of times, and meth once, but had decided that no drug would be his master. He had vowed never to touch drugs again. He was determined he would not end up like his father. Jason had never been told, but he suspected that his father had met Vinnie in jail. The more he thought about it, the more Jason realised that most of his father's friends had also done time. Not one of them was a positive role model for him, nor, as Jason now recalled their faces, could any of the men he had dealt with ever be called a true friend. He remembered how his last girlfriend had described him as a third generation criminal. He cringed at the thought, but knew she had been right. Her judgment had prompted his resolution to come up with a plan to get away from this life.

Jason lifted the lid a few centimetres. He could hear the voices of evening strollers, and he could see it was still not dark enough to risk an escape. His mind drifted again to the day's events.

Late in the afternoon, his father had given him a package and told him to deliver it to Vinnie in his new house at the resort. He gave him the address, but did not bother to mention it was a gated community, and that he would need an access code. It was not a major problem really, Jason just waited until someone punched in the code and drove through the gate, and he walked through behind. He found Vinnie was not at home. He was not going to leave the package on the doorstep, nor was he prepared to come back later. He had plans. He could not take it home again because he would get more than a smack in the mouth from Luke. Jason decided to climb in an open window and leave the package where Vinnie would find it when he came home.

Done, but what he did not expect was to find a deadlock on the inside of Vinnie's door. *No problem,* he had thought, *I'll just leave the way I came*, which was great until he was spotted by two residents on their way to dinner. So, now he sat in a garbage bin, waiting for night to fall so he could make his escape undetected, and report home. He was sure Luke would wonder what had happened to him by now.

An hour later, Jason quietly lifted the lid again and looked around. He gently pushed it back so he could rest it on its hinges. He climbed over the top and dropped lightly to the ground. He closed the lid. He had learnt early in life never to leave a clue for someone else to follow. He stood in the shadows and waited for a couple of minutes. The gates swung open as a car left the resort, and Jason slipped through behind it and out to the street.

******

Back at the clubhouse, the evening meal was still half an hour away. A group of men stood at one end of the room, drinks in hand, and engaged in an animated discussion. The conversation had not moved far away from the criticism of federal politicians, the establishment of a mosque down the road, and the incompetence of the council waste-collection contractor.

"I suppose you're in favour of a multicultural Australia. Well you would be, wouldn't you?"

John Stevens shifted from one foot to the other, then leaned forward and directed his attention to a small man who stood at the edge of the circle. This man tried to make himself heard in response to John's comment, but he could not compete with the noisy conversation in the crowded room.

Contrary to the old saying that politics, religion and sex should never be discussed in public, all three were regular subjects when this crowd of baby boomers met for pre-dinner drinks, before sitting down to the meal. There was only one rule when they met, and that was that there were no rules. Everything was open for discussion.

******

"You look great, love," Charlene said to Vinnie, before they left for their inaugural dinner at the resort clubhouse. He stood resplendent in gold neck chains and bracelets, a 24 karat gold, diamond-set ear stud in each lobe, and a huge, 22 karat gold and onyx ring on the fourth finger of his left hand. Much as she loved them, Charlene thought it was probably best that the more risqué of a dozen or so tattoos, which adorned Vinnie's body, were covered by his body-hugging polo shirt – his formal polo shirt, Vinnie called it – the one with the contrasting collar. Only the cognoscenti would recognise the discreet logo on Vinnie's shirt and realise the shirt was worth more than the weekly old age pension.

Vinnie and Charlene entered the clubhouse for their first dinner with their new neighbours. From the moment he arrived, Vinnie was busy introducing Charlene as his wife, while he established a profile for them that would equate to what he thought a resort style retiree would be. He proudly spoke of his two grown children who had now flown the coop.

He described himself as an ex-mechanic who specialised in classic cars, and retained a Chevrolet Bel Air Convertible 1957 model as a hobby. He went on to list some of the cars he had restored over the years, and found a rapt group of male listeners who hung on to his every word. His audience had expanded to include John Stevens' group, and the conversation abruptly turned to fast and vintage cars. A few of the group resented this ostentatious newcomer, who had taken command of the conversation. Vinnie was completely unaware of the effect he was having on some of the close-knit cliques in his vicinity. He blundered on, in his ignorance, alienating many, but engendering a degree of acceptance from others.

Vinnie looked at the other men who surrounded him, and he silently criticised what he considered their daggy clothes and wondered why they were all so drab. *They wouldn't have a bloody clue,* he thought. He continued to spruik to his audience, while he sucked intermittently on another stubbie of beer that Charlene had placed in his hand.

A considerable amount of the conversation buzz in the room had to do with Vinnie's appearance. 'Understated' was not a word that was used.

"He seems a pretty unlikely type to live in a place like this, don't you think? The reason we live in a gated community must surely be to keep his type out," said a rather dowdy woman, through a mouth that looked like it had just sucked a lemon.

Charlene had no idea she was also the subject of a certain amount of discussion among the women at dinner that night.

"Looks like a bit of a tart to me," was a quiet comment from one of the resort's original settlers.

"Looks like a lot of a tart, if you ask me," answered another, as she looked the new woman up and down.

"Yes," nodded several female heads, but a few pursed lips kept their opinions to themselves.

Charlene could not hear the words, but she knew the men in the room were also making comments about her appearance, but of an altogether more complimentary nature – much more.

This, after all was a place to make new friends.

******

"Why don't you guys wait in my office while I go and see if I can find the owner of this house?"

Jim showed the two constables to chairs in his office and strode off to the dining room. The locals had not yet noted the presence of the police patrol car.

Walking up to a large group standing to one side of the dining room, Jim had to interrupt Vinnie's extremely jovial description of how he once ran over a kangaroo in his old Chevy Impala.

"Fortunately I hadn't started any restoration," laughed Vinnie, "that would really have given me the shits."

Jim tapped him on the shoulder. He swung around so defensively that Jim had to jump back a pace. Startled, Jim thought the look on Vinnie's face would be enough to scare him on a dark night.

"Sorry to interrupt here, Mr. Markwell. May I have a word with you?" Jim stepped back to allow the other man to follow him.

"Excuse me, gentlemen," Vinnie said, as he smiled and waved at his audience, "back in a sec."

"We had a little problem this evening, sir, and I think we need to talk in my office." This sounded uncomfortably like a command to Vinnie, and he did not like it one bit.

"So what's the problem?" he responded abruptly, as they walked back to the office.

15

There, Vinnie saw the two police constables sitting in front of Jim's desk. A shiver of fear shook Vinnie. *Shit, what's this?* he thought. He recovered his composure as they both stood and introduced themselves. Vinnie shook hands but stood back as though they had a contagious disease. The female constable explained that they were responding to a call about a possible break-in at his house.

Bloody hell! Vinnie froze. He had no drugs in his possession at present, but that was an exception. He did not like the thought of cops entering his home, but he had no option but to smile and agree to see if anything was missing.

They all marched over to his place.

"No, nothing missing," he declared, after a quick glance round. "Maybe it was my brother? Marc drops in at odd times – hasn't got a brain in his head. I'll give him a call later and see what's up. Then let you know, how's that?"

The police could see they would get no more cooperation from this man and agreed to Vinnie's suggestion. They reminded him that they could come and take fingerprints, if he so desired. He declined.

"There's bound to be a very simple explanation, I'm sure of that," he said.

"Looks like a false alarm I'm afraid." said Jim, as he returned with the police to his office in the clubhouse. "We may have overreacted and I'm very sorry to have called you out unnecessarily."

"That's okay. Better sure than sorry. Let us know if anything like this happens again," said the police officer. They walked out to the car and slammed the doors as they drove off.

The older constable slipped his seat belt into place. He scratched his head thoughtfully and said, "It was only last year we closed down a drug syndicate which had operatives who were employed at this place." He pointed to the police radio. "We'd better call this in now. This Markwell, we should run a check on him. I'm not sure if he's connected, but he is well known to the drug squad." He nodded as the female officer picked up the hand piece.

The sound of chatter and the clink of glasses and crockery faded, as Jim made his way back to his house. Di looked up questioningly as he walked into the kitchen.

"So, a new mystery begins." Jim laughed as he said it, but at the same time, he shuddered.

\

Chapter Three

Keeala Resort already had a very chequered past, especially for an over 50's resort that was only a little more than five years old. Many of the residents were quite active and some still worked full time. The resort seemed to have more than its fair share of interesting characters, and some of those had been party to crime and misadventure.

Jim and Diane knew most of the residents on a first name basis. A handful, they knew very well, and some of those they called close friends.

Among those friends were Harold Smith and Robert Wieland, a couple who had committed to spend their life together. In the early days of their residency, they had been subject to discrimination from some of their neighbours, but over time, they had become almost universally accepted. The reason for that acceptance was their good nature and reliability in all situations.

Harold and Robert had been part of one of the resort's sadder episodes. They had been part of an unfortunate bus trip that had ended tragically with a road accident. Two people, one from Keeala Resort, were killed, and some, including Robert, were injured. Fully recovered now, he was making up for lost time by doubling his efforts in the gym and on the walking track. He was an inspiration to anyone who needed motivation.

"Can't believe you aren't ready yet," Robert said to Harold, who was still watching the television and tying up his joggers. Harold sighed, clicked the remote control, and followed his mate outside. Once out on the driveway, the two set a good pace as they jogged, absent-mindedly taking in their surroundings.

"Wow! Get a look at that car," Harold said, as he stopped and gazed at the fully restored Chevrolet Bel Air convertible standing in Vinnie's driveway. It took up the entire driveway, and the soft, two-toned yellow and white duco gleamed majestically in the morning sun. Harold walked slowly around the car, afraid to touch it. As he and Robert admired the vehicle, Vinnie emerged from his garage with a big smile.

"Hi," said Vinnie. "She's a beauty, isn't she?"

Harold and Robert had seen Vinnie and Charlene move into their new home a few days previously.

"Some car, mate," said Robert as he looked at the leather upholstery and converted right hand drive.

"My pride and joy," answered Vinnie.

Harold could not take his eyes off the stunning vehicle. "You certainly have reason to be proud of this car. Where did you have it restored?"

Not able to stop smiling, Vinnie proudly acknowledged it was all his own handiwork. He started to tell the men all about his dedicated commitment to the labour of love that was his dearest possession.

Before they realised it, half an hour slipped away while Harold and Vinnie discussed the fine details of the mechanics of his baby. Vinnie had to acknowledge to himself that Harold really seemed to know what he was talking about, and had even made a couple of suggestions that were worth considering, in relation to the long-term smooth running of his engine. Harold and Robert had both been collectors of antiques in the past, and Harold had also collected vintage and classic cars, a hobby he had to give up when it became too expensive and time consuming.

Robert became restless and began to jog on the spot. He nudged his partner and suggested they needed to move on.

"Keeping fit, I see," said Vinnie. He found himself smiling at the two men. "I like to work out myself. The gym looks well equipped."

"You're right," answered Robert. "We also have a good trainer there two days a week." This started a conversation of a different nature, and Vinnie said he had hung his punching bag in the garage and liked to box every day. So now, it was Harold who had to wait impatiently, while Vinnie and Robert discussed their personal fitness programs.

Finally, Vinnie waved them goodbye. He wondered about them as they jogged away. *A bit more intelligent than some of the crims that hang around me on a daily basis,* he thought. Vinnie knew he had made the right decision to move out of the house of degenerates he had inhabited, to live among a much better class of individual. He rubbed imaginary fingerprints from the door handle of his car.

******

Vinnie had stopped distributing marijuana. It was too easily available – every man and his dog was growing it – and the profit had dropped out of supplying it, so Vinnie now specialised in producing a couple of recreational drugs that no one else made locally. They included some ecstasy, but mostly methamphetamine, the latter commonly used for its euphoric and stimulant properties. The main precursor chemical used to make methamphetamine is pseudoephedrine, a drug not easily available, but Luke and Vinnie had a reliable supply chain and agreed that they had made the right decision to concentrate on those two drugs.

To process the ephedrine and cook up the product required a steady hand and an active brain. Jason had excelled in science at school. He was, compared to the rest of the group, an expert, and he produced a high quality product. The meth could be smoked, sniffed, injected, or swallowed. It made no difference to Luke and the others that the fumes from the cook-ups may be affecting young Jason. Vinnie, despite his outward show of bonhomie to those with whom he mixed socially, was a ruthless mongrel when it came to running his drug business. Jason, as far as Vinnie was concerned, was just a means to an end. Vinnie's gang of producers and dealers belonged to a long established criminal network, and the risk to Jason's health was low on Vinnie's list of priorities. He should have paid more attention to it.

Jason did not tell his father about the previous day's incident at the resort. That was a mistake, as Luke found out from Vinnie anyway. It had not taken long for Vinnie to realise where his intruder had come from, after he discovered the package Jason had left. Luke was the only one with Vinnie's new address. Luke confronted Jason when he returned from his rounds, mid-morning. Jason did drop offs before lunch and usually spent the afternoons in the lab.

Neither Vinnie nor Luke acknowledged to Jason that he was indispensible to the venture, but Jason had begun to figure that out himself. Therefore, when a violent confrontation was staring at him in the face of his father, Jason felt a sense of confidence that was new to him. He stood his ground and did not back away when Luke stepped up to his son and threatened him, his face red with rage.

"Wadda you think you were doin'? The cops! Chasin' you, right to Vinnie's door," said Luke, as he grabbed Jason's shirt and shook him.

Jason almost reacted in his usual defensive blubbering way, but something had changed inside Jason's head while he had sat in the bin the previous evening. He could see clearly that he would have the upper hand if Vinnie and his father wanted to continue in the business they had just started. He saw that their clientele was different now, and the number of deals they did had reduced, but the money that changed hands had increased vastly. He knew that his knowledge of chemistry and science was what Vinnie and Luke were completely dependent upon and it was time they gave him his due.

"If you hurt me I'll be no good to work in the lab this arvo," he said quietly into Luke's face. Time stood still while they stared at each other without blinking.

Luke let go of Jason's shirt and turned. He stepped away then turned back and lunged at his son again, his face a mask of anger. Both his hands shook with frustration. He almost spat in Jason's face when he exclaimed, "What the fuck do you think you're playin' at?"

Jason described the incident that had occurred at the resort as simply as he remembered it, and Luke had to acknowledge the outcome had been harmless enough. He calmed down.

He pointed to Jason and said, "Get back to work."

Jason turned and left the room. Jason grinned as he walked out. He knew this was the beginning of a new balance of power and he knew it was time he started to think for himself.

An iridescent silver 4WD pulled up in Luke's driveway. Vinnie was always driven by one of the boys when he made calls to anyone in the business. His own car was far too eye catching to ever leave it parked within public view. Vinnie had the gait of someone who had spent his life on horseback; his arms appeared to be ready for a quick draw. His friends could pick his easily identifiable swagger from a distance.

"Where's the boy?" he said, when he spotted Luke in the kitchen.

Luke kept packaging small white tablets into plastic bags and jerked his head over his shoulder.

Vinnie walked straight to the lab room and found Jason, busy with his head over several test tubes and reading a formula propped up on a bench.

"I gather it was you who paid me a visit yesterday, son."

Jason did not answer. He continued to drop liquid into a vial and focused his full concentration on the activity.

Vinnie waited.

Finally, Jason looked up and said, "Sorry about that, Mr.Markwell. I didn't get caught though."

"You caused me great embarrassment, kid. That place has eyes everywhere, and the last thing I need is the cops comin' around fingerprinting my place." Vinnie paced around the room as he tapped his thigh and looked at the floor. "I have plans for you, so don't do nuthin' to put me off and ruin your chances."

He had slipped into rough speech, as was usual when certain people were around. Vinnie had read in a self-help book that to create a feeling of empathy, one should mimic the idiosyncrasies of the person with whom you were interacting. It was supposed to put the other person at ease because it made you one of them. Vinnie thought he was superior to the people he dealt with, but necessarily had to work with them. He had seen a future for himself and Charlene, when they would be free to live with the right people and take their rightful place in society. He knew it could take a couple of years yet. In the meantime, he was determined to be careful, and that meant he must keep anyone associated with the drug business onside, and stay out of trouble. In this case, he had decided, he needed Jason to think he was a friend.

Vinnie pointed to a couple of chairs and the two men sat. Jason looked at Vinnie, who gazed around the room.

"Do you like the work you do in this new laboratory, Jason?" he waited. "You don't find it too hard or too dirty or too noisy, etcetera?"

Vinnie had returned to his best English and had decided on a different tack with the kid this time. After all, Jason was old enough to share the responsibility for their success or their failure.

Jason sat blinking; obviously, thinking about his answer, while Vinnie wondered what was taking him so long to simply say, 'Yes'.

"Well?"

"I don't want to do this for the rest of my life. I know that, and I've been thinkin' lately that I get an unfair cut of the profits, when you consider my contribution."

Vinnie was completely taken aback. He jumped up from his chair. He spun around, and then looked back at Jason.

"Your dad put you up to this?"

"No. I'm not stupid. You don't have to be a genius to figure out I am now indispensible to the business, and I get paid a pittance for the work I do. If we get raided and I go to jail, I'll end up without a cent."

Vinnie paced around and increasingly tapped on his thigh, as his frown of concentration deepened.

He stepped up to Jason and angrily declared, "I don't know who gave you the idea you were indispensable, son, because you're not. I know a number of blokes that can do exactly what you do here. I gave you the job to give you a start and because Luke and me go way back. You've got the wrong idea completely."

He waited for Jason to respond.

"Well then, you wouldn't mind if I pulled out, would you. I'm thinkin' of going to university. That is, after I can get the dough together."

Vinnie looked horrified. "Yes, I would bloody mind. Your dad has done too much for you, for you to leave him high and dry now. No one just pulls out of our organization, mate. You know too much. And you know that as well."

Vinnie stood over Jason and wagged his finger at the young man's nose. "I'll consider a new deal for you, but I expect total loyalty – no plans to run off whenever you feel like it, and no bloody stupid capers like yesterday. I'll talk to your old man and let you know what I decide."

"Don't bother talking to Luke; I make my own decisions now."

"That fuckin so?" Vinnie raised his eyebrows as he walked from the room.

Chapter Four

Keeala Resort was one link in a chain of over 50's resorts throughout Australia, run by the Sleighmen Group. The founder, Roger Sleighmen, had died a little while ago and his son Andrew replaced him. Andrew's new management had brought many positive changes to the organization, and although the profits had not improved, most employees agreed the working conditions had. Roger had been a tyrant and his son had suffered significantly under his control. At last, his father's overbearing influence was over for Andrew, and now, under his guidance, every employee could feel the positive changes he was making to the organisation.

Matthew Weatherlee had previously been the salesperson at Keeala Resort, under the supervision of Allen Sinclaire, the area manager for the Queensland resorts. Sinclaire had used the resort as a cover to import and distribute drugs, mostly heroin from Indonesia. Sinclaire now, along with his associates, languished in jail after his conviction on trafficking charges. Matthew Weatherlee had stepped up and was now the new area manager. His responsibility covered the five villages in Queensland. He kept a tight rein on the operation of the resorts, and proved to be a good choice by the owner. He drove his white, soft-top Saab through the front gates of Keeala Resort early on Monday morning and parked outside the manager's office.

Jim was delighted to see him and greeted him happily. He shook his hand with vigour. "I can't tell you how good it is to see you, my friend. Come inside, let's have some coffee." This was a great change of attitude for Jim, who had previously had a low opinion of the salesman, but while Jim and Di had been away on holiday, it was Matthew who had managed to keep everything together and sort out the problems.

A few minutes later, Jim placed two cups of coffee on the desk in the office. "So tell me what you've been up to," Jim said.

"Well, Jim, it has turned out to be a much bigger job than I first anticipated. The other four villages had been quite neglected by that toad, Sinclaire, and there is a lot to do to bring the running of them back to standard. I've employed some new people and the wheels are in motion. I'm here today to see how you and Di are faring, and to ask if I can send two prospective managers here to get an idea of how a resort should be run."

"Of course, it would be our pleasure and it's nice to have the compliment. I'm happy to say all is running quietly. Well, pretty much. We did have an incident the other day that involved calling the police."

"Really?"

"Yes, an intruder, we think, but the owner of the house seemed not the least put out and didn't pursue the situation. I have the impression he knows more than he says, but perhaps has his own reasons for keeping quiet. Anyway, I have my eye on him now and I think I'll ask Pekalski to run a check on him."

"And how is Detective Inspector Frank Pekalski these days?" Matthew queried.

"I believe he's pretty good. He's settled into that end house you sold him. He's happy with his privacy and seclusion behind the lilli pilli hedge, and comes and goes like a phantom. I rarely see him; he's such a private man and doesn't mix into the usual resort social life. He seems to like it that way. Mind you, he'd be fair game for two women I can think of and he knows it. I suspect he's not over the loss of his wife and is happy just to work and relax in his own way."

"You think he'd be okay to check on this resident?"

"Sure. I'll ask him this evening."

Matthew nodded and they discussed village affairs until lunchtime, when Di knocked and stuck her head in the door.

"Hi, Matt. It's good to see you," she said with a smile.

"Likewise, Di. So, Jim tells me you had a little excitement here the other day."

"Yes, and to see police here again is not something we look forward to. We've had more than our share of crime and criminals. Nothing has come of it, thank goodness. A misunderstanding, I believe. That's according to Lillian Gossett, one of our well-informed residents. She said Charlene, Vinnie Markwell's wife, said her husband's brother had paid them an unexpected visit. Apparently, he arrived unannounced and thought he'd wait inside when he found his brother was not at home. He entered by an open window and after waiting a while, he decided to leave and found the front door double locked. So he left the way he came in. At this point, someone spotted him and thought him an intruder and he took off, worried he'd caused a problem. All really sounds a bit incomplete to me but, there you are, it's over now."

******

After taking his leave of the managers, Matthew headed back to his motel for the night. He had an early flight to Adelaide booked next morning, where some matters required his presence at the company's head office. He was pleased to have caught up with his friends and his mum. She took less cleaning work than she used to, now that he helped her with the finances. Matthew hoped she would retire but she said she would only get bored, and not know what to do with her days after a lifetime of work.

As he drove along, his mind drifted to his meeting with the new salesperson who had taken over his old position at Keeala Resort. Matthew had employed her himself and had been quite impressed with her.

Ellen Brooks. Tall, slim, with very short, dark hair and a light tan complexion. Ellen had a strong face that reflected her vibrant personality. She had won him as soon as she had begun to talk at their interview. Her easy manner was perfect for dealing with sales to a mature, astute clientele, and he recognised her talents immediately. On this visit to Keeala Resort, they had spent only about half an hour talking before she had to show a potential customer around the resort.

Matthew was not sure about his feelings yet, but he knew he was attracted to her. This, and many other thoughts crowded his mind as he drove along the motorway. So much had happened recently and now, with the previous owner dead, there would be even more changes. He wanted to be part of them. Matthew saw how retirement villages and over 50's facilities were popping up in every state, and he knew he would always be able to get employment in the industry. This was a comforting thought after his recent scrape with the law, and his part in the uncovering of the drug business in which Allen Sinclaire had been involved.

Matthew had discovered he had a friend in the new owner and General Manager, Andrew Sleighmen. They were about the same age and had found lots of common ground when Matthew stayed in Adelaide for training, before taking up his post back in Queensland. He had the impression there was room for promotion if he kept up the good work, and he did not complain about the long hours and travelling. His ambition was to rise above his underprivileged beginnings. After chasing scams and illegal deals, all fraught with anxiety and disillusionment, he could see now that there was another way. He had imagination, talent, and youth on his side. He would be a success. He had no doubt of that.

******

Jason Ethridge was another young man who harboured a great desire to know success in his lifetime. He lay in bed in the early hours of the morning and watched the sun cast its soft light on the torn, dirty old blind at the window. He looked at the peeling paint on the walls of the room he shared with his father's friend. Loud snores filled the room, and the air was almost as foul as he remembered the bin he had sat in a few days previously.

"This is not a home," he said aloud, as he looked around at the clothes on the floor, next to the empty beer cans. "This is a shithole."

He repeated that last statement and quietly began to cry. He wanted out. He wanted all the things he had never had. Like a mother and siblings, a home and friends. He took a deep breath as he stared at the ceiling and fantasised about an ordinary life. The best part until now had been his school years. He had loved going every day and had known the esteem of his peers and recognition by his teachers. However, that was over now, and all he had learned was being put to use in the back room of this shabby old house, cooking up drugs that would eventually kill people. Jason knew his only way out was by his own initiative. He needed a plan and knew that he must dig deep within himself to find the strength to implement it. *What if ... No. What about ... No.* Ideas he had aplenty, but not the means to realise them. He had to acknowledge this was going to take time. A seed of an idea began to germinate in his brain and Jason would allow it to flower in its own time – slowly. He lay back as the tears on his face dried to the sound of the alcoholic snores of the man next to him.

A new day began.

******

Jim usually saw D.I. Pekalski's car pass out the gate around 8am, so he rang the detective early, hoping to catch him before he left for work that morning.

"Yes, Jim, how are you today?"

"As a matter of fact, I need a little favour – if it is within the realms of your portfolio."

"Certainly," answered the detective, who was always obliging.

Jim explained the small incident they had with Vinnie Markwell and asked about whether he thought the man worth checking.

Pekalski agreed and said he would ring Jim later. He thought about the call while he drove into the city that morning. He wondered why any place, especially a retirement resort, should attract so much crime and exceptional behaviour. Right from the start, there had been protests by locals about building the complex there. Pekalski knew that any development of this sort would attract some sort of negative response, but this one had seen more than its fair share. He still wondered about this latest problem when he arrived at his office and sat down in front of his computer. Then, up it popped. *Vincent Markwell, jailed for two years for his part in a drug ring, supplying heroin, five years ago.* Since his release, he had lived locally and kept his nose clean.

Yeah, maybe it's just a case of he hasn't been caught again, thought the detective. *So now he's a neighbour of mine at Keeala Resort. Well, I should pay him a visit and roll out the welcome mat.* Pekalski noted the recent report of the possible break-in at the resort. He thought how hard it must be for someone like Markwell to keep a low profile. He chuckled to himself as he wondered what the man would think about having a cop almost next door. He scrolled down the screen to pick up Luke Ethridge, Markwell's associate in crime. *He might like a visit as well, eh, especially since he's close by.* The detective picked up the phone and spoke to a friend in the drug squad.

"All quiet on that front, mate," said his colleague. "I thought they had all moved on, but maybe he's just lying low at the moment. Mind you, Frank, a fair amount of crystal meth has been circulating lately, we believe probably imported. Your friends have previously been into other stuff, but that doesn't mean they can't branch out. They had a good network established before they went away, so they're all professionals, and could set up again, anywhere. Leave it with me, will you." He rang off, leaving Pekalski thoughtful.

******

Jason was busy, spurred on by his new resolve to be free of his father and the whole drug business. After much thought, he decided to do nothing to alert anyone to his change of feelings. He continued to work away quietly in his lab. Jason had used meth, but had seen firsthand the effects of withdrawal, when long-term users had their supply cut off. In the past, he had also tried marijuana, but Jason did not want to be dependent on anything and he had not continued to use. He had been too close to too many deaths, and lives ruined because of drugs. Jason was very reluctant to betray Luke, but at the same time, he could see no other answer for himself. He began to wonder if there was any way to convince his father to get out of the business. He cast his mind back to the impressions he had of Luke's so-called friends; addicts, living only for their next hit. Luke always had a supply available and used several times, every day. It was killing him. Jason shuddered as he wondered how long it would be before he saw signs of the effects of the meth he unavoidably inhaled himself, with every batch he cooked up.

He wanted to look forward to a better future, without drugs, and without the people associated with them. Jason shook his head and tried to clear his mind of his negative thoughts. He knew in his heart, there was no answer for his father's addictions. He returned his concentration to the job at hand.

Chapter Five

Many of the residents of Keeala Resort knew Ron and Gwen Clarke. The couple cleaned for some of them, and they had been both carers and cleaners to Jessie Thornton. Jessie had died at the hands of her sister-in-law the previous year, and had left her estate to Ron and Gwen. They retired from work and were on the lookout for a new home.

"Ron, you there love?" Gwen called to her husband, as she came through the front door of their rented unit. They had been looking for a house to buy for some time, but so far, Ron found fault with everything Gwen suggested.

"You had better not be still in bed, you lazy bugger." Gwen raised her voice as she made a few long strides down the hall. "Ron?" she called, on her way to the bathroom, which, like the bedroom, was empty.

She returned to the bedroom, stood still, and looked around, first at the unmade bed, then at the clothes scattered around the room. She had a sudden frisson of fear shoot through her. Something was different; a sense of emptiness and abandonment. Her eyes moved to the wardrobe and she could see Ron's end was empty, even the coat hangers were gone. Slowly, she went back to the bathroom and that too displayed spaces where her husband's personal toiletries should have been.

Gwen could feel tightness in her chest. There was a burning sensation in her abdomen and her breathing had almost stopped.

"Ron?" she whispered, as she dragged her feet back to the bedroom.

She sat down on the bed and stared at the impression his head had left on the pillow. Gwen shook her head, stood up and walked around the unit, checking everything.

Why, why? You stupid old man. You know you can't manage without me. Just when we had everything to look forward too. Why are you doing this to me?

The phone rang and Gwen grabbed it from the bedside table.

"Hello." She listened, then pressed off; another real estate agent with something to show them. She couldn't talk, she could barely even think.

What about money? He would need money to go it alone and all we have is in a joint account. Oh, my God, no.

Gwen rushed to the laptop computer on the dining room table. She sat and opened the file on their bank account. Yesterday she had checked their accounts while transferring money to their credit account. They had $743,000 in their main investment account.

There was now $5,000 in their savings account. She looked at the balance of the main account. Ron had removed $738,000. She slumped back on the chair. Her head drooped, and tears dripped onto the keyboard. She lifted her head and stared at the screen. A most incredible sense of loss overwhelmed her, the loss of everything that gave her a reason to live. Quietly she cried, stared at the wall, and sat, unable to move. She was lost in an empty world. The morning reached midday, before she managed to pull herself together.

Normally Gwen was not a sentimental woman and she had weathered many hard times, including separation from her children and the loss of money and friends. She was not expecting something like this now, at the beginning of their old age. She certainly had not seen it coming. As she thought about it, Gwen acknowledged Ron had been his usual self, argumentative and quarrelsome, negative and critical. That was normal for him, and she knew after a lifetime of living with Ron, exactly how to cope with his behaviour.

But why now, Ron ? Why have you left me, you bastard? Why now, when there was plenty of money for both of us. Or was there? Maybe there's someone else in the picture – someone who wants our money.

As Gwen went over recent incidents and conversations, she began to get angry. *It was my money, more than his. I was the real worker, the one who was exhausted at the end of the day after cleaning houses and caring for old people. You went along and pushed the vacuum cleaner around, always saying you did the hard work, you mongrel.* However, it was Gwen who ran from one job to another, making sure of the standard of cleanliness and the approval of her clients. Anger began to bubble up like a volcano inside Gwen, and by the afternoon, she was ready to explode.

She opened the door of the sideboard and took out a bottle of Ron's whisky. She poured herself a triple and topped it up with water, gulped it down quickly, and shuddered. This was not usual for her, as she did not like to see Ron drinking, although he always did. She was surprised he had not taken his supply with him. She was also surprised at how much it steadied her nerves. She had another drink, and then she put the lid firmly back on the bottle and put it in the cupboard. She needed to make plans. She needed a clear head.

The following morning, she looked at the computer screen again. Gwen knew the $5,000 left in the savings account would not last long. The first thing she would do would be to go to the bank. She held little hope of being able to reclaim any of the money her husband had taken, but she would certainly see a solicitor tomorrow. In the meantime, she was going to need a job.

Gwen thought about contacting her old clients at Keeala Resort. She shook her head as she did so; it was a situation, she thought would never arise again. She knew, of course, all those people would have new home help by now, but she could still make her availability known. Perhaps they were not satisfied; she was a hard act to follow. She sat down and printed out flyers she could put around at the resort. She took stock of her present situation and decided she would have to move to cheaper accommodation.

Somehow, she thought, *I will get my money back, even if I have to track that bastard to the end of the earth. You're an idiot, Ron, and we both know it. I'll get you and you're going to wish you were dead.* She smiled at the thought of Ron's face when next he laid eyes on her.

******

Later that same day, Detective Inspector Frank Pekalski drove into the parking bay outside the manager's residence at the resort. "Anyone home?" he called through the screen door. He got the response he was waiting for. A few minutes later, the three were sitting together, enjoying a glass of wine, and Pekalski handed Jim an envelope.

Jim put his glass on the coffee table. He opened the envelope and scanned the piece of paper.

Di watched on curiously. She was reluctant to interrupt in front of the detective, but would have, had she and Jim been alone.

"Well, well, well, I'll be buggered." Jim grinned.

"What?" exclaimed Di, as she jumped up and went to look over her husband's shoulder.

"This is our newest resident?" she looked down, squinting and trying to read without her glasses.

"Sit down, love, and I'll read it to you," Jim said.

By this time, Pekalski was smiling at the thought of being able to share so much inside information about an individual, someone who was trying very hard to present himself as someone he absolutely was not. When Pekalski read about Markwell's record, and how he had been a local drug operator, he immediately decided he would not be showing his hand, not just yet. He knew Vinnie Markwell would probably find out he was a cop, because everyone else in the resort knew, but Pekalski needed the drug dealer to think there was no particular interest in his activities at the resort.

"It says here that he has been in prison and under surveillance on many occasions. Also, he has been charged with conspiring to pervert the course of justice, perjury, and assault, but got off on the last ones – not enough evidence. So," said Jim, "that says it all, doesn't it? What can we do?" Jim looked at Pekalski now.

"Nothing, at the moment. We watch and wait. I don't think this particular leopard has changed his spots. We'll allow him to be himself and let him assume we all accept him in our presence as a reformed member of society. We certainly don't want to go rushing in half-cocked, and have him get away again."

Di sipped her wine, and then said, "I believe drug dealing to be one of the worst of modern crimes. When you see the amount of damage done to the lives of both addicts and their families, as I have in the course of my career, it's unforgivable."

"True, and the associated crime I've seen by way of robbery and assault, and child abuse – the list goes on," acknowledged Pekalski.

They all sat quietly, each with their own image of the cost of illegal drugs.

Before the detective left, he and the managers agreed to be on the lookout for anything unusual and, for the time being, not to say anything to anyone about Vinnie Markwell.

Pekalski said that the incident the other evening regarding the intruder must surely be connected to the man's business.

"Odd types," he said. "You could be on the lookout for more such situations and people."

Detective Pekalski had resisted any involvement in the social activity of the resort, so far. He could see now that there may be a reason for him to become a little more involved. He thought he would go to the next mid-week dinner. *Might be nice to have someone else cook for me for a change,* he thought.

He waved to Harold and Robert, who were sitting on their front veranda in the light of the rising moon, as he drove past. He heard music coming from their unit and envied their companionship and peace. After sharing the company of Di and Jim, he realised he was lonely, and that he had been so for a long time. This was the first time he had openly acknowledged it to himself, but nowhere in his mind could he imagine ever finding anyone like his wife. No one else would do.

******

Gwen sat alone in her rented unit. She felt abandoned, as she reviewed her day. She had been to the bank, had seen her lawyer, and now held out little hope of recovering the money. Her lawyer had given her the business card of a private investigator. Gwen planned to ring him the next morning. Using the last five thousand in the bank, she would offer it as a start in the pursuit of her ex-partner. She had already put her name down with a cleaning agency as a casual cleaner, and was starting work for them on the following Friday. She would have money coming in, and gave her the confidence to rise to the challenge of chasing what was hers. *You'll expect me to just let you get away this with, won't you, but with your limited imagination, you won't think I'll get a private investigator, will you? But more fool you, you bastard,* she thought, as she sat and contemplated her microwaved dinner. She had no appetite and pushed the meal away. She poured another drink.

Gwen was right when she said her husband, Ron, had no imagination. At that particular moment, he sat in a pub, alone, and pondered what he was going to do next. Thinking about the past few days, he wondered what had given him the idea to up and leave when he did, since he had thought about it many times before, but never acted. He knew he was the type of personality that saw escape as the best alternative in any uncomfortable situation. There had been many of those in the past, but Gwen had managed to steer them through to better times, with her stalwart character and determination; not to mention her commitment to hard work. Ron was not prepared to suggest to himself that she was also the brains of the operation, but he did acknowledge she might at least be his match.

He picked up his glass, threw down the last of his whisky, and called the bartender for another. He had eaten in the bistro several hours ago, and knew he really should push off home. *But what for?* he asked himself. *I don't have to answer to her, anymore. I can stay out and get pissed and who cares. I'll do what I like from now on, and won't have to put up with any more shit from the dragon. I can sleep all day if I like, and eat what I like. And no more bloody cleaning. She can get stuffed.* He smiled to himself, and began to feel very happy. He chuckled aloud, and caused the barman to look at him curiously. The barman shook his head. He saw many strange characters; this was just one more.

Ron finally shuffled off to his motel room down the street. The last thing he thought before he drifted off to sleep was that he must make a plan. He did not want to run into Gwen, who lived only a few blocks away.

Chapter Six

Jason opened his eyes to another dawn, and realised he did not feel well. He blinked to clear his vision, but without success. He raised his head from the pillow and looked around the room. Not one, but two bodies lay inert on the floor, surrounded by the paraphernalia of meth smoking. Empty beer cans littered the floor. When he had gone to sleep, he had been alone. *So, these dickheads must have come in and flopped, without wakin' me,* he thought. He could see they had been smoking in his room; that meant he had been exposed to the secondary smoke in his sleep. Then he vaguely remembered someone giggling in the night. He had rolled over, and gone back to sleep. Jason now threw the cover back and stood up, and he swore as he tripped on the bodies on the floor. He staggered to the bathroom.

After he splashed cold water on his face, he moved to the shower. Ten minutes later, he emerged from the bathroom. He was not prepared to attempt the obstacle course across his bedroom floor again. Piles of clothing lay around; that was nothing new. He hated having to rummage for something to wear, but finally found his own jeans and tee shirt, dressed, and made his way to the silent kitchen. He prepared percolated coffee, and then held the fridge door open as he looked for something edible. It was not that he was hungry, but he thought it might help to straighten his head out and clear his vision.

He reached for a slice of pizza, saw the teeth marks on one side, and left it alone. He picked up a carton of milk, sniffed the open top, and shuddered. He threw that in the kitchen sink and closed the door to the fridge. He realised there was nothing safe to eat. He walked to his father's room and glanced around at the mess, almost identical to the one where he had slept. He saw Luke sprawled on his bed in a tangle of old bedding and beer cans, as well as drug equipment. Jason shuddered as he reached for Luke's pants hanging on the bedpost and rummaged for the car keys.

Jason drove to the convenience store a couple of minutes down the road, and parked outside. He rubbed his hands over his face and wondered how he looked. He was a good-looking boy, but did not know it. Jason saw himself as looking like his father and normally was inclined to avoid mirrors, but on this occasion, he peered into the rear vision mirror and dragged his hand through his hair.

For a moment, while he looked at the image in the mirror, he had the impression he was looking at someone else. At first he was confused, and then realised it was his mother. *Mum!* He had no idea that he even remembered what she looked like, but there she was, looking back at him through his own reflected eyes. A sense of sadness overtook him. *I look like her, not him.* He wondered why he had not noticed the likeness before, and why he could see it now, but he also felt her presence near him. He knew then that he was being looked after, that he was not alone. In a flash, his mother's face was gone, and he slowly tilted the mirror back into position. He stared out the windscreen, but felt somehow different, almost as though an unfamiliar force, or someone else, was now in charge, directing his thinking.

He walked into the shop, his mind blank, and he wandered around aimlessly, picking up some things and keeping them, taking other things off the shelves and staring at them, not knowing why he had handled the items. He was on automatic pilot when he returned to the car, and he sat and stuffed dry bread into his mouth and drank directly from the milk carton.

Must be the drugs. Either that or I'm goin' mad. Maybe I'm already dead and I'm lyin' on my bed at home. Maybe. Just then, a car pulled up beside him and he looked at it as the driver got out and went into the shop. *No, I am definitely alive,* he said to himself. *It has to be the drugs. This is serious now, and I need to think.* Jason started the car and drove out of the parking area on to the road. He headed for a park a few streets away, and pulled in there underneath a tree. He got out, walked around for a few minutes, before he sat on a bench which overlooked a small lake.

Never in his life had he felt like this. *What's happenin' to me? Maybe it's a spiritual experience and I'm wakin' up and seein' my life as it really is.* He looked up at the sky, half-expecting to see God looking down, and perhaps pointing an admonishing finger at him, but puffy, white clouds scudded across the blue background of the sky and the sun's rays warmed his back. He could not see God.

Then strangely, his mind began to clear. He took a deep breath and began to make decisions – several, in quick succession. *I'll write them down*, he thought, and he pulled out a note pad and pen from his shirt pocket and started to write .

1. Get out of that place.

2. Get my own place.

3. Get money.

4. Find out about uni.

He stopped; pen poised, and looked at the list. He knew it would not do. For a start, getting away was going to be a major undertaking and he would have to move to somewhere where they could not find him. Jason realised that the third item on his checklist should have come first. Before he could do anything, he had to have money, and that wasn't just lying around, waiting to be picked up. He scrunched up the list and threw it on the ground. *But it was a good exercise,* said the voice in his head, and he began to re-arrange his plan. He noted first that he would need money, and then everything would be easy. *Yes, it really is that simple. I must get at least five thousand dollars to kick me off, then, when I leave, I'll have rental bond money and livin' money while I look for work. But what job can I do? I've only ever worked for Vinnie and Luke. I need to go to Centrelink. Shit, this isn't goin' to be easy.* Jason scratched his head as he stood up, and walked around in circles. *Money, then at the same time, a job. I'll take a look online this arvo. I'll find somethin'.* Jason walked back to the car and made his way home. He tried not to think negatively about all the obstacles. He began to try to focus on his mother's face again, to see her smile at him. As far as he knew, she was dead, so Luke had said, but what if she was not? He shook his head to eliminate any further stupid thoughts.

Luke was prowling around the kitchen, opening and closing the fridge door, when his son returned.

"You get bread and milk?" he asked.

Jason nodded as he handed over the remains of the bread and half a carton of milk.

"Fuck! That the best you can do? You're an idiot, you know."

"Yeah, I know," answered Jason, as he walked out of the room.

Jason sat on a stool in the lab room, and tried to keep a positive attitude, despite the pall of depression that hung over him. He turned to the computer and began to bring up work possibilities. He had no training in any trade, and the only subject that interested him was science. *Lot of good that'll do me,* he thought, as his fingers punched in 'Hospitality'.

I guess I could go work for Maccas, or some fast food place. He let his mind drift and saw himself in the kitchen of a fast food restaurant, cooking, and taking orders. *I could do that. Maybe get a loan and study at uni at the same time. If I could just rent a room somewhere, maybe.* He turned to the boxes and jars on the bench in front of him. He had no desire to make another batch of crystal meth or any other type of methamphetamine. In his head, he was moving on and found it hard to focus on the job at hand.

One of the boys walked in, looking decidedly hung-over from the night before.

"Startin' a new batch, huh, Jase? I could help if ya like."

"Well, you could drag that bag over there, and dump it up on to the bench where I could reach it. Thanks, Nat. When you've done that, you could measure out some of that powder into the bucket, three cups. You'll find a measurin' cup on the bench. Be exact."

"Sure, sure," nodded Nat, as he huffed and puffed while he dragged the heavy bag into place. "I was hopin' ya could show me how ya do this stuff; I hear it isn't too hard. And you never know when you might be glad of a bit a help, eh? What if you were to get sick, or somethin'? Who'd produce the product then? We'd all starve to death."

"Or go into the heebie jeebies," Jason said with a grin.

"That's right," laughed Nat, shaking all over to demonstrate. "We can't have that."

"It's not that it's so hard, mate, as it is touchy," said Jason to his helper. "There are plenty of people who've had bad accidents makin' this shit. It's quite volatile, and could blow this house to smithereens, very easily."

Nat raised his eyebrows and pulled a face. "Well, I'd just have to be a bit careful, wouldn't I now?" He was obviously not going to be dissuaded. He moved in closer to watch what Jason was doing.

A seed of an idea began to flower in Jason's brain. *What if there was a terrible accident here?* he thought. He shuddered as he imagined how destructive such an explosion could be, but he could see how he could eliminate more than one problem at the same time.

Jason became oblivious to Nat's presence in the room, as his brain started to go into overdrive. *Poor Luke would be out of his misery, once and for all. The equipment and fingerprints and any evidence would be blown to kingdom come. No one could blame me for an accident, especially if my apprentice here was the one to be workin', while I was out doin' errands. Vinnie couldn't blame me, and he'd have no idea that I had collected all the cash and walked out with it before the place blew up.* His thoughts raced and his hands flew around while Nat watched.

"Hey, take it easy, mate. I can't keep up with ya. I'll have to write some of this stuff down." Nat left the room to look for writing material.

Jason sat on his chair and tried to get his thoughts in order. He could easily imagine the right day would be when they had the takings in the box, before Vinnie came round for the pickup. Jason could set Nat up in the lab, and have everything in place so he could not avoid an explosion as soon as he started to mix the chemicals. By then, Jason could be long gone with the cash and return home to find a charred mess, and these poor unfortunate buggers out of their misery. *It could work, it could.* He shook his head as Nat came back with a biro and a dirty scrap of crushed paper.

"Now, tell me from the start." He leaned on the bench, ready to write.

Nat maintained his interest, and several days later the two worked quietly in the lab, enjoying each other's company. Jason decided to get the other man onside so no one could suspect anything, and he would be able to call on him for a favour in the near future. At lunchtime, they sat outside together on the grass, and leant up against the house in the shade. They ate leftover cold fried rice. They were becoming firm friends.

"Ya know, ya not the mongrel yer dad makes ya out to be. I don't think he 'preciates how lucky he is. Anytime I can give ya a hand, just call out. Okay?"

"Thanks, Nat, I appreciate that."

They finished eating in companionable silence.

Chapter Seven

Ellen Brooks had strong, athletic limbs, and the heart of a long distance runner. At least that was what her dad used to say, when he was alive. Now that he was gone, she still tried to live up to his expectations. She wanted to make him proud. She set a high standard for herself, as he had, and was only happy when she met her own personal goals. Whether it was success in business or personal relationships, she worked equally hard and was always moving the goal post further away.

Her mother had said, "Good luck to you." but she had no understanding of what drove her daughter to work so hard at everything she attempted.

Her mother and father had parted when Ellen was twelve, and she had stayed with her father. He said their family was dysfunctional when Ellen's brother had chosen to leave with his mother. No amount of counselling could put the family back together again, and they had drifted further and further apart.

Now at twenty-nine, Ellen had some satisfaction in looking back and seeing herself rise from being a diligent school student, to becoming a successful salesperson in the Sleighmen Group, as well as being a gifted speaker as a life coach. Becoming a life coach had been a long and expensive journey for a young, penniless girl alone. She had to sell real estate to make a living while she studied at university. She found she loved it, and was very successful, so now, she did both, despite her original plan to give up selling when she started to get life coaching clients. It was a good balance and she had enough energy for both, knowing that when she was earning enough from coaching she would have to let selling go. The fact that she knew how to keep her life uncomplicated, and was extremely healthy in mind and body, made all the difference.

Men had played a very small part in her life, and although she had a few boyfriends to look back on, she had never been in love. There had been little time for meeting men socially and her liaisons had come from the people she either worked with, or met through her studies. Her father was her role model for her partners, and he was a very hard act to follow, but now there was Matthew Weatherlee. She was taken unawares when he popped up in her life and she found she was so attracted to him. While they talked on the phone and had a regular online connection, she had seen him only three times since he employed her. She was very impressed, despite her strongest reservations. She wanted to see more of him and was happy to talk to him when he rang, which was several times a week, whether there was any business to discuss or not.

"Hi, Matt, it's good to hear your voice. I'm afraid that last sale, the one I told you about last time we spoke, fell through. But I have someone else waiting in the wings, and with luck, they'll be here tomorrow, and I'll go in for the kill." She laughed at herself; she was the least forceful salesperson he had ever met, but she had techniques and skills others did not, and had a good success rate.

Matthew spoke for a few minutes about some of the changes going on within the organisation, and then returned to talking about Keeala Resort, one of his favourite subjects. He finally got around to the real reason he had rung. That was to ask if she might come to Adelaide for a sales conference, all expenses paid, of course.

"I'd love to!" she said, then thought perhaps she had slightly over reacted and been a bit too anxious. "Oh, I'll have to clear it with a couple of clients I have. But that's cool; let me get back to you in the next day or so."

After she rang off, Ellen realised she had several commitments that would need rescheduling, but she knew, no matter what, she would be in Adelaide for the conference in three weeks. She sat smiling at the phone, after it had gone dead. *He's so nice,* she thought.

******

Ron Clarke had a hangover, again. He woke in his motel room. *Where the hell am I?* he wondered. He had no idea where he was for a minute or so, and then he remembered. *What the bloody hell have I done? Why have I walked out on Gwen?* As he sat, alone, confused, trying to make sense of his circumstances, he could not rationalise his actions. He knew it had seemed like a great idea a couple of days ago. It had seemed so clear; half his life he had laboured under the idea that he would be much better off without Gwen, whose presence seemed to hang round his neck like a ball and chain. For some reason now, he was unable to think of a single advantage. *Who's going to do my washing?* He began to scratch at his groin and realised he had not changed his underwear since he left home. *And who am I going to talk to? Like now, when I have to decide what to do and where to go next.* He stopped asking himself questions and decided to act. *I have to get going, out of this town and interstate, before she finds me and takes all the money.* Then he laughed. *She can't do that because it's all in my name now, and I have my own bank account. So sue me! Yeah.* He laughed as he made his way to the shower, and later packed his bag.

I've never seen Western Australia. That's where I'll go. With a bit of money I can get myself a girl, whenever it suits me. I'll go fishing, maybe charter a cruiser and find out what other blokes see in deep sea fishing. Shit, there's heaps I could do and eat and drink whatever and whenever I like. Ron was smiling all the way to the airport and did not mind waiting three hours for a flight. He was doing mental arithmetic when his flight was called, and he figured he would have enough money to last him for the rest of his life. He realised he would have to be sensible, and not just throw it away. Gwen was good at making money last, and he wondered for the second time that day, why he hadn't just taken her along. *She had her uses. Too late now*, he shrugged. *She really was a pain in the arse a lot of the time.*

******

As Ron was flying across the cloudless western skies, Gwen was explaining her story to a young man who advertised himself as a private detective. She did not have much confidence in young people, and this particular one looked a bit too smart for his own good.

"Can you describe Mr. Clarke to me, or better still do you have a photo of him?" Tom Heart smiled.

"Naturally," Gwen said, as she handed the investigator a photo of Ron. It had been taken in front of a property they were looking at recently, and one that Gwen had been keen on. She had been disappointed when Ron had given it the thumbs down, and she had kept the photo in case he might change his mind.

"You say he had no close friends, and as far as you know, there was no other woman in his life."

"That's right. He wasn't the type of man to attract women and he was too mean to spend money on anyone. Personally, I think he took the money and left, just to see if he could get away with it. I'll bet he already regrets being on his own. He won't be able to look after himself, you know. He rarely remembers where he left his car keys, let alone his wallet and his glasses. Honestly, he has trouble getting himself out of the house in the morning, without me to get him organised."

"I suggest this may be the time he learns, don't you think? It's in his interest to do these things for himself now that you aren't there to wait on him. A lot of men find they have hidden talents when their wives either pass on or leave."

Gwen grimaced; so far, this man failed to impress her. "Well anyway, can you see any hope of finding him?" she asked.

"Absolutely. He can't be too hard to locate, with what you tell me about him. Give me a week and I'll get back to you with my findings."

Gwen stood and Tom put his hand out to her to shake. She grudgingly responded, then walked to the door. "Please remember he has taken almost all our savings, so keep me informed of the costs."

"Certainly."

******

It was Gwen's first day back at work. She now had an office-cleaning job through an agency, and had one response to the flyers she had put in the letterboxes at Keeala Resort. The thought of cleaning for a living once again, appalled her. However, she did look forward to the human contact, especially at the resort where she had so many old acquaintances.

She thought about some of them now as she drove to her appointment at the resort. Usually, the residents who had their homes cleaned, waited for her, and stayed to oversee the work. Many were very fussy, and would not dream of leaving her alone in their houses. Most office cleaning was lonely; after hours work and there was no human contact. Gwen liked to talk and loved to hear about how other people managed their lives. She had heard many secrets in her time, much like a hairdresser, and she considered herself a good confidant. *Ron used to say I was a gossip, but what the hell would he know,* she smirked.

The gate code at the resort came to mind quite automatically when Gwen pulled up in the driveway. She punched it in and drove slowly to Unit 41. She waved to Robert as she passed him, walking Gypsy, their King Charles spaniel. She pulled up in the driveway of Freya Holman and had not turned the engine off before someone approached her and tapped on her window.

"Hello, Gwen, do you remember me?"

"Yes, of course, it's Joy Rayne, isn't it? How are you, Joy? Are you over your eventful bus trip at last?"

"Indeed I am, and wasn't that the event of a lifetime." They both laughed. "Freya tells me you are going to start cleaning for her again."

"That's right. Ron and I have split up, so now I need something to keep me entertained."

"I'm sorry to hear that, love. If you have time to do another unit, please consider mine. I'll get rid of the couple of girls who are presently wasting my money. Useless, they are, and you can't trust anyone these days, can you?"

"That's true, dear. I'll call on you when I've finished here this arvo. Okay?"

"Great, see you later then." Joy moved away from the car and Gwen walked up to Freya, who stood at her open front door. They talked for five minutes and Freya said how sorry she was that Ron had left, but guessed Gwen would be 'just fine' on her own. Gwen wasted no time getting started; she surprised herself at how quickly she slipped back into her old routine.

Later that evening, as she drove home, Gwen decided she would not do any more office cleaning. She actually enjoyed meeting up with so many old friends again, and she could see she would have no trouble picking up enough work. She wondered where Ron was now, as she thought about how they used to share the work and how much he grumbled about carting out rubbish and vacuuming. She did windows and showers, while he stood around talking to anyone who went past. Ron considered he was the PR man, and constantly urged Gwen to hurry up with the actual cleaning.

What a dope I was. All those years, doing his share as well as my own. He so took me for granted, and obviously he never loved me, or the bastard would still be here now. She shook her head in an effort to clear out thoughts of the man she would never forgive.

******

That same night, Ron landed in Perth and checked himself into an inner-city hotel. Before he left Brisbane, he had taken the advice of the salesman, and bought several new outfits. He looked at his reflection in the mirror, before going to the dining room for dinner. He had dressed carefully for a change, in a new outfit; navy jacket, pale blue candy striped shirt, and grey slacks. He beamed as he checked out his new shoes, and then returned to admire the new Ron in the full-length, mirrored wardrobe door. *I look great*, he said to himself. *No I don't – I look fabulous*! He felt a little embarrassed about the socks, but thought probably no one would see those old things under his pants. He resolved to buy a few more pieces to complete his wardrobe. Ron strode off confidently, feeling better than he had for a long time.

Chapter Eight

"Ellen is going to be away for five days, next week," Jim said to Di. She had joined him in the office on Monday morning.

"Really? What's happening?"

"A sales conference in Adelaide. She was just in here telling me about it. Actually, she seems to be really looking forward to going over, but I suspect there's a little more attraction than just sales talk."

"Like what?"

"Matthew Weatherlee."

"Really? Well, that's news to me, but I can see why they would make a good couple. How come you know everything, anyway?"

Jim tapped the side of his nose and nodded sagely. They grinned at one another, as Di reached over to answer the phone.

"Thanks for keeping us informed," she said before she hung up. "That was Pekalski; he's still watching our friend, Markwell, from afar. Nothing new at this point in time, but if anything happens he'll let us know."

"Good," said Jim. "Now, back to the sales next week. Do you want to do them, or would you like to share with an expert?"

"Well, I think you should leave the sales entirely to the one with the best record. As you well know, I have outsold you on every occasion in the past. My record speaks for itself."

"Yes, and no," Jim returned. "It was only because we had a run on women buying alone. Naturally, they would prefer to buy from another woman. Given the same situation, I would win, hands down."

"Yeah, yeah," Di laughed as she walked out with her hands full of lists for the notice board. She really enjoyed doing the selling when she had a chance. Because she was a registered nurse, Di felt she was type cast in the same old jobs all the time. She had excellent counselling skills and was a good listener to good news, as well as tales of woe. She enjoyed the variety at the resort and felt she had done her share of helping and healing in her career. She planned to call and see Ellen Brooks, later in the day. *Wouldn't hurt to get a few pointers before next week*, she thought.

On her way to the sales office, Di ran into Charlene Markwell who was striding along the path to the hairdresser. Charlene spent several hours, at least twice a week at the beauty parlour.

"I've got the type of hair that needs a lot of attention, you know. Not like yours, that you can just pull back any old how, and be happy with it."

Di grimaced at the inferred insult but smiled, "Yes, some of us are lucky that way, mine takes no time at all."

"Well, I suppose I could just do that too, but my husband, Vinnie, is so fussy about how I look. He says I'm beautiful and I can't afford to disappoint him, you know."

"I do, I do," nodded Di, "You mean you have set a very high standard for yourself and now you must maintain it."

"That's right. My mother used to do my hair in curlers when I was young, and she brought me up to make the best of myself."

"I can certainly see that, Charlene." Di patted the other woman's hand and they both smiled at one another. "How are you settling in?" Di asked, by way of digging into Charlene's vulnerable background.

"Oh, I love it here, Mrs. Watersen. It's so peaceful, and the gardens are beautiful and everyone has been so nice, welcoming us and all. Vinnie says we should have come here years ago. Much better than hangin' out with those dead losers he used to hang around with. Well, you know what I mean; we're in a class of our own here now, respectable and Vinnie says intelligent people of our own kind. We can't afford to hang around with riff raff, if you know the type I mean and all."

"I do, I do," said Di again. "Did you find out who your intruder was, the day after you moved in, Charlene?"

"Oh, for heaven's sake, it was his stupid brother, Marc, just a total mix up that was. But it won't happen again, I can promise you that. He has warned all his old friends off. He'll go and see them, from now on. They won't be coming here, and that's for sure and certain."

"Good to hear," Di said. "Well, I hope you'll be very happy here at the resort, dear, and please consider my door always open if you have any problems, or you just want a chat. That's what I'm here for and I can see we're going to be great friends."

Charlene blushed to the roots of her dyed hair and squeezed the manager's hand. "You're so kind. Thank you, and I hope we will be good friends. You know what Vinnie always says?"

"No," answered Di.

"He says, 'You can't have too many friends, and that's a fact, Jack'," she laughed, "and he even says that if your name's not Jack." Again, she laughed at herself.

As Di walked away, she had to hold her hand over her mouth in case Charlene heard her laughing. When she arrived at the sales office, she needed to sit in the chair and compose herself before she was able to talk sensibly to Ellen. "One day I'll tell you why I'm like this," she said, "but not today."

Ellen was her diplomatic self and sat patiently. "I can wait, but I'll keep you to your word and ask again one day."

"I hear you're going to Adelaide to a sales conference," Di said, when she was fully composed.

"Right. I was hoping you would be taking over the sales in my absence – not that I think Jim won't do a good job, please understand, but I'm a firm believer that women have the last say when buying real estate. I do believe men tend to defer to their wives, because they know their spouses have an intuition about such things."

"I agree, wholeheartedly," Di said, as she nodded and smiled. "Not only that, I want to beat him with the overall sales, after you of course, at the end of the year. We must stick together; we cannot have men thinking they are better at anything, least of all, sales." They both laughed raucously and enjoyed the joke at Jim's expense. "Aside from that, I think he's great," Di said.

"I'll give you the story so far," said Ellen, conspiratorially. She moved over to the computer and made room for Di to sit next to her. "Now, I'll just bring up the sales I have in progress at the moment." Ellen was generous with her advice and had an easy manner when explaining anything. Di's mind wandered to the image of Ellen and Matthew, getting married, and she smiled at the thought, realising that Jim would accuse her of matchmaking again. She loved to see people happy in the way she and Jim had found happiness. She brought her attention back to the matter at hand.

******

Charlene returned to the house, where she found Vinnie relaxing. He had his feet up on the lounge, with the sun streaming in on him as he sipped a glass of beer.

"How do I look?" she asked.

"Bloody beautiful, as always." Vinnie belched, and blew her a kiss, as if to emphasise the sincerity of the compliment.

"You know, beer never tastes the same from a glass. I always prefer it straight out of the stubbie," he said, as he lifted the glass to his lips.

"It doesn't look nice, darl. Drinking out of a bottle, I mean. We're civilised now, as I said to the manager before."

Vinnie perked up at the mention of the manager. "What exactly did you say to the manager?"

"I said we don't hang out with riff raff anymore. I told her those people are in the past, and if we want to see them, we go there – they won't be coming here."

"You said what?" Vinnie almost exploded out of the lounge. He went to stand in front of Charlene as she turned away. He pulled her round by the arm to face him.

"We were having a chat, on the path. Mrs. Watersen and her husband are both very nice people, and happy to talk about anything."

"I bet they are," growled Vinnie. "Tell me what you were talking about again."

"You know, just passing the time of day, talking about how much nicer it is here than some of the places we've lived."

"I don't want you talking about the past – not yours – or mine – not where we lived – or who we were with. Hear me? Keep away from the managers and mind your own business." He shook her arm and looked deeply into her eyes, trying to impress upon her the need for discretion, especially about their past.

"Okay, okay, let me go," she said, as she shook free of Vinnie's big hand. "You don't trust anyone, that's your

trouble. You wouldn't know a friend if you fell over one."
She left the room.

Vinnie picked up the magazine he had been reading, as he flopped back on to the lounge. His peaceful morning was shattered now, as he wondered what Charlene might have inadvertently let drop to Di Watersen. He began to wonder how he could get Charlene to keep her mouth shut. Vinnie thought she was just a dumb blonde; well, not just a dumb blonde, but a very attractive dumb blonde, who made a spectacular accessory hanging off his arm on social occasions. She did make him feel more of a man. He guessed he was stuck with her.

Vinnie had more problems than he wanted right now. Although Jason tried not to show his hand, Vinnie was astute enough to detect that he was losing interest in the drug manufacturing business. Vinnie knew he could not afford to let Jason slip from his clutches; the young man was a crucial part of Vinnie's network. Having Nat as Jason's apprentice was good insurance, should Jason decide to leave, but Vinnie was well aware that the manufacture of meth was a hazardous venture. To make it safely was more about knowing what not to do, rather than what to do. Vinnie did not like to get involved in rough stuff, but there were times when it was unavoidable. He had a couple of bikie mates who had no concerns about eliminating someone, for a price. In the past, his associates had eliminated a couple of problem characters on his behalf; the incidents that led to their deaths simply reported as 'single vehicle accident – no known cause'. The problems died at the scene. It was quick and clean, at least for Vinnie. He may have to resort to that solution again with

Jason, but not yet. For the moment, he would watch and wait. Nat was not ready to go it alone yet – but soon.

******

As he continued to ply his trade in the laboratory, Jason gave his exit strategy a great deal of thought. The more he considered the practicalities of it, the better it sounded. When he envisioned his father dying in the explosion, he had little sense of self-reproach. The odium engendered in him by years of neglect and abuse by his father, overrode any compunction about committing patricide. Guilt, if he had any at all, he felt for not having done anything to save his father from himself, all these years. He believed now, Luke was in no position to be dragged out of the mire of drug addiction, which consumed his life. His father's enslavement to the chemical demons had gone on for so long, Jason thought, that going into rehabilitation was not an option. Most of Luke's mates were in a similar position, and Jason could see they would all meet an unhappy end. At least this way, death would be quick.

Jason had a rough plan formed and he wanted to keep it on the boil, until he was sure it would work. *If I never do another thing right in this lifetime, this must be the exception.* He thought this to himself, repeatedly, day and night, and he became increasingly preoccupied with his plans. Ultimately, those around him noticed he was becoming withdrawn and absentminded.

******

Grant, one of Luke's distributors, stood at the drug lab sink. He held a freshly rolled joint between the thumb and index finger of his left hand. It was poised in front of his pursed lips. In his right hand, his thumb was resting on the striker of a cigarette lighter.

Luke came into the room. He could not believe what he saw. He lunged and knocked the lighter flying from Grant's hand.

"Shit! Tell me you weren't goin' to light that in here, were you?" he said. "Which part of the 'NO fuckin' SMOKING' signs don't you understand?"

"Oh, sorry mate, I forgot."

"Yeah, that so? Well, you'll be bloody forgettin' in a pine box if you do that again. Shit! I can't believe it!"

"Look, calm down, okay? I said I'm sorry. Anyway, there's somethin' I need to talk to ya about."

"Yeah? Like fuckin' what?" Luke was still shaking his head in disbelief.

"Well, it's about young Jason, mate. Me 'n' a coupla the other boys are gettin' a bit worried. He used to 'ave a joke with his friends, and 'e's always been so business minded, don't ya think? Nowadays, you can't get boo out of 'im. Do ya think 'e's becomin' depressed? I've known a couple of blokes what 'ave been depressed. One ended up in the loony bin, and the other topped 'imself. We just 'ope 'e ain't 'eadin' in that direction."

Luke looked sideways at the man who could have just ended their lives. *Shit, I suppose we all make mistakes*, he thought. *Guess he's learnt his lesson. Anyway, I'd better listen to what he's sayin' about Jason.* Luke had noticed the same things about Jason's recent demeanour. Conversations he had had with his son recently, had given Luke the impression that Jason was not happy at all. Luke hoped it was just a phase, but now, it seemed everyone was noticing changes in Jason's attitude. Luke was worried.

"I'm a bit worried about him myself, Grant. He told me he wanted to go to uni and he didn't want to keep working here anymore. But what can I do? I can't give him that kinda dough and I can't pay someone else to do his job either. I've been trainin' him for this work, all his life."

Grant shook his head, and said, "Not much of a life for a smart kid like that, mate. I'm real glad I never 'ad any kids; I wouldn't wish this on 'em."

The room went quiet as the men thought about the conditions that they all lived in.

"I'll try to talk to 'im if ya like, maybe later when the others go 'ome; 'e might listen to me, I'm younger than you, and maybe I can give 'im some advice."

"Sure, mate, give it a go. Maybe you can find out what the problem is. Give him the message that things will change, as soon as we get a bit more dough comin' in, and he can start to save some for himself."

"Sure, leave it to me." Grant headed for the door.

"Oh, and Grant," said Luke as he turned.

"Sorry about before, but you scared the shit out of me."

"No wuckin' furries, mate." Grant laughed at his play on words.

Chapter Nine

The gloss of returning to paid work, in the form of house cleaning, had worn off. *I can't believe I've come back to this drudgery,* Gwen thought, several times a day. She began to remember all the things she did not like about working for someone else, and how much stress it was putting on her old body. *Since leaving this place, I had really begun to enjoy sleeping in past 8am, and sitting with my feet up for a coffee break whenever I felt the urge. Now, having to take instructions from someone younger, not to mention being told how to do it, is really sticking in my craw.* So, after two weeks, she was becoming short tempered and touchy.

"Be sure to air out the second bedroom, will you, Gwen, I'm expecting a visitor next week."

Gwen shook her head and mimicked her employer, Freya Holmen. She did not bother to say she had already done just that. Gwen only knew how to work one way, and that was the right way – no shortcuts – everything done to perfection.

"I'm going out now, Gwen," Freya called to her from the front door.

"Okay, I'll lock up behind me when I leave."

Gwen heard the door slam and the car start up in the garage. She wandered to the lounge and watched through the fine curtains, as the other woman drove off. Gwen turned to pick up her duster and walked over to the polished sideboard in the corner of the dining room. She flicked at dust and picked up small ornaments then placed them back on their tiny doilies. She closed drawers and doors securely, and wiped her finger marks as she went along.

One drawer popped back out again and Gwen slammed it shut. She had neither the time nor the patience for anything that did not conform. The drawer flew back out and on to the floor with a thump.

"Damn, bloody damn", she exclaimed as she bent down to pick up the mess.

She noticed one piece of paper caught as she tried to ram the drawer home again and Gwen pushed the drawer and the piece of paper back hard. Again, it poked out, refusing to lie down and her patience was wearing thin. Several sheets fell on to the floor, and she bent over and shuffled them back into a small pile. She looked for the first page to put them back in order. Her eyes scanned the writing and then, suddenly, the words drew her attention to the content. She began to read slowly, and at the same time, she walked to the big chair nearby and sat herself down.

She read all ten pages and then held them in a trembling hand. She looked around in a daze, and wondered exactly what she had discovered. *What does all this mean, though?* she wondered.

Gwen leaned back in the chair and held the bundle up to her eyes. She began to read selective paragraphs ... *Dear Brenda ... I'm only pleased my parents never lived to see me go to jail ...* also ... *remember the price I'm paying for our comfort and the fact that, at no time, did I ever implicate you* ... and ... *"When I get out, I think we should leave the country and make a completely new start. There will always be someone who will recognise us here, no matter where we go* ... Finally ... *I'm having this letter smuggled out so there is no chance of the authorities ever reading it. I know our money is safe with you, my love ... .*

When Gwen saw the endearment at the end of the letter, underwritten with the name Brett, a small bell rang in the back of her mind. She stood up, and with the duster in her hand, began to flick it around. She attempted to dig down deep in her memory. Suddenly, she had it. *Of course, yes, it must be.* She turned around in a circle, as she tried to remember the details. *This has to be a letter from the famous Brett Simpson.* Gwen cast her mind back about five years and recalled the embezzlement case that had been front-page news at the time. She remembered he had been jailed for seven years, and that he supposedly had no accomplices. Most of the money had never been recovered. Simpson had gone bankrupt, and despite the efforts of forensics and the assistance of the best accountants in town; no one could find the money. But now, Gwen knew who had it. Brenda ... somebody-or-other, also known as Freya Holman. Now it made sense. Freya had become the custodian of the embezzled money when Brett went to jail. Gwen reasoned that he probably had it in some sort of a trust or overseas account; some place untraceable, that only Freya could access.

Well, well, well, what do you know about that! Gwen had a smile from ear to ear. She had been involved in a few, less than legal schemes in her life, but had never even been close to anything of this magnitude. She had no particular respect for the law, and was a firm believer that the most corrupt people in society hid behind some kind of authoritative badge of rank or privilege. "So, what can this do for me, I ask you?" she said, out loud. There was that smile again. She tapped her foot and ran her hand over the pages of writing, thinking, and thinking, and thinking.

A copy. That's what I must have first. Several copies even, insurance you might say. She jumped up and strode into the guest room where Freya kept her computer and printer/copier. She made half a dozen copies, thinking as she did so, *Well, my dear, you really should have been more careful about where you stored your valuable correspondence. After all, I didn't go looking for it; it literally jumped out at me.*

Next, she went out to her car and took off in a hurry. She decided to put a few copies of the letter away as insurance. She hid them in several hiding places at home and included a covering letter for the police, explaining her situation. She was not sure how to get a copy to the police, should something unforseen happen to her, but Freya would not know that. *Details,* she thought, *I'll get back to that.* She then drove back to Freya Holman's, to await her return.

Gwen sat comfortably, although excitedly, on the woman's lounge. She went over, step-by-step, what she would say when Freya returned home. *That should do it. I think she should get the message if I spell it out for her. The woman will just have to learn to share.* She waited.

"Good heavens, what are you still doing here? I thought you'd be finished and gone home hours ago." Freya was startled to see the cleaning woman sitting at ease in her front room, when she returned at five-twenty that evening.

"Well, I was waiting for you. There's something we need to discuss."

"Oh, surely it could have waited, I'm tired out. Nothing could be that important."

Freya had put her handbag and parcels down on the dining room table. She turned to the kitchen and went to the fridge. She brought out a bottle of wine and one glass.

"Yes, what a good idea, I'd love a glass of wine, thank you."

"What!" Freya curled up her top lip in disdain, as she looked at the cleaning woman, then at her wine. "I don't believe I offered you one, and I'd like to see you get up from my lounge and be off home."

"Not until we've discussed some very important business."

"Important to whom?"

"You, really. But if you're too tired to talk now, I guess there's always tomorrow." Gwen stood, and took a couple of steps toward the front door. She hesitated, turned around to stare her employer straight in the eyes, and said emphatically, "Brenda."

Gwen turned, and started to the door.

"What did you say?" The other woman, almost screeching, said behind her.

Gwen turned. The smile on her face betrayed her menace.

"I said, Brenda. That's your name, isn't it?"

Freya took several hesitant steps toward Gwen and spoke very quietly.

"How do you know that name?"

"Brett Simpson is your husband, right? Your name is Brenda Simpson – famous disappearing woman of the 2007, $10,000,000 embezzlement case in Brisbane. If my memory serves me correctly, you and the money disappeared not long before your husband was locked up in the Arthur Gorrie correctional centre, for seven years."

The bottle of wine slipped from Freya's fingers, and landed softly on the carpet. She stared down as Gwen looked at her, picked up the bottle, and went to the kitchen, coming back with another glass and a corkscrew. Freya watched Gwen open the wine and walk over to fill her glass.

She stood, frozen to the spot, until the cleaner said, "Take a seat, we have business to discuss."

They both sat down.

Gwen allowed Freya to drink a glass, and then topped it up again, as well as her own.

"Feeling better?" she enquired politely.

Freya nodded. "What do you want?"

"Money, of course. I'm finding this work too much for me, now that I'm getting older, and, I have to say, it's not as much fun as it used to be. You may have found that yourself, if you have ever done any cleaning."

Freya didn't answer.

"I'm thinking in terms of a little pension. As you know, Ron took our savings ..."

Freya interjected, "You mean the money you squeezed from old Jessie Thornton."

"Not at all. Not a bit of it. We inherited that estate, fair and square. I worked like a navvy for that old girl and she was like a mother to me."

Gwen stood up suddenly and splashed her wine on the arm of the chair.

"How dare you say that!" said Gwen. "I know for a fact that no one believes that." She walked around the room, taking several large gulps from her wine glass. "Anyway, I'm not here to talk about me. This is about you."

Freya seemed to have begun to get some colour back into her face.

"You haven't got a hope of getting any money out of me. It's all tied up in trusts, and there is no way I will help you to access it."

"Well, my dear, I didn't really expect you to just hand it over, and you may not even have to break into your trusts for little old me. The fact of the matter is, I'm not greedy, and you can be very grateful for that. If I were anyone else, I would be asking for a share, but just quietly, I don't want to wait until hubby gets out of prison in a couple of years. No, it can all be a lot simpler than that. Do you have any elderly parents, dear?"

Freya shook her head and kept her eyes on Gwen.

"No," she said.

"Well, if you did, you'd probably be the type to help them out a bit in their old age. I tell you, living on the pension is not much chop. One can barely afford to pay rent, let alone the cost of utilities and food, but you seem to manage pretty well. I notice cartons of the best wines in the garage, and some very nice seafood defrosted for your dinner tonight. How on earth do you manage to eat so well? I suppose you have a little more than the trusts put aside – maybe enough for a couple of holidays? Perhaps overseas holidays? Of course you do. And why not, there was a great deal of money taken from those poor people. I believe more than $10,000,000. Correct me if I'm wrong."

Gwen was really beginning to get into her stride. She was loving this whole encounter now. As Freya seemed to become more uncomfortable, Gwen reached over and filled up her employer's glass, then her own.

"The way I see it, Mrs. Simpson, is this. You could make up for some of the hardship you caused those poor people you stole from, by assisting me. I must fulfil the role of someone in need, a very worthy cause, you might say." Gwen leaned close to Freya and looked her in the eyes as she said, "Now, wouldn't that help to relieve you of some of that horrendous guilt you're carrying around?" She straightened up, "Course it would, course it would."

A silence followed and the two women sat looking at one another, each wondering what to do next.

Finally, Gwen stood and put her empty glass on the coffee table.

"Must be time I was off. There's so much for you to think about. I'll be back tomorrow, and I hope you'll have a proposition for me. Bear in mind that I'm not a greedy person, but I would like to live out my remaining years in something like the comfort you enjoy now. I would like to live in my own, small home without the threat of eviction hanging over my head. I'd need a healthy diet and one or two holidays each year. Occasionally I'd like to entertain some friends and buy new clothes. Nothing lavish, just a civilised income, and the opportunity to live out my remaining years with dignity. You get what I mean?"

Gwen had reached the door, and with her hand on the knob, she turned and smiled at Freya, "Try to get a good night's sleep, love; one shouldn't make important decisions when tired. Good bye."

Chapter Ten

Luke was not happy about having to do the deliveries, as well as keep the details of the one and only book. His hands always shook and his vision was cloudy. He found it hard to concentrate. They called the account book the 'Bible'; it was a complete history of all transactions carried out with clients and suppliers. Up until now, Luke had kept it up to date, but he had made several mistakes lately.

Vinnie was the one who found them. His face was red with rage when he confronted Luke. He grabbed him by the front of his shirt, and shook him so violently that what was left of Luke's teeth almost rattled.

"I'm takin' the shortfall out of your share, mate," Vinnie said. "I'm givin' you the benefit of the doubt this time, but I'm warnin' you, anythin' like this happens again, you'll wish you had never been born."

Luke was slowly coming to the realisation that his memory was not what it used to be. He was not going to panic about it, because one of his mates had told him once that if you could remember that you could not remember something, then there was nothing wrong with your memory. Luke had laughed about it at the time; now, it did not seem so funny. He had not been trying to cheat Vinnie. His mistakes in keeping the records were genuine, and it had taken Vinnie's threat to make Luke take stock of his situation. A couple of days after the altercation with Vinnie, Luke thought maybe he could hand the 'Bible' on to Grant.

When he suggested this to Vinnie, his boss said that would mean he would be doing almost nothing for his keep. Vinnie told him to lay off the drugs, wake up to himself, and get on with the job he was paid to do. Vinnie was not aware of the extent of Luke's brain damage, or he would have put him out of action before now. With Nat and Jason in the lab, and Luke, Grant and Artie on the street, they had a good system. Jason often did deliveries also, and between them, they had the business covered.

Luke was the only one available to do the overdue deliveries one afternoon, and he grudgingly shuffled out to the car. As he opened the driver's door, something caught his eye. He looked down. *What the?* Luke bent down and peeled a piece of paper from the sole of his shoe. He glanced at it, and was about to throw it on to the ground when, out of curiosity, he held it up in front of his eyes and squinted. There were four bullet points, in his son's handwriting.

1. Get out of that place

2. Get my own place

3. Get money

4. Find out about uni

Oh shit! He scrunched the note and threw it back down with the rest of the food scraps and rubbish in the passenger footwell. *So now he really is gettin' serious.*

Luke started the car. He turned on the radio, selected a heavy rock station, and gave it full volume. The doors of the car vibrated to the beat of the pounding bass, as he drove off to his first delivery. The explosion of sound reverberated inside the cabin. Luke could not hear himself think, which was exactly what he wanted. It was much easier to let the wall of sound overwhelm his senses, than try to work out what to do about things. He had enough on his mind just remembering where to go, without having to worry about what Jason was up to.

******

Jason was in the lab. His mood of late, had improved. He found Nat good to talk to and Nat was happy to help with anything Jason asked of him.

"Where do ya see yourself in five years time then, Jase?" asked Nat, as he bounced around on his toes.

"Out of here. Long gone. Haven't you noticed how Luke has been looking lately? He won't last much longer, and if you keep using the amount of stuff he does, you'll go the same way."

"I won't, I won't, mate. I've got plans for meself. You should get serious about gettin' away as well. When I came here, I was only gonna stay a couple o' days. I was between jobs and Luke invited me to hang out with youse."

"Well, that's how it goes, one day you wake up and find you can't think anymore. But by then it's too late – you have irreversible brain damage and you die a shit of a death."

"I know, I know," said Nat. "But that ain't goin' to happen to me. As soon as I get clear of a few debts, old ones, I'm outa here. You should come wiv me. We should go together. Take some product wiv us, and shoot off one day, real soon."

"And take drugs with us? How is that an escape? I can just imagine Vinnie lettin' us go. Pig's arse! No, you want to think outside the square for a change, mate. Pack your bags and go. He who hesitates is lost. Know what I mean?"

Nat shook his head in agreement and smiled. "You're right, ya know. As soon as I get my head sorted, I'm outa here. Wait and see."

"Sounds like an excuse to me, Nat, but you do what you like. Don't say you weren't warned."

"I know, mate, I know. I 'preciate your interest, I really do."

Nat scratched his head and his groin, then shuffled around the other side of the bench, tidying up and moving things around.

Jason knew all the signs. Nat was already unable to consider a life without drugs. He was still in his twenties, but looked much older. His skin was dry and wrinkled, and he was an unhealthy colour. He looked as if he weighed less than 60 kilograms. Jason shook his head; he had to acknowledge that Nat was a lost cause as well.

Tom Heart had taken over his father's private investigation business a little more than a year ago. He had planned to join his father sometime in the future, but then Tony Heart had been diagnosed with lung cancer. It was discovered at a check-up for a persistent, ticklish cough that just wouldn't go away, and so they both had to change their plans. It was eighteen months, since Tony had stood in the office of his GP, and heard the results of pathology tests that verified the diagnosis. Then it all began; the biopsies, the surgery, the chemotherapy, and finally, the radiotherapy. However Tony was terminally ill, presently at home, but soon to enter a hospice since there was no one to care for him now that Lottie, his wife, was dead. Tom had moved back home, but he had to earn a living and he kept long, irregular hours.

"I'm still getting a handle on this business, Dad, I can't see my way clear to work, and look after you as well," he said.

"Son, you're doing the right thing. I'm just sorry I couldn't be around to show you the ropes. We would have made a great team." Tony held Tom's hand, as his son stood next to him in his old recliner chair.

"What would you like for dinner, Dad?"

"Nothing, son. As usual, no appetite."

Tony turned back to the television and Tom made his way to the kitchen. Later that evening, they discussed the tactics to find Ron, Gwen's absent husband.

"You have one cruel sense of humour, my dear." Jim shook his head and listened to his wife's tale of how she and Charlene met on the path earlier that day.

"You have the poor girl at a disadvantage; she probably counts you as one of her friends, and here you're making fun of her." Jim threw back the best part of a glass of gin and tonic. He did not notice Di's observation of his consumption. Some days, he made no attempt to monitor his intake of alcohol. Some days, his thirst seemed insatiable.

"Well, I may be her only friend. If I hadn't been there, I really wouldn't have believed anyone could be so stupid. If her husband has any secrets, then I'm sure ten minutes alone with our friend, Pekalski, and he will have them all. I'm going to ring Frank and suggest he run into Miss Charlene, sometime after Mr. Markwell has left the premises and she is looking for someone to talk to."

Jim sighed, and thought, *Oh, no. Here we go again. Another bunch of suspicious characters and an as yet, unknown crime. That's all I need - more excitement and subterfuge of the kind that could only be found in Keeala Resort, crime capital of Queensland. God grant me the strength to keep doing this job.* Jim could see Di seemed to thrive on it, but all he wanted was a quiet life and time to play golf occasionally.

They walked together into the lounge and Jim turned on the television. He had heard enough intrigue for one day. He sat down with his glass of gin at his elbow, and watched the news. One half of the world seemed to be trying to kill the other half. *Ah, a little light relief,* thought Jim, as he sipped his gin and smacked his lips.

Di sat silently in her chair. She was absorbed in her recollection of events of the last couple of days. She had spent some time over the last two days at the home of Robert and Harold. They were busy putting the finishing touches to the novel they were writing together. Not many people could collaborate in the way these men did, but they had found the secret of give and take, and were rarely at odds with one another. Their story was of murder, drug running, abduction, and a road trip gone horribly wrong. Di had been asked for her input, and she had been flattered at the invitation. She was anxious to see if they could publish their tale.

Di also had a sense of waiting for something big to happen now. Her intuition was not often wrong, and the arrival of Vinnie and Charlene Markwell in the resort had triggered her suspicious mind. Her pulse raced every time their name was mentioned.

"I'm glad we have Frank living on the premises," Di said. "It's comforting to know we don't have to go further than the end of the road for help, if needed."

"I can't imagine what could go wrong around here that hasn't already happened," replied Jim. He was exasperated. He had become impatient with his wife's hunger for ever more excitement, and struggled to understand her. The thought of the Markwells being the source of more disruption and mayhem only filled him with horror. In the past, he had managed to make a joke of those things that were out of his control, but these days, more trouble just made him feel old and cranky.

Di had begun to notice Jim was not the happy-go-lucky man who had come with her to Keeala Resort. He talked less now and did not seem interested in the family or the residents, as he had in the past. At first, she thought it was only a passing mood, but now she could see he was more withdrawn, rather than less. Their holiday gone-wrong of last year had not brought about the improvement in his attitude that they had both hoped for. Di considered having a talk to Harold about Jim; Harold, particularly, was a very insightful man.

"Would you like a nice steak for dinner tonight, love?" Di asked.

"Whatever," he answered, without lifting his eyes from the television.

******

"Is your room comfortable?" asked Matthew. "Do you have everything you need?"

"Absolutely," smiled Ellen, as she stood back to allow Matt to enter the suite he had arranged for her in the Adelaide Hotel. "I assure you this is more luxury than I'm used to. Not that I'm suggesting it's too much. No, no, it's all lovely, thank you very much."

Matthew smiled. He had a great sense of happiness when he looked at Ellen. She filled his heart with warmth. He had never known a feeling like this before, and he wanted to hold on to it. He stood there for several minutes before he realised he was staring. She seemed to be waiting for him to speak next.

"Oh, so did you have a good flight over?" he asked.

"Sure, sure, please sit down." She pointed him in the direction of the lounge. They sat and stared at one another, neither knowing what to say next.

Matthew's mind began to race, yet he did not feel uncomfortable with the silence between them.

Ellen offered him a drink, but Matt declined.

"We really should get going; dinner starts in a few minutes," he said.

Ellen picked up her jacket. They walked out into the hallway and toward the elevator, looking at each other but neither speaking. She, wondering why she couldn't think of a thing to say, and he, not wanting to say a thing.

The following day, the sales conference began with an address by Andrew Sleighmen and the introduction of the sales people in the organisation. They all appeared in high spirits and it was the first time such a group had gathered since the death of the founder, Roger Sleighmen. There had been a great deal of changes in the short time since Andrew's father had died. A majority of the staff agreed that most of the changes were for the better, and although the country's economy had not improved, the sales of houses in the resorts and retirement villages had been consistent. The future of the industry looked bright, so jobs were secure and employees happy.

The day moved along in a positive atmosphere, with stirring talks, enthusiastic testimonials about success, and helpful hints for newcomers, like Ellen Brooks. All this stimulating talk appealed to her and it was the essence of what she thrived on. At lunchtime, she found herself seated next to a middle-aged man from New South Wales, who dropped into the chair she had been saving for Matthew.

"Oh, that chair is reserved, for a friend." She looked at the salesman, as he pulled the chair up to the table.

"Yes, I'm your friend," he smiled, "a new one." He held his grin and stared her down. Ellen's mind raced to think of what to say next.

"A lovely lady like yourself shouldn't be left alone with so many wolves around. I'm sure you've noticed them circling."

Matthew strode up behind Ellen and put both his hands on the back of her chair. "Ellen," he said, "I have someone waiting to meet you at the next table." He helped her to slide out of her place and then he nodded to the man, who looked them both up and down.

"How's it going, Brad? Still the state's top man, I see. You're a hard man to beat." Matt winked, and turned to direct Ellen to the next table.

"That was neat," she said. "I was beginning to wonder how I was going to get out of there. Not a real savoury character, I suspect." Ellen looked up at Matthew. *My saviour*, she thought.

"Not one of my favourite people, actually. We go way back, and I'm really surprised he's still with the Group. I'll tell you all about him one day, when we have time, but for now we have many more pleasant things to talk about."

They pulled their chairs close and played with the food in front of them. Neither really had an appetite; not a great deal of conversation either.

"What time is it?" Ellen asked Matt, as the crowd made its slow procession back to the elevator at the conclusion of the day's events.

"Still early," he smiled.

"How about a drink, before you go back to your room?" Ellen said quietly, as they stood shoulder to shoulder, looking anywhere but at each other. She had never felt shy in the presence of a man before. She had no idea what was going on.

"Thought you'd never ask," Matt smiled.

They closed the door of Ellen's room quietly, but not before Matthew put the DO NOT DISTURB sign on the outside.

Sometime during that night, Ellen and Matt became aware they were beginning a special relationship. It felt right, they were both at ease and stimulated in each other's company. They felt as if they were at the beginning of a long journey.

The next morning, they were late for the seminar.

"How time flies, when you're having fun," commented Matthew. He winked as they slipped into their seats at the back of the convention room.

Chapter Eleven

Freya stood, mouth agape, and watched her nemesis walk out the front door. She had felt secure, until now, that she and Brett would indeed live to see the fruits of their labour. She was also a practical woman, much like Gwen, and quickly realised she could not let this problem interfere with their plans. When she heard Gwen's car drive off, she came back to her senses and lifted the wine glass to her lips. As was her nature, she would face this situation and deal with it in a thoughtful and systematic manner.

Gwen did not sleep when she went home that night. There was too much to think about. Plans had to be made. Gwen had researched Brett Simpson and his wife Brenda on the internet, and now she thought she had the whole story.

The court case had played out in 2007 and Brett had been doing time since then. He had a few more years to do and the case appeared to be closed, but the money had never been recovered. Gwen believed it must be in someone's interest to be watching from a distance, and waiting for the man's release to see if he led them to the money.

Gwen made herself a cup of tea and sat in the tiny lounge of her shabby, little unit in western Brisbane. Most of her belongings were still packed and much of her new furniture was stacked in the garage. She could not picture herself staying for long where she was.

"Temporary accommodation," she told herself. "I'll be out of here soon."

She thought about Brett and Brenda, as she now called Freya. She guessed they must have a very trusting relationship and she began to think that one, or both of them, could be dangerous to someone threatening their future. They had survived so much, and still they had the money hidden and would no doubt get back together. If she were in Brenda's shoes, she would not let anyone interfere with her plans.

A very good reason to be cautious, she told herself, as she looked at the many pages of information she had printed out concerning the embezzlement. She took a sip of her tea and re-read the description of Brenda, as described by a reporter during the trial in 2007. Gwen could see that this woman, Freya, had made changes to her appearance since the trial. The case had created a great deal of speculation and interest at the time. It was alleged that Brenda was complicit, but it had not been proven. She had disappeared right after the case finished, although she was in big demand to tell her story to the press. She had given no interviews, and dropped out of sight very effectively.

Gwen wondered now about what other interested parties might be out there, who would value her intelligence as to where Brenda might be hiding out. Gwen pondered whether she stood to gain more from Brenda directly, or get a bigger slice of the pie by pointing her finger. The problem with the latter scenario was that she had no idea about whom the other interested parties might be, nor how to find them. *I'd need to be a ... a private investigator?* She froze in the middle of the room with her cup half way to her lips. *A private investigator who was not averse to making a little extra money himself, and knew his way around the criminal world. Well, I may know just the man.* She smiled and sipped her tea.

That man would have been very surprised to hear himself described as knowing his way around anything in the criminal world. He often felt out of his depth in his father's occupation, and he had developed a healthy respect for the old man since he became more aware of how much his father knew. He wished with all his heart that they could have worked together. Tom Heart carried a small tray into his father early the next morning.

"How's it going this morning, Pop? Think you feel up to giving me a few clues about this case I'm working on, before I have to leave?"

Tony Heart turned his head toward his son. He had not slept much, but seeing his son brought a smile to his lips.

"Sure, mate, sit down here and we'll talk it through."

Tom turned and grabbed his folder from the dining room table, then sat next to his father's bed. As he pulled a pen from his pocket, he looked at the grey face and wasted hands of the man who used to be so fit and vital. Tom desperately wanted to make a go of this business; he wanted his father to be proud of him, in the little time he had left.

******

The phone rang in the Heart Investigations office not long after Tom arrived and turned on his computer.

"Gwen Clarke here, Mr. Heart."

"Morning Mrs. Clarke, I was just thinking about you. I have a few leads to follow up today regarding Mr. Clarke, and I'm optimistic we will track him down by the end of the week."

"Good. However, I now have another little matter I'd like to discuss with you. I would like to see you as soon as possible."

"Of course, you can come round now if you like."

The call ended and Gwen sat for a few moments with the phone in her hand. She went over the situation again. She knew that to share her secret would lessen its value immediately, but, at the same time, she could probably not source the person she should be looking for by herself. Gwen reasoned that to simply blackmail Brenda may turn out to be very dangerous, because the woman would feel threatened, and may try to remove that threat.

Well, any money is better than none at all, half of something is better than all of nothing, she reasoned. She also felt more inclined to trust Tom Heart, rather than Brenda Simpson. Gwen gathered all her research information and stuffed it into her shopping basket. She left for her appointment with the private investigator.

Twenty minutes later, Tom listened as Gwen outlined her plan. For several minutes, he did not move in his chair. He stared at Gwen while she told him about her meeting with Brenda Simpson. This was way out of his league; he had no idea how to respond, and so he sat and hoped something would come to him.

"Well, so what do you think?" she asked, as she leaned toward the young man.

He shook his head and licked his lips. "I wish I knew," he said. "No one has ever suggested something so blatantly criminal to me before."

Gwen's chair flew back as she stood and grabbed her handbag.

"I can see I made a mistake, telling you. I thought you would appreciate the opportunity to earn some easy money, but I was wrong. Forget I mentioned anything." She turned, and then froze. "But now you know the story you can go off and take advantage of it yourself. Can't you? You don't need to share it with me; I'm just the fool that handed you an opportunity on a plate."

Tom shook his head and walked around his desk. With both palms held up in a sign on peace he said, "Please, please sit down. I have no intention of doing anything with this information. You caught me completely unawares, that's all, and I'm not yet an old hand at this business."

Gwen took a deep breath and searched the man's face for any indication of deception. She sat down again, and began tapping on the edge of the desk.

"What about a cup of tea or coffee? And please, call me Tom," he said, in some attempt to defuse the situation.

"Yes, good idea, tea please. A couple of biscuits too please, if you have any. I haven't eaten this morning."

"Sure, sure."

Tom walked into a tiny back room and turned on the electric jug. He lifted down an old biscuit tin from a shelf where he remembered having his father's favourite shortbread. *Possibly a bit stale,* he thought. A few minutes later, he carried a small tray back into his office, his mind racing, but still without a response for the woman. He handed a steaming mug of tea to her and pushed the plate of biscuits across the desk.

"Now, let me see if I have this correct. You say you know the identity of the wife of an embezzler, who is now serving time in jail. You say she is in possession of the $10,000,000. You are telling me that you have confronted this woman with your discovery, and as yet, no deal has been made. You also believe there will be a person or persons, somewhere out there, who will pay for this type of information."

"That is correct!" Gwen firmly nodded her head. "I know we could just go to the cops, or to the company that lost all the money, but I believe we stand to benefit a great deal more if we sell the information to the highest bidder."

"Deal with crooks, you mean?"

"Possibly; I can't see how I can find that person on my own. I wouldn't know where to look. I am prepared to split whatever we make 50:50 with you. What do you say?"

"Right now, all I can say is, I will have to think about it – overnight – and get back to you tomorrow. I'm not ruling it out at this stage, but I also don't know how I would go about sourcing this person. I can spend today continuing my search for Mr. Clarke, and do a little research of my own tonight. How does that sound?"

"Sounds alright, but remember I won't be able to put Brenda off for longer than tomorrow. She may take action herself to avoid any nasty consequences, and I'm sure I don't need to tell you that this whole discussion is private, absolutely."

"Of course." Tom stood and put his hand out to Gwen. "You are my client and anything you discuss with me is confidential."

Gwen turned to the door, stopped, and looked back over her shoulder.

"You know this could make us both rich. You may even be able to afford some fresh biscuits." The woman smiled broadly then chuckled and closed the door behind her.

Tom flopped down on to his chair and picked up his pen. He began to chew the end of it while he thought about what Gwen had said. He could not sit still, and eventually he picked up his keys and left the office.

"What are you doing back home so early, son, surely you haven't wrapped up that case already."

"Hi, Pop. No, I have a big problem and really don't have a clue what to do about it. I'm hoping you can give me a couple of ideas." He pulled up a chair next to Tony and sprawled on it, blowing out his frustration.

"I expect the nurse to be around here in the next hour, so let's have the conversation before we get interrupted."

"That new client of mine – I told you about her this morning – Gwen Clarke. She came in a while ago and blew my plans for the day."

Tom hesitatingly explained what Gwen had presented him with.

Tony whistled then began chuckling; it ended in a coughing spasm. He bent forward and tried to adjust his pillows. Tom leaned over and gave him a hand.

"Geez, son, you'd better give me all that again. I got a feeling I may know this bloke you're talking about."

When Tom finished his second recounting of the story, Tony was already nodding his head. "This really is an amazing coincidence, son," he said.

"There was a private dick, used to work with me occasionally, gone out of business now, I believe. Well, he was involved in the investigation back in 2006. Unofficially, that is. He discussed the case with me at the time, but it all ended very inconclusively. Actually, he was never paid for his part in the investigation. Anyway, as you know, they never found the money and the company that had employed him was not very generous, in the end. It's much more complicated than that, of course, and my mate was way down the line when payments were handed out. He was pretty pissed off about working for nix."

Tony coughed.

Tom handed him a tissue.

"In the office, you'll find a large, black note book – in the bottom drawer. That's if you haven't chucked it out. Well, cruise through that until you find the name, Charlie Savka.

That's our man and he's the one to consult. I'm presuming he's still alive and kicking. He'll be able to give you all the key names in the case of Brett Simpson, and I suspect he'd have a personal interest in getting something back after all these years. One other important thing though, son, I really don't recommend you get involved with any criminal elements to sell your information. Surely, the insurance company would be the best ones to deal with. Even then, I suspect you won't be staying on the right side of the law. Know what I mean?"

"Sure, I think so. Okay, well thanks, Pop, you've been a big help, and I'll call you later today if there's any update. Do you want anything before I take off again?"

"Yeah, give us a hand to stand up. I feel like sitting in the chair for a while."

Tony threw the covers back and swung his legs over the side of the bed.

Tom settled his father into a massage chair and handed him the controls.

"I'll leave you to set which mode you want, Dad. You know which setting you prefer."

As Tom left, he waved to Tony's nurse, who had just pulled up in the street and was waiting to park in the driveway after Tom left. Tom's head was full of questions and thoughts about Brett Simpson. He felt a little excited now; he could also see how much his father had enjoyed his job. Once again, he wished his father could be around for a while, he felt as if he was just getting to know him.

Inside the house, Tony's face broke into a smile of pure ecstasy, as the vibrations of the massage chair kneaded and slapped their way along his spine.

"Bugger!" he said, a few seconds later, as he heard the nurse call his name.

Chapter Twelve

Brenda Simpson was worried, but she was also very angry with herself for allowing the situation to occur in the first place. *Why the hell didn't I burn that letter from Brett? I left myself wide open.* She had done nothing but worry all night, and still she had no idea about what to do with the cleaner when she returned. She ruled out killing her, but only because she did not know how. She considered giving her a nice glass of wine and arsenic, but that too was a bit messier than she wanted. She finally considered just paying up, and hoping the woman would go away. She sat in her kitchen with an untouched cup of coffee in front of her, and mulled over how to go about paying up and assuring the woman would shut up afterward. There did not seem to be an easy answer. She knew if she could talk to Brett, he would know what to do.

Brenda could not afford to share her secret with anyone, least of all someone who would be quick to see the advantage in the situation. She considered ringing Gwen, then changed her mind. The one thing she felt sure of was the fact that Gwen was too greedy to share her knowledge with anyone else. She decided to sit tight and wait until the other woman got back to her. In the meantime, she would check her bank balance and see how much she had to play with, without touching the bulk of their carefully hidden haul.

Brenda's hands were shaking when she tapped out her customer number and password on her computer. The screen came alive with words and numbers. $450,000 was her balance in her working account.

"I thought it was more," she mumbled to herself, but she always had the security of knowing Brett had allowed for her to have more than enough to live on until he was released.

So, she thought, *I could give away half of that and would still have enough to get by for the next, almost three years.* She closed her computer down and started to tap her thigh as she wandered around the small lounge room. After some thought, she decided to offer Gwen $75,000 to begin with. That would give her room to negotiate and she would stop at $200,000. If that did not keep the cleaner quiet, then she would have to resort to another tack.

The suspense was beginning to unnerve her, and she now wished Gwen would make contact. She wanted to get this problem over and she knew she would not share it with Brett, on her next visit. He was already suffering enough.

Brenda sat and began to think of how to treat Gwen. *How can I keep the psychological, upper hand? How can I put the "fear of God" into the woman?*

The first thing that came to mind was a gun. *That would scare the shit out of her.* She almost laughed as the thought flashed through her head. After scrolling through several other ideas, she decided a gun was still the best deterrent. *Where to get one?* was the next question.

Without a good reason, she was unable to buy a gun and get a licence, but her mind kept drifting to a gun that her father had owned when she was young. *Whatever happened to it?* It was like running her fingers through files, thinking back, then forward again, from where she had last seen that gun. After her parent's death, her sister had taken the responsibility of attending to the sale of the house and disposal of all their effects. She rarely spoke to her sister these days, not since Brett went to prison. She was amazed when she realised it had been that long.

Her sister had been there for her, offering support, but as usual, Brenda had not shown the least interest. *Perhaps it's time I rang my little sister. Could do no harm anyway.*

Brenda consulted her file, and five minutes later she was talking to her sister, Lesley, who was surprised by the call.

"My God, Bren, I was beginning to think you didn't want to speak to me. I've left heaps of messages on your machine, did you get them?"

"I did love and I would like to come over today and see you. I need to explain in person about what's been happening to me."

"Sure, come over now, I'll be waiting. See you soon."

Later that day, Brenda sat with Lesley, sipping tea and trying to explain away her long absence. "Firstly, I have had to remain hidden. As you know, after the court case I was hounded by the press and I really had to take on a new identity."

"But why didn't you respond to my calls? I certainly wouldn't have exposed you."

Lesley looked at Brenda, who was close to tears as she dabbed at her nose.

"Depression. Really bad," said Brenda. "I've been taking medication and I'm so much better now, but for these last few years I just couldn't relate to anyone. No one could help me. I just had to wade through it myself. It's an awful condition. If you've never had it, you just couldn't understand how low you can feel. I really was on the brink of doing away with myself on several occasions. Thank God I survived, and I'm so much better now."

Brenda reached across and squeezed Lesley's hand.

Lesley rose and stood behind Brenda with her arm over her shoulder. She patted her with sisterly affection.

"I wish I had known, and all this time I had been taking it personally. I'm so sorry. What matters now is that we're both okay and you don't need to be alone anymore."

They talked about the past and even their childhood. They laughed over some of the standout events of the teenage years then talked about their mother and father.

Brenda finally apologised for not being there to help Lesley deal with their parent's estate.

"How on earth did you finally get rid of all that stuff? It must have been a horrific job to dispose of a lifetime of rubbish," said Brenda.

"Some of it is still down in the garage. Most of it went to the Op Shop, but a lot I just gave away to friends. I think it's actually time I took a look at that garage. No use keeping it just to take up space."

"Oh, let me. Please. Perhaps it would help with my healing, to go through things that belonged to Mum and Dad. You never know, there might be something I want to have for a keepsake."

"Why not. Do you want me to help you?"

"Certainly not. Some things just have to be confronted. It's high time I faced the fact that our parents are gone, and now is as good a time as ever. Is the garage locked?"

"Yes, I'll give you the key and leave you to it, if that's what you'd like. I'll call you at five and we can have a drink. Of course, you'll stay for dinner. I'm not letting you get away without a fight, this time," Lesley said, as she smiled broadly.

The sisters hugged and Brenda wondered why she had not contacted Lesley sooner.

******

Vinnie Markwell worried over his present situation. When he thought about the fact that he had a neighbour who was a cop, he cringed. It was not as if this was an ordinary community and one could ignore one's neighbours for no reason. Everyone was so damn friendly. It was impossible to go for a walk and not nod or smile or have a chat.

"I see you've made friends with that cop down the road," Charlene had said, when they sipped their morning coffee on the tiny, front veranda earlier that day.

"What are you talking about?" He glared at her as he asked the question.

"That bloke you were having a yarn to, a while ago. I saw you having a great old yak when I was collecting the mail. It's good to see you making friends with everyone. But I really never thought I'd see the day you'd be chatting to one of them."

"How do you know he's a cop?"

"Ask anyone. It's common knowledge."

Charlene had taken the coffee cups away and left Vinnie to worry about the incredulity of the situation.

He was making good money these days and there had been absolutely no problems recently. He had congratulated himself many times for the decision to make the present move. He had begun to feel good, almost normal, and when he consorted with his old friends from the drug house, he couldn't get away quick enough. The money was rolling in, and the group he had working for him were close knit and reasonably happy.

"S'pose it was a bit too good to be true," he muttered to himself. There was no way he could change the present situation, short of moving again. *Maybe it's the best place to be – right under his nose.* A smile spread across Vinnie's face when he considered the fact that a cop probably would not look so close to home for someone like himself. Vinnie could not believe that bloke could have known who Vinnie was when they had had their conversation. They had really hit it off. He considered that maybe they could be good friends. Vinnie slapped his leg and laughed as he pictured the two of them playing bowls together.

"Get real," he said, and released some of the tension he had been holding onto.

Then he brought himself up short when he remembered Charlene. *How the hell can I possibly keep her quiet?* When Vinnie thought of how she had gabbed off to the manager, he shuddered. He sat down on his recliner and thought hard about what it would take to keep her quiet. *To threaten or to bribe, that is the question now.* He knew he might only get one chance, so he had to get it right. He called from the lounge, and at the same time closed the sliding glass doors that led to the veranda.

"Yes my love," she answered sweetly, as she returned wearing an apron.

"What you got that on for?" he asked.

"What this? This apron? I'm doing some cooking, of course."

"You can't bloody cook. Don't come the raw prawn with me, girl"

"Who says I can't cook, eh?"

"I do, and I know from firsthand experience, don't I? That's why we eat out, or order home delivery every night."

"Well, I've been given a new recipe, and tonight, I'm cooking."

Vinnie shook his head. "Sit down, we have to talk."

"What's wrong?" Charlene looked worried; she straightened her apron and sat on the edge of the chair.

"Is something on the stove?" Vinnie sniffed.

"Oh yeah, you distracted me." She jumped up and ran to the kitchen.

"Just turn it off and come back here," he shouted behind her.

"Damn, look what you made me do already."

She came back and held out a burnt saucepan, full of onions, stuck to the bottom.

"Just put the bloody thing back and come in here."

He could feel himself losing it.

Charlene banged the saucepan back on the stove and turned it off. She returned to the lounge room.

"I'll have to start all over again now," she huffed, and sat down.

"I want your full attention."

Vinnie sat a few feet away, and looked closely at Charlene's face. "Do I have it?"

"Yeah, yeah, get on with it, will you."

"Don't speak to me like that. Just bloody listen."

"I'm listening, I'm listening."

Now, they were both getting feisty.

"The cop!" said Vinnie.

"The one down the road?"

"Of course the fuckin' one down the road. How many bloody cops do you know?"

"Well, what about him?"

"I don't want you to talk to him. Not ever."

"Ever?"

"No, not ever."

"What if he talks to me?"

"Don't give him the chance. If you see him, disappear. I want you to have no discussion with him. None at all."

"Yeah, okay, okay."

Charlene got up and was about to walk away.

"I'm not finished!" Vinnie yelled.

Vinnie grabbed her by the elbow before she could leave the room.

"What else? I've got stuff to do, you know."

"If I find out you have said a single word to that man, I'll shoot your dog."

"You wouldn't?"

Charlene's eyes and mouth flew open.

"I would. Right between the fuckin'eyes."

Charlene burst into tears. She ran to the bedroom, where her poodle lay curled up in a pink satin basket.

"Don't listen to him, my baby. I won't let that bastard touch you. I'd kill him myself first." Charlene looked up to see Vinnie fill the doorway.

"All you have to do is remember, girlie, not to open your trap to the cop. It can't be that bloody hard. Pretend you've lost your voice if he speaks to you, but don't say a bloody word. Hear?"

Charlene shook her head, then turned her back on the man she thought she loved.

"You cruel bastard," she mumbled.

He walked away and sighed. He really wished there could have been another way to deal with this situation.

"I'm just getting too bloody soft; that's my trouble," he said.

Chapter Thirteen

Luke returned from his deliveries, tired, and in a bad mood. He went straight to the laboratory and helped himself to a snort. He really needed that, and he sat down while it permeated through his body. Jason watched from the other side of the workbench, aware there was no point talking to Luke until he settled. He waited for Nat to come back with coffee for them both. Nat arrived, a couple of minutes later, with two mugs in his hands.

"Get it while it's hot, hey." He passed a cup to Jason, and noticed Luke, silently sitting on a chair with his head flung back and his hands on his knees.

"Oh, didn't see you there, mate," he said. He glanced at Jason to see if something was up.

"He okay, Jase?"

"I think so." Jason nodded and walked around and put a hand on his father's forehead. "Yeah, he'll be right in a minute."

The two sat on the floor, backs against the wall, and sipped their coffee. "You do see how bad he's gettin', don't you?" said Jason quietly. "I don't think he should be drivin'. Could end up killin' someone else, besides himself."

Nat nodded, and said "But what can ya do, mate. He's ya dad, and he doesn't listen to no one."

Jason stood and looked at his father again.

Luke's head had dropped forward and his limbs twitched.

"Help me get him to his bed will you please, Nat."

"Sure mate, sure."

Nat jumped up and between the two of them, and they walked him to his bed and helped him to lie down. They closed the door and went back to the lab.

"Pretty bad, hey, Jase. The old man. He looks real sick. It's a shame we can't do nothin' for him."

"Yeah. Listen, I'm goin' out for a while, mate. Can you keep an eye on things here, please?"

"No worries, mate. Go for it. I'll be here when ya get back."

Jason went to the car. He knew he could not visit Vinnie at the resort, but he had to talk to him. He grabbed his mobile phone, punched in Vinnie's number and waited.

"Yeah?" Vinnie growled on the end of the line.

"It's Jason, Vin. I'm a bit worried about Luke."

"What do you mean?"

"Well, he's out of it most of the time, and he's not fit to drive. I'm real worried he'll have an accident, and as you know, that would bring the cops to our doorstep, real quick."

Jason knew that any mention of cops would make Vinnie sit up and listen.

"Where is he now?"

"In bed. Me and Nat put him there, but he looks real bad."

"Shit! The stupid bastard is ready for the chop. I'm coming over."

Vinnie hung up.

Jason sat with his phone in his hand. Silent tears dripped from his eyes. All he could think of was how Luke used to laugh, or how he looked when he had given Jason his first pushbike. *So long ago, so long ago.*

Jason felt the great well of regret rise up inside him. He felt as though Luke was his responsibility and now he had failed him. Jason saw Vinnie's car drive by him, and pull up in the driveway of the house. Vinnie would not normally ever use his car for this kind of situation.

The two walked inside without speaking.

Vinnie walked to Luke's bedroom and stood in the doorway.

"Shit! Why the fuck didn't you tell me he was this bad?"

Jason stood behind Vinnie, and said, "I thought you knew." Jason backed away to the kitchen.

Vinnie followed him. He lowered himself down on to a chair and leaned toward Jason.

"I had no idea he was this bad. How much is he using?" Vinnie asked.

"I've got no idea, but he can't think straight most of the time, and we have to do all his work. Today he went out to do the deliveries, and it was more than he could handle. He's lucky to have got home in one piece. We should take him to hospital."

"Nah, mate, too many questions. He should stay here and we look after him. I know where we can get something to knock him out, but then we'll have a body ..."

Jason jumped up and grabbed Vinnie by the front of his shirt.

"That's all he is to you, isn't it? A bloody nuisance, an inconvenience." Jason was shaking and spitting, his face red as his breath came in gasps. Slowly he let go of Vinnie's shirt and turned to the wall. He banged his fists and cried loudly.

Vinnie looked at the boy's back and shook his head. He had known father and son for almost fifteen years and did not want to see it end like this either. Vinnie stood and walked over to Jason and touched him on his shoulder.

"Take it easy, son," he said. "We don't want to watch Luke suffer any more than you do." He turned Jason to face him, and hugged him to his broad chest.

Jason sobbed and then went limp and flopped in a nearby chair.

Vinnie stood behind the chair with his hand on Jason's shoulder, for once at a loss for words.

"I can't let him go on like this, Vin, there must be some way we can help him. He's not a bad person, he's weak, but not bad. He never hurt anybody and he's tried to be a good father to me."

"I know, son, I agree, but I can't see what's left open to us. He's used drugs since I met him years ago, and that habit's increased. Its times like this I wish I had nothing to do with any of it. Some people can use drugs, for a bit of a hit, and then there are others, like your dad, that just can't leave the stuff alone. Let's take another look at him."

The three men walked back to Luke's bedroom and filed along the side of his bed.

Jason leaned down close to Luke's face.

Luke's breathing was very shallow and rapid. Rivulets of sweat ran down his face and fell in drips off his chin. His whole body twitched.

Jason began to cry again.

"I can't just do nothing; I have to take him to the hospital."

He turned to see Vinnie nodding.

"Okay. We'll do it," said Vinnie. "You take him in and leave him at the emergency department. All you have to do is drive him in to the entrance and park out front. Then run in and tell them you found him in the street. As soon as they get him on a stretcher, you drive off. Tomorrow, we'll ring up and see how he's going."

Jason could see they had no other choice. He turned and picked up his car keys. The three of them carried Luke's limp body out to the old car.

"I'm comin' wiv ya mate," said Nat.

He jumped into the passenger side and Jason got behind the wheel.

Vinnie stood and looked after them as they drove off. He had a feeling that something was changing. Luke was dying and that marked the end of an era. He walked back to the house and made sure everything was secure, before he drove home with a great sense of emptiness, also dread. He had no idea he had harboured any sentimental feelings for Luke, before this day.

Nat rang Vinnie an hour later, as he and Jason sat in the car in the driveway of the drug house. He said they had taken Luke to the hospital and both run in to seek help. The attendants had had brought a trolley out to the car, and Luke had been wheeled inside. They had driven away. Nat had driven back.

"Do you want me to come back there now?" Vinnie asked.

"No, I'll handle Jase from here, mate."

Nat rang off, and went round to help Jason inside.

******

Detective Frank Pekalski had seen Vinnie's car leave the resort. He knew his colleagues would tail the car, so he made contact to find out the result of the surveillance. He was told Markwell had travelled to an unkempt house, a short distance away, where he entered. A few minutes later, he had come out, accompanied by two young men carrying a person who appeared unconscious. That person had been placed in a vehicle, not Markwell's, and driven away. The detectives decided to follow the second vehicle and tailed it to the hospital. Pekalski grimaced when he heard that the two men had virtually dumped the unconscious man at the emergency entrance and had left the scene hurriedly. They had returned to the house.

Pekalski rang the hospital and was informed that Luke had died, shortly after his arrival in emergency. He had to decide whether to suggest they move on the house now, or wait for an opportunity to apprehend them in the act of dealing. There was so much more to gain if they could follow this group to other contacts. He decided to wait, but rang his superior to keep him informed.

"Patience," said his boss. "We can do better than this; we're right on to them now. Just a couple more weeks and I reckon we'll get the lot."

Pekalski had to agree, but he always worried when they got this close to a bust and had to just sweat it out.

He saw Vinnie's car return and he wondered what he could do to push things along. He felt restless all afternoon.

******

The Sleighmen Group sales convention was a great success, according to the new Managing Director.

"Worth every cent," he said to Chief Executive Officer, Andrew Sleighmen.

A small group stood in the fast, emptying convention room at the end of the fourth day. The new managing director came well qualified, and Andrew hoped his worth would be borne out in the coming months, certainly by the next financial year. He knew he was taking another risk by employing this highly qualified young man, but so far his decisions had proven themselves and he was becoming ever more confident in his own ability.

Ellen Brooks and Matthew Weatherlee would be going home, radically changed; not because they had gained so much from the sales convention, but because they were both in love. They stood, facing one another in Ellen's room, next to their travelling bags. Neither knew how to say goodbye, or how they could possibly take their leave from one another, now that they had discovered their true feelings.

"Will you call me as soon as you get to the airport?"

Matthew reached for Ellen's hand and drew it to his lips. Their eyes locked as they leaned together.

She nodded, and whispered, "What about you? What will you do today after I leave?"

Matthew sighed and blinked rapidly as he tried to clear his vision.

"I don't feel much like working, but they need me here for another couple of days."

A broad grin spread across his face. He bent down and picked up both their suitcases.

"We'd better move or you'll miss your flight."

He dropped the bags again and grabbed Ellen by the arms; he pulled her close to him and buried his face in her soft hair.

"I'm going to miss you," he said.

She hugged him back and sighed deeply.

"We aren't going to be much good to anyone like this," she said.

She lifted her small bag to her shoulder and Matt picked up the bags again. They walked to the lobby in a silence that continued all the way to Adelaide airport.

Ellen felt like a different person when she touched down in Brisbane. As promised, she rang Matt and he had been waiting for her call.

"I'll ring you this evening." Matt said as he leaned back in his chair in the office. His thoughts were not on his work at all.

Chapter Fourteen

Tom Heart had no problems tracking down Charlie Savka. He found him exactly where his father had suggested.

"Come in and take a seat, Tom. I can't believe Tony would have a son your age. How time flies, huh?" Charlie offered Tom a drink, whisky, but Tom declined and watched as Charlie dashed a big shot into a glass for himself. "Sit down, man, can't have you standing round like a shag on a rock."

It took Tom a few minutes to bring Charlie up to date with his father's terminal illness, and his own involvement in his father's now flagging business.

"I didn't really expect to be running the business, single-handedly. Well, to be honest, I had no idea I'd be working in it at all, until I found out how hard jobs were to get for a not very talented artist." Tom smiled.

"I'm real sorry to hear about Tony, but I'm guessing that's not what your here for, son. So, tell me why I find you sitting on my lounge now," said Charlie.

"Well I was talking to Pop about a new case that turned up on my doorstep and he suggested the best person for me to contact would be you. He said the name of Brett Simpson would ring some bells, and you may be interested in joining me on the case."

A smile spread across Charlie's face at the mention of Simpson. Tom could see he had the other man's undivided attention, as he told Gwen Clarke's story. Charlie nodded constantly, and as the story continued, he became more restless. When Tom had finished, Charlie started to ask questions. He wanted to know every detail Tom knew about Gwen, and about the embezzlement case.

"I will have that drink now, if you don't mind Charlie," Tom said. He felt drained.

"Course, mate." He got up and splashed whisky into another glass. His attention to his own thoughts distracted him, and when he handed the glass to Tom, he almost missed the young man's waiting hand.

"That sort of information is very valuable, you know," Charlie said. "If anyone could have followed Brenda Simpson after the trial, they would probably have recovered the money by now, but she was better than Houdini. She completely disappeared, dropped out of sight without a trace. I personally spent six weeks following false leads and ended up drawing a complete blank. I had nothing to show for all that effort at the end. To make matters worse, I never was paid by the bastards at the insurance company. They still owe me."

He stood up, walked over to the whisky bottle again, and hefted it back to his glass.

"Gees, what I wouldn't give to at least get back what's owing to me."

"Maybe you can," said Tom, as he too served himself another drink.

They were both well on the way to getting over the limit. Fortunately, Tom thought of this and sipped his second glass slowly.

"Do I get the impression you might like to join me on this case, then?" he asked.

Charlie stopped as he drew level with his chair. He turned and looked at Tom, and for a moment, he said nothing. He appeared to be thinking. He sucked in his breath between his clenched teeth and sat down. He swilled the liquor in his glass and stared at it.

A clock ticked. Tom imagined it was getting slower and slower.

"Yes, I do believe I would, Tom, I do believe I would."

Again, he was lost in thought. He took a small sip from his glass. Tom waited again. Tick – tock – tick – tock.

"Right, let's talk business, eh?"

Charlie jumped out of his chair and started pacing about the room. A few minutes later, they came to an arrangement. Charlie wanted to meet Gwen.

Tom suspected she would not be too happy about having anyone else in on the deal, but she would have to accept it. This was the only way he could track down that money and they all stood to benefit.

"I'll come in to your office tomorrow morning, son. I don't know whether you are aware, but I no longer have a licence. Any work I do for you is off the record."

"Can you get your licence back?"

"No, no way. It's a long story and I'll not bore you with it now. Maybe some time when your dad is with us we could talk about old times. Please give him my regards, and thank him for thinking of me. Hopefully I'll see him soon."

As he drove home, Tom wondered about the best way to get Gwen on side. He had a sense of increased confidence now, almost as if he had joined the big boys' club. He sensed he could gain a great deal of respect for old Charlie. He was looking forward to working with him.

******

The following day, Jason was up early. He had spent a restless night. He was anxious to ring the hospital and find that Luke had improved. Maybe they would let his father come home. He wondered about the best way to get this information over the phone. He rang, but had no luck at all; the staff could give no information. He decided he would have to go into the hospital, maybe give a false name and tell them he was the interested 'Good Samaritan' who had found Luke lying in the street, and he wanted to know how the man was doing.

He picked up his car keys, and walked out through the side veranda, where two of the boys were watching television. He could not possibly have avoided hearing the news item; the volume was up, as usual.

"An anonymous middle aged man was yesterday brought into the emergency department of the hospital suffering a drug overdose, and has died within minutes of his arrival. Information is sought ... "

Jason staggered and turned to stare at the television. Grant and Artie looked at Jason as they too had grasped the full meaning of the report. Jason stood and shook his head. He tried to speak. His lips moved but nothing came out.

Artie left the room and came back with Nat, who went straight up to Jason and helped him to sit down.

"I'll need Vinnie's number, mate," said Nat.

Jason put his hand into his pocket and pulled out his mobile phone. He handed it to Nat. He hung his head and put his hands over his face. His eyes were dry but he began to cough, and then hyperventilate.

"Calm down, mate, look at me."

Nat knelt down and looked up into Jason's face and he tapped him on the cheek, then, a small slap, and then another one. Finally, Jason made eye contact with Nat and he took a deep breath.

"I'm okay, Nat. It's okay. He's dead. Did you hear it? My dad's dead and no one was even with him. He died right after we left him. He's been dead all night. He's dead Nat!"

"I know, but he's outa pain now, mate. He was sufferin' somethin' awful. You didn't want him to go on like that, did ya? He's at peace now. He's happy. He's got lots a old mates to meet up wiv, up there. He'll be happy now Jase. Honest."

Jason acknowledged with a shake of his head, then stood up and went to the bathroom. Nat looked at the mobile phone and wondered how to find Vinnie's number. Artie noticed his dilemma.

"Give it to me, you idiot," he said, as he snatched the phone. A moment later, he was speaking to Vinnie. "It was on the television, Vin, just a minute ago. ... Yeah, Jase is not too good himself. ... Yeah, we'll all keep an eye on him till you get here ... Okay." He handed the phone back to Nat and they both walked into the bedroom to see Jason stretched out on his bed, staring at the ceiling.

Nat turned to Artie and said, "You stay an' keep an eye on him, Art. I'm goin' to check a couple a things." Nat went to the lab to make sure everything was in order before Vinnie arrived. He would have to check the messages too, but decided to give that job to Grant, as he hated most technological instruments like smart phones and computers. He saw himself as more the hands on type of operator, and a decision maker. Unfortunately, the others just saw him as stupid.

"We're all going to have to do some extra work round here for the time being," announced Vinnie, when he walked into the house about half an hour after he had spoken to Artie. He strode to Jason's room and saw that he had gone to sleep. He gently closed the door.

"That's good, for the time being," he said to Nat. "Let him be."

"I gave him a sedative, I did. He needed a rest. I dissolved a couple a pills in some juice and feed it to him. He'll be right when he wakes up."

"Bloody hell, mate. What the fuck did you give him? Can't you lot do anything without drugs?"

"Sorry, Vin, I was just tryin' to help. The boy was in a bad way, you shoulda seen him."

"Yeah, yeah, okay. Let's go to the lab and see what needs doin' today."

The four men went to the lab and discussed the division of the work. Vinnie could see he needed to stay around to make sure things ran smoothly. He also wanted to be sure that Jason did actually wake up. One thing Vinnie did not need was another body. *Speaking of bodies*, he thought, *what the hell am I going to do about Luke? Shit, that's all I needed.*

It was past seven that evening when Jason finally walked out of his room, rubbing his eyes. Vinnie nodded at the sight of him and then ushered him into the kitchen and sat him down.

"Put that water on to boil," he said to Nat, who was busy filling his mouth with the Chinese fried rice. Vinnie had shouted for their meal.

"Last of the big spenders," Artie had commented when they saw what Vinnie had come back with.

"How are you feeling, mate?" Vinnie looked closely at Jason.

"A bit better thanks. I'm thirsty and I've got a bit of a headache, but I do feel better." He sighed deeply. "When I woke up I was just lyin' there thinkin' about Dad. It really is the best thing that could have happened to him, considerin' how bad he was. At least he just went to sleep and then it was all over. He never believed in goin' to gravesites and so on. He figured when he was finished with his body, he'd just step out of it, like an old suit. So, I'm not even worried about a funeral. He wouldn't have wanted one. Wherever he is now, it couldn't be worse than where he was when he was here.

Drugs are evil. That's what I believe and I've got to get out of this business."

Vinnie opened his mouth to speak, but stopped as he saw Jason raise his hand and shake his head.

"No, don't say a thing to me now, Vin. We can talk about this tomorrow, but I'm getting out, mate, no matter what you say. I'm getting out."

He accepted the cup of strong tea from Nat, who was listening to the conversation.

"Thanks Nat. And we all should do the same. It's a shit of a life. And then you die."

Vinnie stood up and left the room. They heard the squeal of tyres as he drove away.

Chapter Fifteen

Ron Clarke was missing the attention Gwen had always given him. He had never realised how little he had done for himself, even to laying out his clothes, so Ron never had to worry about what to wear.

He had been living in the Perth Hotel for two weeks, and when he got around to checking his bank balance, he was astonished to find how much it was costing him. He had never used a computer and always got his updates from Gwen. On this Monday morning, he decided it was time he went to the bank. It had not occurred to him at any time that his wife would pursue him across the country, or that she would have the means to track him down.

Ron had not changed banks, but simply opened another account in his name, and transferred all their money to the other account. Forging Gwen's signature on the transfer form had not been a problem.

When Ron had left, Gwen suspected that Ron had forged her signature, and she had contacted the bank, requesting to be informed if her husband made contact with them. Fortunately, the bank manager had been very sympathetic to Gwen's situation and had agreed to co-operate. Forgery was a criminal offence and the police were informed.

Tom Heart received a phone call from Gwen's bank manager to say Ron had been into a branch in Perth, about half an hour earlier.

"Thanks very much," he said. He put the phone down and tapped the desk with his pen. *So, our friend is in Perth, but for how long, and where? Maybe it's time I took a plane ride.* He made a booking on the next flight out of Brisbane. He then rang Gwen to tell her his plans.

"But what about Brenda?" she asked. "Don't we have to keep an eye on her?"

"We do, and we are. I haven't had an opportunity to discuss that with you yet, but rest assured, it's all in hand."

"What's that supposed to mean?"

"It means, don't worry. Since I last spoke to you, I've made contact with an interested party and we are watching her closely."

"We? Who's we?"

"Look, you may get a visit from a friend of mine while I'm away. His name is Charlie Savka. He's okay. He's going to help us. I'll keep you updated and our agreement stands. You get half, and I get half, and if I have to split my half, then them's the breaks, as they say. Have a good day, Mrs. Clarke.

I've got to get out of here to get an afternoon flight. I'll be in touch as soon as I have anything to tell you."

Tom arrived in Perth later that evening. He booked into a motel not far from the CBD. He sat in his room, going through the phone book and the accommodation guide. He tried to keep in mind what Gwen had told him about Ron's behaviour; 'not too smart', she had said, 'and probably still going under his own name'. Tom began his search.

"My name is Ron Clarke, and I have a booking for later today." That was Tom's opening statement to the people he contacted at every form of transport Ron might have booked on. Within an hour, he was almost certain that Ron had not hired a car, or booked on to any other form of transport. He decided his quarry must still be somewhere in Perth.

******

Ron was still in Perth, and he was none too happy. He was miserable. He had left the Perth Hotel and now sat on his bed in a cheap motel room, on the outskirts of town. He wondered what the hell he was doing there. *Why did I think this was all going to be such fun*, he thought. *I've got no one to talk to, no friends and nothing to do. Bloody hell, this was supposed to be the best time of my life.* He realised he was missing Gwen. He put his hand on the phone with the intention of ringing her, and then hesitated. *She's probably got the shits with me good and proper.* He made himself a cup of coffee and walked around the room, trying to decide what to do next. He imagined himself sitting on a lounge, by a pool, with several young girls fawning over him. He laughed and realised it was never going to happen. The money he had would run out eventually and then what would he do, he wondered. Ron lay on the bed and fell asleep. Thinking really did his head in.

******

Gwen sat at her computer, but stared past it to the brick wall that was her view from the small window in her lounge. She thought it was symbolic of where she was in her life right now. *Up against a brick wall and I've painted myself into a corner.* She knew she had shown her hand as far as Brenda Simpson was concerned, and she would have to act on that situation, now that she had involved other people. There was no going back, and she was beginning to lose her nerve. She was actually wishing Ron was still around to lighten the situation. In the past, his sense of humour always managed to lift them out of even the deepest holes. She wondered if Tom had come any closer to finding her wayward husband. For some strange reason, she had ceased to be angry with Ron. Maybe it was because she was now distracted with Brenda Simpson, she thought, but she was remembering some of the good times she had shared with Ron, and she wondered if he had taken up with another woman. She quickly dismissed that thought and looked down at the keyboard in front of her.

There was a knock on her door. Gwen responded.

"I'm Charlie Savka, Mrs. Clarke. Tom Heart said you would give me a little of your time."

"Oh, yes, come in Mr. Savka."

For the next hour, the two sat and talked about Gwen's involvement with Brenda Simpson, and Charlie put forward ideas about how they could all benefit, while bringing the woman to justice.

Gwen said, "You know, Charlie, I feel a lot better now we've talked. It's as though we are doing a community service and not a criminal act, as Tom has suggested."

"Indeed, and why shouldn't we be rewarded for our efforts? There are some very unscrupulous people around who would have blackmailed the woman, and then just let her go. No, we will be sure her crime reaches the authorities, after we have been rewarded for our work. I plan to deal with the insurance company involved, and they will pay up this time, or else."

******

Tom had no idea where to start when he opened the accommodation directory and began his search for the elusive Ron Clarke. *Alphabetically,* he thought, *it's as good as any other way, but I've got a feeling this is going to be a long day.*

He was down to the R's when he hit the jackpot.

"Rellington Inn," the receptionist answered. "Yes, Mr. Clarke is staying with us, can I connect you with him."

"No thank you, I'll call and see him myself," Tom slammed the phone down, grabbed his wallet and dashed to the taxi stand out the front of the motel. It was a ten-minute ride, but he didn't take in the scenery; he was fully occupied with his plans of how he would handle Ron.

Tom was not prepared for the sight that met him at the motel room door. A bedraggled, pathetic looking person opened the door and simply stared at him.

"Yes?"

"Mr. Clarke?"

"Yes."

"My name is Tom Heart, and I have been employed by your wife to find you. May I come in?"

Ron made a half-hearted effort to close the door on the other man, and then to Tom's surprise, Ron stood back and allowed him to enter.

"So how'd you know where to find me?" Ron sat on the side of the bed, while Tom sat facing him on the only chair.

"Couldn't give away trade secrets, now could I?" Tom smiled. "Mrs. Clarke has been very worried about you, sir. She has been concerned that perhaps you've met with an accident, or even been kidnapped. Oh, yes, very worried. Is there some reason you haven't contacted her?"

"I've been in a very bad mood. A mid-life crisis, you might say."

"Bit old for that, don't you think, sir?"

Ron did not answer but got up and went to the bathroom. He slammed the door behind him. Tom looked around at the depressing room and wondered why Ron had chosen such a lonely place.

After a couple of minutes, Ron came out of the bathroom. He had washed his face and wetted his hair back from his forehead.

"So what can I do for you?" he asked, with renewed vigour. He swallowed a gulp of water from the plastic cup in his hand.

"You could start by ringing your wife, sir. She is in great need of hearing that you are okay. After that, you will need to sit down with me and work out an arrangement whereby you return the money that belongs to her. I believe it will be as simple as transferring the money to an account in Mrs. Clark's name. Unfortunately, you may have to face charges for forgery. Not a smart move to sign your wife's name."

"Has she told the police yet?"

"She has. She had no alternative since you didn't make contact with her, and she was left without an income."

"She could go back to work."

"She did, but it's not a good substitute for retirement, wouldn't you say?"

Ron sighed. He stood, punched his fist into his open palm, and walked in circles around the small room.

Tom no longer felt at risk from this man; he even began to feel sorry for him. He sat silently and watched while Ron moved around, obviously considering his position. Tom could see it was a difficult process.

Ron stopped moving, looked at Tom, and said, "I'll ring her." He reached for the phone and began to dial a number.

"Hold it," Tom said.

"What?"

"Your wife doesn't live there anymore."

"Why not?"

"She couldn't afford to pay the rent," Tom said smugly.

"Oh, so where is she now?"

Tom dug into his pocket and pulled out a notebook. He flipped it open and handed it to the other man.

Ron stared at the numbers as though they were hieroglyphics. He eventually dialled the number. When Gwen answered, he was silent.

"Hello, hello. I can't hear you. Is anyone there?"

Tom could hear Gwen's faint voice from where he sat. He could sense the exasperation.

"It's me, Ron."

There was silence for a few seconds on the other end, then, "Ron? Hang on, I've got to sit down."

"Sorry I haven't rung, but I had a few problems I had to sort out, and I haven't been feeling too well either. I needed to get away by myself for a while. You know what I mean?"

"Sure, Ron, I know exactly what you mean. And you had to take all my money with you, as well. It wasn't enough to just take your own, but you had to take mine as well. You didn't ring me once and you forced me to have to go back to work, scrubbing for a living. I know exactly what you mean, you bastard." Gwen burst into tears.

Ron stared at the phone. He was speechless.

Tom took the receiver from him.

"Gwen, it's me, Tom. I'm here with your husband and I'm confident we can work something out. Don't you worry now, take it easy. Has Charlie been to see you yet? ... Good, good. Well look, I'll talk to you again before I leave Perth, and you'll need to email me your bank details, so we can have that money returned to your account. Rest easy, it's all going to work out. Ron is being most co operative. Goodbye."

Tom hung up and turned his attention again to Ron, who was now sitting on the side of the bed again, with his head almost in his lap.

Chapter Sixteen

Vinnie Markwell returned to his home at the resort. He was a worried man. He could see he was going to lose Jason and maybe even one of the other blokes as well. This did not suit him at all; he had worked too hard to arrive at where he was, to give it all away just when he was making some real money. When he walked in the front door, he found the house empty. He cursed under his breath.

Charlene returned a few minutes later. "You look tired, babe," she said. "Can I get you some breakfast?"

"Where have you been?"

"Having coffee at the club house with a couple of friends." She looked at him and smiled.

Vinnie was glad to see Charlene had forgotten about their previous altercation. He acknowledged to himself that she was never one to hold a grudge. She was quick to forgive and forget.

"What friends?"

"A couple of very nice ladies I play Bingo with. I'm pretty good at that, you know."

"I will have something to eat. Seeing as you can cook now how about some bacon and eggs?"

"Yes sir." Charlene hurried past Vinnie into the kitchen. "Scrambled or fried?" she called out.

"Fried, soft. Don't cook the hell out of it – and make that bacon crispy. I can't stand fatty bacon."

He flopped on to his favourite reclining chair and recommenced his worrying. Vinnie knew he would have to make changes at the house now. Nat, Artie, and Grant were all users, and couldn't be trusted to be left alone at night, or any other time for that matter. He wondered how they had managed this long, seeing Luke was always out of it and there was only the kid. Vinnie surmised that he had underestimated Jason, and that he must have been the glue that had held the place together.

"He's not going anywhere," he mumbled to himself.

A few minutes later, Charlene called from the dining room table. She had laid the table with tea and toast and a big plate of bacon and eggs.

Vinnie sat down. "Where's the bloody salt?" he asked.

She turned back to the kitchen and returned with salt and pepper. She smiled as she put them down gently on the table.

"Where's the tomato sauce? Can't expect anyone to eat eggs without sauce, for Christ's sake."

A small frown spread across Charlene's face as she turned to the kitchen again. She returned with the sauce.

Vinnie vigorously shook the salt and then splashed tomato sauce onto his fried egg. He lifted knife and fork, cut into the bacon, and carried it to his mouth. He spat it back on to the plate.

"Are you deaf as well as stupid? I specifically asked for a soft fried egg! This bloody thing is as hard as a rock. Go and get me an axe, and I'll give it a go with that."

The corners of Charlene's pursed lips turned down and her eyes narrowed. She went to the kitchen and returned a few seconds later. Her body tensed and the knuckles on both hands turned white on the handle of a frying pan.

Vinnie turned back to his plate and again pushed around his food.

"This is nothing like crispy bacon, woman; didn't your mother teach you to do a single thing?"

Vinnie's mouth was open, ready to continue to voice his criticism when the pan came down on his head. His whole surprised body fell forward and his face landed in the middle of his plate. His attacker stood behind him ready to hit him again if he moved, but he was out for the count. He started to breathe heavily, and blew bubbles in his tomato sauce.

"Taste alright now, fatso?"

Vinnie hated that name. He was very sensitive about his weight. He had developed a sweet tooth in recent times and the good life had begun to show. Charlene picked up some of the things from the table, and she continued until the table was cleared, except for Vinnie's plate. Finally, she brought a folded towel and lifted his head by the hair. She quickly pulled the plate out and put the towel under his face. He moaned and sat back, his head rolling from side to side, he continued to groan and put his hand to the lump that was developing on the top of his head,

"What the fuck happened?"

He slowly pushed his chair back and saw Charlene as she stood and looked down on him.

"I hit you," she said, with some degree of satisfaction.

"You? What for?"

He tried to stand but crumpled back to his seat. He tilted his head back to see her.

"No one says anything about my mother and gets away with it. Not even you. Next time, go to the fast food joint down the road for breakfast. Complain to them. See how they feel. Or, better still, get your own. I'm going for a swim."

Charlene turned and headed for her bedroom. She reappeared a few moments later in a fussy swimsuit, a towel over her arm.

"You can wash up," she said. "I've done enough domestic chores for one day."

Vinnie watched her walk out. He breathed a sigh of relief. Anger was boiling in the pit of his stomach but he did not have the energy to pursue it. *First Jason, and now Charlene. I can't take a bloody trick.* He wondered if his judgement of people was not all he had previously thought it was. He ground his teeth and slammed the table with his fist.

Slowly, Vinnie stood and made his way to the kitchen; what he saw, took his breath away. *No amount of home cooked food could be worth this.* He surveyed the mess, then rolled up his sleeves.

******

Ellen Brooks returned from Adelaide, and was at the office by 8am the next day. She was ready to come to grips with all the loose ends that waited for her. She was happy to find everything in good order. She had guessed Di would not leave her a mess to sort out, but she was pleasantly surprised at how well organised everything was. She read the page from Di on her desk, and set about following up the leads that Di had left her. The manager had made one sale and completed another that Ellen had commenced.

She could not have asked for more. Ellen picked up the phone to ring Di, just as the woman walked in the door. They hugged then leaned back and examined each other.

"You look well satisfied with yourself. And so you should, I found everything in peachy order." Ellen smiled broadly and they both sat down.

"And you look ... I'm not sure, but you look different. Very healthy, or is it happy?"

"Both," answered Ellen. "The convention went off just great, and the weather was perfect. I slept well and ate everything not nailed down."

"In other words, you're in love!" Di clapped her hands together then threw back her head and laughed. "Don't lie to me now, I know all the symptoms."

Ellen sat comfortably back in her chair and allowed the smile to spread slowly across her face. She bit her bottom lip and nodded.

"Matthew Weatherlee, I presume." said Di. It was more of a statement, rather than a question.

"Who else? We had a great time and ... I believe he feels the same way about me. He says he loves me ... so I can't ask for more than that. Can I?"

"Oh, yes indeed you can. There's always getting married. You can ask for that."

"Well, I do believe I'll wait until I'm asked. I know how Matthew feels about his mother. He has a sense of responsibility toward her. I plan to visit her in the next few days and introduce myself. They obviously had a struggle when he was young, and there is a strong bond between them."

"Yes, that's the impression I had, too," answered Di. "I think she should be very proud of her son."

"Now," said Ellen, "tell me how things have been around here this past week – off the record, I mean."

"Hell, where to start? Sales, or residents, or gossip?"

"Oh, gossip please, of course."

The women laughed and huddled together. They were still giggling when Detective Inspector Frank Pekalski put his head in the door and interrupted them.

"So this is where you all hang out. I should have known I'd find all the staff in one place. May I come in?"

"Take a seat," said Di, with a sweep of her hand.

Pekalski pulled out a chair and sat.

"Jim's not in his office," he said. "I wanted to discuss a few matters with him."

He looked at Di, a soft smile creasing his rugged face.

"He's out today, Frank. Can I help you?"

"Unfortunately, no. Secret men's business, I'm afraid. I'll catch up with him tomorrow, if that's okay."

"Sure," Di answered.

Pekalski departed and the women went on to discuss the sales convention in Adelaide.

******

Frank waited outside Jim's office the next morning.

"Morning, Frank."

Frank saw Jim check his watch, as he approached the office.

"Hi, Jim. I know I'm early – just wanted to catch you before I left for the city. Got a couple of minutes?"

"Sure, mate, come in."

Frank started to tell Jim the Luke Ethridge story. "His name was Luke Ethridge, and he was dropped off at the local emergency unit of the hospital. He was the father of Jason, who also lives in the house, and he may well be the major chemist in the business."

Jim listened with interest. "So, are you going to close them down now?"

"Not yet. We believe there's more to be gained before we go in. I saw the man's body – it was awful. Most people have no idea of the damage long-term drug use does to a body. Mind you, an almost nonexistent diet, no exercise, and constant personal abuse in the form of lack of sleep and so on, all add up. This man's whole body was ravaged. No one has come forward to claim him, not that you would expect them to. He came with no I.D., but we had them under surveillance so we already knew who he was."

"Anything happened with our friend, Mr. Markwell?"

"We're still watching; that's why I wanted to see you. He comes and goes from the drug house, more so since the death, but we're hanging close to him. He's undoubtedly the brains and the one we want. The others are all killing themselves without any help from us. I wanted to ask you to keep a note of any vehicle that brings visitors to Markwell's house, alternatively, if they walk in, can you note their description?"

"Sure, Frank. I'll let Di know what you're after."

"Thanks, mate. Oh, listen, would you apologise to Di. Yesterday, I might have appeared to be a male chauvinist pig when I told her this was men's business. I just didn't want to discuss Markwell in front of Ellen."

Pekalski took his leave.

As Jim watched Pekalski walk to his car, he saw Charlene strolling back from the pool. He could not help thinking she looked like such a nice, ordinary person. Again, he wondered about the pall of crime that hung over this resort, and yet there were so many lovely people. It just didn't make sense.

Chapter Seventeen

Charlie Savka tried to convince Gwen that to simply blackmail Brenda would come with its own problems.

"What if the woman became desperate," he said, "and caused a fatal accident for you? All the money in the world wouldn't be any use to you then, would it? Look, the reward posted by the insurance company is ten percent of the recovered money. Surely that is still an attractive figure – and the bonus is, you'll live to enjoy it."

Gwen's eyes expanded and her mouth fell open. "Tha ... that would be one million dollars. Oh my God, that's much more than I would have gotten from Brenda directly or in monthly instalments. I had no idea they were prepared to pay so much." Gwen was astounded.

"If you and Tom split that fifty-fifty, you would each receive five hundred thousand. That's not a bad return for the cost of a couple of phone calls."

"But how do you ensure we get that money, after we have given them the information?"

"Legal document. They sign a legal document to the effect that they pay ten percent to anyone leading them to the ten million, and we get that when it's been recovered. This means that we get paid when they get paid – simple. I'll be your go between, if that's satisfactory with you."

Still dazed, Gwen nodded. "How do they get her to tell them where the money is hidden?"

"That's the technical part, my dear. Of course, she probably won't tell them, but once they have her in their sights, they can track it down through computer hacking, unbeknown to her. She won't know they are on to her until they have the money, or at least located it. There's no question that it's in a hidden account or safety deposit overseas. Whatever she knows, they will soon know. Up until now, they've been unable to track her down. This is due to her changed appearance and new identity documents and so on. What you have to realise is, that on the one hand, the wonderful world of computers makes these frauds possible in the first place, but equally, modern technology also makes it possible to backtrack and trace the money anywhere in the world. All the insurers need is a starting point, and you, Mrs. Clark, have that information. You can do that for them. Despite the fact that her identity and appearance have been altered, which we agree is the case, they will pursue her relentlessly, and not stop until she is in jail with her husband. In this case, he may be out before her."

Charlie could see the whole picture, in vivid colour, in front of him. He knew exactly who he would contact and how he would approach the insurance company. Gwen had given Charlie a copy of the letter Brett had written to Brenda. He agreed there was no question as to the true identity of Freya Holman.

"I'm wondering now about how you should handle Mrs. Simpson," said Charlie. She will certainly feel threatened, but at the same time, you will have given her a terrible scare. Does she know where you live?"

"No. It's only temporary anyway. But I haven't given her my address."

"She may follow you home. It would be in her interest now to keep tabs on you. You should keep cleaning for her. You have to tell her you've changed your mind."

"Do you think she'll believe that?"

"No."

"Well, what can I do?"

"I think we should talk this over with Tom, but my reasoning tells me that she will only believe you are more corrupt, not less. By that I mean you should suggest to her that you have thought it over, and decided to take a share of the loot when her husband comes out of jail, rather than a regular pittance now."

"This is getting so complicated. Why would I do that?"

"Because you're greedy – and Brenda would rather pay you when her husband is out and can deal with you, rather than deal with you herself."

"I see."

Gwen sat back in her chair and thought about what Charlie said.

"So, I have to change my demands, and keep working for her as well? This doesn't let me off the hook at all, does it?"

"No, not at all. Your life will still be at risk, as long as you have information that you can sell."

"Well, I certainly didn't know what I was starting when I set all this in motion. Perhaps I'm naive, but I can see it's much easier to earn your money honestly. I'm too old for a life of crime." Gwen smiled at her own comment.

They had most of the details nutted out and Charlie was ready to leave. He said they would have to run it past Tom, when he returned from Perth, but he felt sure it would be sanctioned. Next move would be for Gwen to go and see Brenda – clean her home and do her bidding, as usual. All this meant another sleepless night for Gwen.

******

Tom Heart was looking at a broken man – or a very good actor. Ron Clarke was quietly sobbing into a bunch of tissues and Tom was standing by, feeling helpless.

"I'm really sorry about all this. I didn't want to hurt Gwen. I just thought it was time I went it alone. I'm a fool, like she used to tell me. I'm a bloody fool," he sobbed.

Tom sat and listened; this was all new to him. Having to deal with human emotions, especially those of the quarry, was far in excess of what he saw as his duty. He reached out and patted Ron on the back.

"Okay, mate. Take it easy, I'm not going to cause you any problems. All you have to do now is agree to hand back what you owe to your wife."

Tom sat next to Ron on the bed, and put his arm around the man's shoulder. He gave him a manly shake.

"Pull yourself together now, mate."

Ron nodded and tried to stop his snivelling. He pushed Tom away.

"I'm okay, give me a minute," he said.

He blew his nose, then stood up and opened the fridge. He took out a bottle of brandy and dashed a measure into two glasses. He handed one to Tom, not asking if he wanted it, then tipped his head back and swallowed his.

Tom took a sip and realised it was exactly what he wanted.

They sat together in silence for the next few minutes.

"I'd like to get this business settled tonight, if possible Ron. I know you're upset, but you'd think me a fool if I left now and hoped you'd be here when I came back tomorrow."

"I want to go home."

"What?"

"I want to go back to Brisbane with you, and try to sort this mess out. With Gwen, I mean."

"Oh. Well, I'm sure that's possible. Let's give her another call now and see what she says."

Ron was silent while Tom, once again, dialled Gwen's number. There was no answer. He hung up.

"Let's see what flights are available, shall we?"

Tom made a booking for later that night, which would get them home before breakfast. He decided to collect his gear and wait with Ron, just in case Ron reconsidered, and decided to go it alone again. They were both on their way to the airport by 9:30pm. Tom marvelled at the fact that he had wrapped up a case in such a short time and with so little fuss.

******

Tony Heart was beginning to feel like his old self. His spirits had received such a boost since the visit from his long-time friend, Charlie Savka. *Lying in bed, waiting to die, had a way of depressing a fellow.* He thought about his friend and smiled.

"What the hell are you doing lying down on the job, old son?" That was how Charlie had greeted Tony when he turned up at his house the previous evening. "And how come you never tried to contact me?"

Charlie had walked in the unlocked front door and made himself completely at home immediately.

Tom had asked Charlie to visit his dad, as he had to spend the night away from home and Tony needed someone to look after him. Charlie had agreed without reservation, saying, 'Leave it to me, son, I'll sort him out.' And he did.

"Now, tell me the routine, so I can ignore it, mate."

Charlie laughed as he said it, although he felt like anything but laughing when he saw the condition of one of his oldest friends. Tony was a shadow of his former self. His emaciated body was bad enough, but his hair had gone and he could barely stand and support his own weight.

"Tom said you might need a little company, since he had to stay in Perth overnight. Not a bad kid that, huh?"

Charlie was walking around Tony's room. He took in the plastic urinal, the lined-up medications, and the half-eaten food on a tray. The water bottle and the phone nearby, all painted a picture of an invalid who had been left alone for most of the day.

"I'm cooking dinner tonight, mate."

"That so?" answered Tony. "If my memory serves me correctly, you can't cook water – or have you taken cooking lessons since I last saw you?"

"Get a look at this." Charlie lifted his hand to display a Chinese food container. "We're having omelette and prawn cutlets. Now, what do you say?"

"I say, you haven't changed. That's exactly what we had the last time we ate together. Come over here and give an old feller a hug."

Tony held his arms open, and with tears rolling down his cheeks, he grabbed his friend and hugged him to his heaving chest.

All this display of emotion was a little more than Charlie was used too, but he could not refuse those open arms and stepped over to Tony. He ran his hand over Tony's rough head of half grown stubble.

"I wouldn't go round recommending your barber to anyone, if I were you, mate," he said.

They enjoyed a laugh together, and Charlie helped Tony to sit up in the chair.

"I'm going to prepare dinner," Charlie said, "but not before we have a couple of slugs to improve our appetite. What do you say? Oh, is it okay to drink with all that medication you've got lined up there?"

"The one thing about being in my condition, mate, is nothing matters. I'm going to die anyway."

Tony seemed to think he was being funny, but Charlie didn't see it that way.

"Fair go, mate, you're not dead yet. I could get run over by a truck before you piss off."

"Sure, okay, whatever you say. Now, where's that drink?"

Chapter Eighteen

S omething about standing at the kitchen sink, washing dishes, is very conducive to thinking. Vinnie could not avoid it while he, for one of the few times in his life, cleaned up. He realised he did not know what to do about Jason. If it were anybody else, he would call in some friends and sort out the problem with a heavy, blunt instrument. Then he would take the person and his car and run it off the road so it looked like a motor vehicle accident.

He had to acknowledge to himself that he had known Jason and his father, Luke, too long to dispose of him so simply. He sensed he was getting soft. However, he just couldn't do it.

He worried the problem around in his head and became angrier with himself and Charlene, as he slopped hot water and threw soapsuds around the sink. When he finally picked up the frying pan, the one that had so recently had been used as a weapon to give him the gigantic headache he now had, he slammed it to the bench. He spun around, wet hands on his hips and looked at the wall behind him. He gritted his teeth and swore repeatedly. *Shit, shit, fucking, bloody hell.* None of this helped and he finally walked out of the kitchen and kicked the chair that stood in his path. He flopped down on the lounge, nursing his wet hands in his lap.

What if I simply let Jason go? he thought. *Would the boy expose me, either inadvertently or on purpose? Would he influence the others to leave as well?* Vinnie began to wonder if this was the end of his new business. He thought about his income and scratched around in his brain for an idea as to how he could salvage it. After a couple of minutes, he stood up and walked back to the kitchen. He knew he needed an inspiration from somewhere, but was aware none was forthcoming. He used his pent up energy to clean the stove and all the kitchen surfaces. Strangely, he began to enjoy his exertions, and he looked around for anything else he could clean.

At that moment, Charlene sashayed into the kitchen, with her towel over her shoulder and her hands on her hips. Her hair was damp, as was her swimming costume; her tan was perfect. She looked pleased with herself and wore a very provocative grin.

"Feeling better, big boy?"

Vinnie's jaw dropped, all the anger in him had dissipated, and he stared at the woman who had so recently assaulted him.

"Wha ... wha ... " He was almost speechless.

"My poor darling."

Charlene walked over and gently stroked his head.

"I'm so sorry. Will you forgive me?"

Her face was very close, lips parted, eyes like pools of blue.

"Come and lie down, you need to rest."

She led him by the hand to the bedroom. He sat on the side of the bed while she removed his sandals, then his sleeveless tee shirt, and then helped him to stand, while she removed his shorts and undies. She pushed him back onto the pillow then walked over and turned the phone off. She closed the door and pulled the curtain so the room was almost dark. She slipped out of her costume and lay next to the man, who watched her every move.

"You're going to be alright. I'll look after you, I promise." She kissed him and he reached for her.

******

Tom looked at the man sitting next to him in the airport lounge. He leaned over and patted Ron on the back.

"It's okay, mate. I think you'll find you'll be alright."

Tom grinned to himself when he said that, because his father Tony had said that to him a million times when he was growing up. No matter what the occasion, the remark came – 'I think you'll find you'll be alright.' And very often, Tom wasn't. It was a platitude he could well have done without.

Ron looked up at Tom and said, "You think so?"

"Yeah, I do. Now, start thinking about what changes you'll need to make when we get home."

"Changes? What do you mean?"

"Well whatever the problem was that you had with your wife, you need to do something about it. I'm no psychologist, but I can see you disappeared with all your joint savings. You didn't consider how that would affect her, and you've made both of you miserable into the bargain. Surely, something will have to change, if, and it's a big if, Gwen decides to take you back."

"So you think she's going to kick me out?"

"I have no idea, but if I were you, I would allow for the possibility."

Ron sighed. He was already nervous at the prospect of facing Gwen again, but having this fellow along made him feel more confident; sort of like a buffer. He did not know if he could handle being told to leave.

"She should be just glad I'm coming home and she's getting her money back," he said, barely above a whisper.

"What was that?" Tom asked.

"I said she should be glad that I'm coming home and bringing the dough."

"With that attitude, you won't last long. Take my advice Ron, and go home prepared to apologise, ten times, if necessary. Try to see what you put your wife through, and how much pain you have caused her."

"And what about my pain? What about me?"

Tom was getting very frustrated with Ron. He was fast losing patience with the man. His teeth were clenched when he turned to the other man and grabbed him by the elbow.

He said, "I don't want to hear another word about you, mate. You sound like a bloody great sook. You're only sorry for yourself. If I were your wife, I'd be bloody glad you left."

Ron pulled his elbow from Tom's grasp and turned his back to the other man. He had nothing to say. A moment later, their flight was called. They exchanged only the minimum of words on the flight home to Brisbane.

******

Brenda found her father's gun. She found it in a small trunk where Lesley had stored their parent's valuables. There were photo albums, small ornaments, and several cups and medals from achievements in golf, swimming and tennis. The whole family had excelled at something, and it had made Brenda quiet nostalgic to unearth these old mementoes. She took out her high school swimming medal and dropped the lid on the trunk.

"I was about to come and get you so we could share a drink before dinner," Lesley said, as she turned to her sister, who came in with her hands full. "So what have you found there?"

"Well, I have my old school medal for swimming and I have this gun and some bullets, of Dad's."

"What on earth could you possibly want with that gun?" Lesley stared at the object in her sister's hands.

"I have been considering buying one lately, but found it is difficult to do, so I just thought it was quite timely that I should come across this one now."

"But why on earth would you need a gun. I thought you felt very happy and secure, living in a gated community with security and live in managers. You've got the lot, haven't you?"

"You might think so, but still I feel insecure. Having a husband, as you do, is completely different to living alone. As you know, I was harassed something terrible after Brett went to jail, hence my name change. By the way, I really appreciate your respecting my confidence and not telling anyone about my whereabouts."

Lesley waved her hand to acknowledge the comment and pointed to the glasses of wine poured on the coffee table. They sat down together and sipped in silence for a few minutes.

"Have you decided what you're going to do when Brett is released from jail?"

"Not really. We will have to find a way of avoiding all the media again, and slip out from under all the attention. They still believe we know where that money is; of course it's no use saying again that we don't. They may never give up. We have to get away, somehow and try to pick up our lives – somewhere – far from here."

"So I may never see you again, once Brett is home?"

"Possibly not. But we'll keep in touch, somehow. I'd like that."

"Me too."

Lesley got up and went to her sister's chair. She bent and hugged her. She had tears in her eyes when she sat down.

"You've had an awful time with all this money business. I can't imagine what it must feel like to be accused of something you didn't do. And to think the real criminal is out there somewhere, getting off, scot free."

Brenda decided to spend the night with her sister, because she knew that as long as she avoided Gwen she would not have to make a decision. Continually turning the problem over in her head had not brought her any closer to a resolution. To pay the woman out seemed the obvious choice, but she could not rid herself of the thought that it may not mean the end of Gwen's interest in her. If she were Gwen, she would not go away so easily, but then, she reminded herself, not everyone was like her, and Gwen was an amateur.

The next morning she had decided to pay Gwen out, and at the same time, warn her off about coming back for more. She would grab the upper hand by flashing the gun and making it clear that she was not afraid to use it. *I'll just get really tough and scare the hell out of the blood sucker.* She grinned as she thought it.

Brenda took her leave of Lesley and agreed to return soon.

"I am grateful for your loyalty, Lesley; I'll never forget how you have always supported me and Brett, even when the rest of the world didn't."

They hugged and parted with smiles; Lesley still aware that she knew so little about her sister.

******

Earlier that same morning, Tom and Ron touched down at Brisbane airport. It had been a very long, nonstop flight, and they were both ready for a good sleep.

"I been thinking I should check into a hotel or something. If you think I'm going to be told to piss off again, I might as well get a sleep in first, then go and see Gwen later today. We can sort out the money stuff and that should be that. At least I know a few people around here, and if I'm going to go it alone, it might as well be where I feel comfortable."

"Not a chance, mate!" Tom grabbed Ron's elbow in case he decided to make a run for it. "We're going to see Gwen - right now. All the money your wife had to spend to get you back, and you're worried about being comfortable? Get real, mate! When we see the bottom line of her balance sheet returned to where it previously was, then, and only then, can you go and get comfortable."

"Yeah, yeah. Alright, let's get a cab."

They were soon on their way to Gwen's home. Ron could not help taking in the atmosphere of the neighbourhood as they pulled up in front of a shabby block of units.

Since Charlie had visited Gwen, she had felt a lot more positive about her future. She had confidence in the man, in a way young Tom had never inspired. She smiled as she opened the door, and saw Tom and another person standing behind him. Tom stepped to the side and Ron cringed, just slightly. Gwen's mouth fell open, and she felt an almost irresistible desire to lean over and knock his stupid head off. She clenched her fists and stared.

"May we come in?" asked Tom.

Gwen stepped back. The two men walked past Gwen and she pointed them both to a chair. She finally found her voice. "So ... I really never expected to see you again."

Ron looked around the room before he responded.

"Yeah, it's a bit of a surprise to me too. You can thank your cop friend here. He really didn't give me a choice."

Gwen looked a question at Tom.

He shook his head and sighed. He could see this was going to be like drawing teeth.

"Actually, it was Ron's decision, and I agreed that these things are better worked out in person. If you're unhappy about him being here, we can sort out the money and I'll take him out of your hair."

Gwen put up her hand, and said, "It's okay, I'm just surprised, and that's all. I'm really happy to see you have returned to the scene of the crime, old man." She gave him what looked like a sarcastic smile.

Ron opened his mouth to respond but thought better of it, especially when he looked at Tom and he clearly shook his head.

"We could certainly go a cup of coffee, before we begin," Tom said to Gwen.

"Sure, would you like something to eat as well?"

"No thanks, Gwen," said Tom, "we ate on the plane."

"I would, I'm starving," interjected Ron.

"Course you are, Ron. I'll find something, an arsenic sandwich maybe, even though I'm living on the bread line."

Gwen laughed this time and left the room.

The two men could hear her rattling about in the kitchen and Ron stood up and walked around, noting all the old familiar furnishings.

Chapter Nineteen

Jason filled his mind with a new resolve. He began to have a sense of confidence he had never known before. From the moment of Luke's death, Jason became a man, and he was no longer afraid; not of Vinnie, nor of life.

He felt Luke was still with him, as he walked around the laboratory. As he touched the surface of workbench, he sensed a presence around him. He thought back to several weeks previously, when he had looked into the rear vision mirror in his car, and he had seen his mother's face. He wondered if they were together now, his mother and father, both looking after him.

"How ya feelin' today mate?" Nat hovered and tried to read Jason's expression.

Jason sighed and then smiled. He turned and looked straight at his friend.

"I'm okay. Actually, I feel pretty good. I do appreciate your bein' there for me Nat. I consider you my friend, and I'm grateful for the support you've given me."

"S'okay Jase, you've been a good friend to me too. So what we doin' today?"

Jason stared at Nat, and took some time before he answered, "I'll set you up to get started here, then I'll give Vin a call and tell him I'll be takin' over the drop offs, for the time bein'. Luke really wasn't doing much, so we can manage. Grant can come and give you a hand, if necessary."

"But aren't ya help'n in the lab no more, mate?"

"No. I've got plans now, and you should just get used to doin' without me."

Nat's jaw dropped as he realised what Jason was telling him.

"So I guess you really are leavin' then," he said.

"I am, mate, but please don't say anythin' to anyone else for the time bein'. I want to choose my time and I don't want to cause anyone any problems."

"Sure, sure, mate," said Nat, as he looked around the lab with new eyes. *Soon to be my own work place,* he thought.

The two walked together to the kitchen. Jason filled the kettle and flicked the switch. He spooned coffee and sugar into two mugs and filled them when the water boiled.

"There you go, mate," said Jason. "Wanna bikkie?"

"Nah, I'm good," Nat said, as he tried to pick up his cup without spilling it. His hands shook.

"Geez, Nat, how much are you using now?"

"Oh, not much, just occasional, ya know, like when I feel like I need a lift."

Nat had turned his head away and walked out of the room ahead of Jason. He was not a good liar.

"What have you had today?"

"Umm ... actually ... "

He stopped and took a deep breath. He turned and faced his friend. His face betrayed the guilt he felt, as his expression crumpled and he looked close to tears.

"I ain't strong like you, mate, but I'm tryin', honest. I'm cuttin' down, every day. I reckon I'll be off all this shit by next month, maybe even sooner."

Jason shook his head and looked into Nat's eyes, as they made their way back into the lab.

"The point is, you're still lyin' to yourself, mate. You have to start tellin' yourself the truth. Have you considered goin' into rehab?"

Nat looked around the room. He was uncomfortable talking about this.

"No, I'm pretty sure I can knock this off without all that trouble. I just haven't been ready till now. Maybe, it's not as bad as you think, Jase. Just because Luke couldn't control hiself, doesn't mean we're all that bad. Stop worryin', and show me what we're doin' today and put a smile back on ya dial. Okay?"

"Right, nuff said. Let's get started."

Jason picked up Nat's notebook and read what he had written so far. He started to write instructions, in point form.

Nat looked over his shoulder.

"Yeah, yeah, that's good, I can get that," Nat said, as he pulled up two chairs.

Jason began to explain the process of making methamphetamine from the basic ingredients.

It was past midday by the time Jason got away. He set out on the delivery run and expected a good cash flow from the afternoon's activities. He had cleared the run with Vinnie and they planned to have a meeting the next day.

******

The sun had set by the time Detective Inspector Frank Pekalski came home and poured himself a cold beer. He sat down heavily on his favourite chair. He had a good view up the street, through the well-established night jasmine shrubs in his front garden. He could see out, but it was difficult for anyone to see in. It suited him well, and he could not help thinking that he had made a good decision to buy into the resort. He was happy to leave the lawns and gardens to someone who liked that sort of work.

He had made a new start when he moved to the resort. He had tried to leave memories of his wife behind, in the old house. He made a concerted effort to go beyond his grief. Largely it had worked, and he was beginning to feel like a single man again. He had even begun to notice some attractive women at work, and at the resort. One particular woman walked her dog by his house about this time, most evenings. At first, as he would watch her walk past, he found himself subconsciously comparing her with his deceased wife. Then, two days ago, she had walked up behind him, as he wrestled with the empty garbage bin that was still standing out the front of his house.

Frank smiled as he recalled the encounter.

"Hello, how are you settling in?" she said, to his back.

He swung around to face her.

She smiled, and he realised she was beautiful. She had thick, blonde, shoulder length hair, tied loosely to one side with a ribbon. He noticed she wore makeup, but it was only light, and very flattering. Her large eyes were blue and smiling.

She waited for him to respond, and finally he did.

"Um ... good ... yes ... very well, thank you. My name is Frank."

He put his hand out.

She put her hand in his, and smiled again.

Frank realised he was holding her hand; the soft, warm, delicate touch was like a magnet to him.

Frank cleared his throat. "You been here long?" he said.

"Almost two years. I love it. I've met so many nice people, I'm never lonely like I had been, living in my old house. Here, everyone makes you feel welcome and treats you like family. My name is Joy."

"Well, Joy, I haven't been here long, but I also haven't made much effort to mix in as yet. Probably the job I have – long hours – and I've lived alone for so long that I've just got used to my own company."

"I can understand that. It's what you get used to. After my husband died, I didn't expect to ever be happy again, so I wasn't, but when a friend talked me into coming here, I really didn't care too much, but then I was pleasantly surprised, and now I'm into lots of things."

"Like, what do you mean?"

"Well, I'm in the writers group and I enjoy art classes and dancing classes, also I go to the dinners and the movies. I can't go to anything and not have a conversation with someone. It's not possible. So like it or not, I have many new friends and it has made a world of a difference to my attitude, and my happiness."

"That's good to hear. I think I'll have to make an effort to join in more." Frank nodded and smiled.

"Why don't you join me at dinner next Wednesday? The people I usually sit with would welcome you, and we have a vacant seat at our table. Five-thirty for drinks and closely followed by a nice baked dinner. What do you say?"

"I say it's a date."

"Nice meeting you, Frank," she said.

"You too, Joy."

She turned and walked away. After a few steps, she looked back over her shoulder, smiled and waved.

Frank felt like an awkward teenager. He felt his face flush as he self-consciously raised his hand and returned her smile. He stood, rooted to the spot, as he watched her walk up the street. He wished he had asked her to stay and have a drink with him, but he was a little rusty with the pick-up lines. He felt that might be pushing his luck.

"Next Wednesday," he mumbled quietly to himself. *Oh, God,* he cringed, *did I really say, 'It's a date?'.*

A car drove past and interrupted Frank's recollection of his encounter with Joy. He peered through the shrubs and recognised Vinnie Markwell's vehicle. He saw that Markwell was alone, and heading back to his house. His cop mentality wondered where he had been and if he had recruited anyone new to fill the vacancy left by Luke. His mind drifted to the drug house, as he now called it. He wondered what sort of an impact Luke's death would have on those who worked with him, especially his son, Jason. Frank had a file on all the inhabitants of the drug house, and was keen to see the place closed down. He knew he must be patient though, and take his lead from the drug squad. They had a much broader agenda, with the possibility of catching some very big fish in due course. Frank went to his kitchen and took another beer from the refrigerator, unscrewed the twist-top, and walked back to the television. His mind flashed up an image of Joy and he found himself smiling, *Roll on Wednesday*, he thought again.

******

Vinnie slid his car gently into the narrow garage space. There was never enough room for a vehicle like his anymore. The spaces at the shopping centres seemed to be smaller, and reversing was a nightmare, even for an expert like him.

"What's for dinner, Charlene?" he shouted, as he came through the connecting door into the hallway.

They had been having lots of home cooked meals, now that Charlene had found her true calling. Some had been edible and some had ended up in the garbage. She was adamant; it would be just a matter of time before she mastered all the dishes she attempted. With flour on her face and apron, and a dripping spatula in her hand, she appeared in front of him.

Vinnie had a feeling her expression did not portend well.

"What's all the shouting about?" she asked.

"I'm starving. What's for dinner?" he asked again.

He walked directly to the kitchen to see for himself. What confronted him was one of the biggest messes Charlene had managed so far. Vinnie stared and his jaw dropped.

Charlene tapped her foot for a moment, then walked around in front of Vinnie and looked up at him.

"I guess you'll just have to wait and see, hey?"

Vinnie turned and made his way to the lounge. He had learned his lesson now, he would not criticise Charlene while she had an instrument in her hand. The lump on his head she had given him with the frying pan, had not long disappeared.

"I can wait. I'm not really that hungry," was all he said.

Charlene smiled to herself in the kitchen.

The phone rang and Vinnie picked it up. He barked into the handpiece, "Yeah, yeah, okay."

He listened to Jason as he gave him a rundown of events that day in the lab, and on the street. They were making good money now, and Jason was keeping the book and taking over the control of the business, far better than Vinnie had expected. Vinnie was surprised at the way Jason's attitude had improved, and at how well he was keeping the rest of the group in hand. Despite the fact he wasn't much more than a kid, he had come to grips with all aspects of the drug business, and Vinnie could see he would not need to make the changes he was considering, after all.

"Nat's doing well, and he enjoys cooking up the stuff. He's careful, and I think he should keep on with it," Jason said.

"I'll think about it. In the meantime, just continue, and I'll let you know what I plan to change, when I'm ready."

Vinnie wanted to keep the upper hand; he wasn't ready yet to let Jason know he was pleased, but he could not help feeling that Jason sounded forceful and sensible – a leader in the making.

Jason was being a lot more careful now. He made sure he was never in the house when Nat was cooking up a new batch. He had seen what the fumes had done to his father and he did not want to end the same way. Jason also started to look after his own income. Whenever he got a new customer, he added a small percentage for himself. The extra cash he skimmed went into a safe place. Vinnie would never know about it. He had no definite plan yet as to how he was going to make his escape, but ideas came and went all the time and he knew he would soon be ready to make his move. Jason wondered if his father would have approved of his plan to clear off as soon as he had enough money. He thought about his father often, he hoped one day to be someone Luke would have been proud of.

Chapter Twenty

Ron made himself comfortable very quickly, after Gwen bought him a cup of tea and a toasted cheese sandwich. He had been relieved when she had not abused him or thrown him out. Instead, she had smiled at him when she had handed him his snack, and then given him the remote control for the television.

"Why don't you watch the footy while I have a talk to Tom," she said, with a neutral expression.

"Thanks, love."

Thanks, love? I'll give you 'thanks, love', you bastard. Gwen turned and sat at the table with Tom Heart. She sucked her breath between clenched teeth, exhaled a long, slow breath, and took a few seconds to compose herself, before she said, "So, Tom, you had a good trip home?"

"We did. I must say this whole situation was wrapped up much more quickly than I anticipated. I suppose the fact that Ron was not really trying to remain hidden did help."

"Yes, I suppose so." Gwen looked over at her husband.

Ron was wolfing down his snack, as his eyes remained glued to the television. He was oblivious to what was going through Gwen's mind at that moment.

Gwen's temperament was a long, long way from forgiving.

"I spoke to Charlie this morning," Tom said to Gwen. "I hear he paid you a visit. I wonder did he have any suggestions as to how to proceed with Brenda Simpson?"

"He suggests we go to the insurance company and try to make a deal. He believes that if we were to blackmail Brenda, we may end up with the worst end of the stick. Also, it seems there is a lot more to gain that way. Apparently, we could get ten percent of ten million. Did you realise that?"

"No, but it sounds like a much better idea to me. We wouldn't be doing anything illegal and we may end up looking like heroes." He smiled broadly. "Charlie stayed with my dad last night and it sounds like he has cheered him up no end. I'm going to shuffle off now; I don't like to leave the old man alone. We need to arrange a meeting and decide what our next step will be in relation to Simpson. What would you like me to do with our friend here? He looks pretty relaxed and comfortable, doesn't he?"

"You – leave – him – to – me," said Gwen, as she waggled her index finger and looked in Ron's direction. She was not smiling. Gwen could see the worried look on Tom's face as he opened his mouth to speak. She held her hand up and stopped him before he could utter a word.

"It's okay; I'm not going to shoot him. I don't plan that his punishment should be over so quickly as that. You leave that bugger here. I'll sort him out. Looks pretty content now, doesn't he?"

They both turned their attention to Ron, who looked up from the football, his mouth full of toasted cheese sandwich.

"What? What's happening?" Ron spluttered the question.

"I'm off now, Ron," Tom said. "I'll leave you in the hands of your grateful and loving wife, here. Is that alright with you?"

Ron stood, looked first at Tom, and said, "Sure, mate. No worries." He then looked at his wife.

Gwen nodded back. She still had no smile.

Ron began to look a little uncomfortable, and even switched off the television, as Tom let himself out the front door. When the door closed, Ron and Gwen looked at one another. Ron's bravado seemed to have slipped out the door as well.

He stood opposite Gwen, and bit his lip. His eyes were lowered.

"We need to talk, mate," said Gwen. "Sit down!"

It was not a request.

Tom drove off up the street.

******

Brenda was restless and agitated from the moment she returned to her home at Keeala Resort. She looked around her lounge as she came through the front door. She would not have been surprised to find her house cleaner and arch enemy, sitting, waiting. She felt very defensive.

"So where are you, you bitch," she said aloud, to the empty room.

She remembered the gun, and took it from her handbag. She walked around the room and wondered about the best place to hide it. After a couple of minutes, she put it down on the dining room table; she did not like the feel of it in her hand. It was not loaded. She put the packet of bullets next to it.

The phone rang a couple of hours later, just as she was beginning to calm down.

"This is Gwen. I've been thinking about our situation and decided I don't want anything to do with you."

Brenda listened with her mouth agape.

"You won't be hearing from me again."

The phone went dead.

Brenda stood still, the receiver still clutched in her hand. She shook her head in disbelief, as she tried to digest what she had heard. She replaced the handset and sat down.

"What on earth made her change her mind? Who's she been talking to? I can't believe this." Brenda realised she was talking to herself. She went to the kitchen and put the kettle on.

Gwen sat and grinned at nothing. She had enjoyed that little talk, brief though it was. Now, she looked forward to the next episode in the Simpson saga. She had spoken to Tom on the phone, and he had suggested she ring Brenda to put her off her guard. Tom agreed with Charlie that they would approach the insurance company next and see what sort of a deal they could get. In the meantime, no one wanted Brenda getting desperate.

That night everyone slept well, except Ron. He had a feeling that his welcome home had been too easy.

******

Vinnie looked down at the plate in front of him.

"So what is it?" he asked.

"Well, what does it look like?"

Vinnie would have liked to have said, 'It looks like shit to me.', but he was an intelligent man, so he said, "Could it be steak?"

"Certainly it could – but it bloody isn't. Try again."

"Mushrooms?"

"Have another go, you mug."

"Why don't we just drop this guessing competition and you tell me what this delightful looking plate of food is."

"Ratatouille."

"Rat-a-bloody-what?"

"Ratatouille! Try it, go on. I promise you, you'll be pleasantly surprised."

Vinnie stared at Charlene, then back at the plate. He was reluctant to pick up his fork. She poked him in the back, and then sat down and started eating her own serving.

Vinnie watched her and saw her nodding in approval, so he picked up a fork and placed a little of the dark, squashy matter in his mouth. He held it there a moment, made a gagging sound, and spat the food back on his plate.

Charlene's loaded fork stopped halfway to her mouth. Her body froze, except for her steel-blue eyes, whose focus shifted slowly, but menacingly, from her plate, and drilled into Vinnie's watery stare.

Vinnie blinked the tears from his eyes.

She was still watching him.

He tried again. This time, he swallowed.

"See what I mean. Like it, don't you?"

At first, Vinnie did not know what to say. He was not one of the world's great gastronomes. He had spent a lifetime eating fast food or counter lunches. The Holy Grail of Vinnie's dining expectation was the perfect plate of steak, two eggs, fried onions, red-wine gravy and hand cut, deep-fried potato chips – with tomato sauce. He had never seen anything that looked or tasted like what he was in front of him.

"What's in it?"

Vinnie tried to make the question sound as if he was genuinely interested, and he tried to keep his tone light-hearted.

"That's for me to know, and you to eat."

Vinnie ground his teeth. Inside, he was seething. *I've popped guys for less insubordination than this,* he thought.

Charlene continued to shovel the food into her mouth with a Splayd, and pointed to the bowl in the middle of the table with her other hand.

"What's that?"

"Cous cous."

"I see. Oh, well, why didn't you say so?"

Vinnie had no idea what cous cous was, but he spooned the substance on to his plate, mixed it in with his rat-a-bloody-touille, and began to push the lot down as fast as he could. He swallowed again, and again, trying to get it from his lips into his throat so fast that it would bypass his taste buds. He almost succeeded, but a small portion lingered in his mouth for a couple of seconds. It reminded him of slime, mixed with granulated cardboard. He realised that was a silly thing to think, because he had never eaten slime mixed with granulated cardboard. *But that's probably what it would taste like*, he thought. Finally, he wiped the back of his hand across his mouth, belched, and leaned back in the chair.

"So, any dessert?"

"What do you think?"

Vinnie had no idea, so he shut his mouth, sat back, and marvelled as his partner thoroughly enjoyed the rest of her main course. He wondered how he could avoid this sort of food in the future. Maybe he could make a diplomatic request, or tell Charlene there were a few things to which he was allergic – especially anything beginning with rat.

Charlene went to the kitchen. Three minutes later, she returned.

"Close your eyes, lover," she said, as she stood behind his chair and brushed her breasts against his shoulders. She slid her left hand inside the front of his shirt, and ran her fingernails through the mat of hair that covered his pecs. With her right, she leaned around and placed a dessert plate on the table in front of him.

"Open wide, big boy!"

Vinnie looked. In front of him, were four scoops of butterscotch-brickle ice cream, smothered with caramel sauce, garnished with a layer of crushed nuts, and the whole lot drizzled with a brandy liqueur. Vinnie's heart sang. It was his favourite.

"Now, if you're a very good boy, and eat all your dinner, I might have a surprise for you after."

Bloody hell! Man, maybe I could get a taste for rat-a-bloody-touille after all!

******

After Di Watersen left Elaine Steinberg's home, she strode out along the path, but felt the creaks and twinges of old age. She had just finished telling Elaine how proud she was of her wonderful recovery from her stroke. It had happened when Jim and Di were away on holiday. Di was impressed with how Elaine had attended rehabilitation, and later, when Elaine returned to the resort, had attended the gym four days a week. Di quietly acknowledged to herself that her own fitness level had gone down. She was not exercising regularly and she had a list of excuses why she was too busy. She thought about how well Elaine looked, and began to consider coming to grips with her own laziness. Di picked up the pace and was almost running by the time she arrived back at the office. She was walking up the path when the general alarm sounded. She looked around and then saw one of the cleaners running toward her.

"For God's sake come quickly, Mrs. Watersen. I just went in to see Mr Watersen and he's lying on the floor. He's fallen over," she said.

Di ran and brushed past the cleaner. She threw the office door open and stopped in front of Jim's prone body. His head was against the metal filing cabinet and lying in a pool of blood.

"Call the ambulance," she shouted at the small crowd that was gathering behind her. She knelt down, and for a moment, all her usual responses were frozen by the shock of seeing her husband in that state. She quickly gathered her wits and reached out to feel for a pulse at Jim's neck.

"No, no, no, yes. Oh God, yes, I feel a pulse." She gently lifted his eyelids to check his pupils but the light in the room was in the wrong position. She placed her hand on his chest to see if he was breathing.

"Move out of the way," said a voice from behind, and she looked up to see a resident and friend, Peter Kaminski, pushing his way to her side. He knelt down on the other side of Jim and began to check his pulse, breathing and pupils, as Di had just done. Suddenly he shouted and pushed Jim over on his back. "CPR right now, his pulse has stopped."

Di's eyes widened and she helped Peter to position Jim, then she started artificial respiration while Peter counted then began chest compressions. They worked together, and remained focused on counting the breaths and heart compressions. Sweat ran down Peter's face and into his eyes, and Di took her lead from him when he stopped to check for a pulse. The crowd behind was almost silent as they waited and watched this life and death scene playing out in front of them.

The onlookers stood back when they heard the ambulance pull up outside. Paramedics rushed in and evaluated the situation. They took over from Di, with a mask and hand held respirator, then connected Jim to a cardiograph. Both Peter and Di stood back as the professionals took over.

It was not looking good. They defibrillated Jim several times before he responded, and they connected him to an intravenous tube. It must have been twenty minutes before they finally wheeled Jim out to the ambulance and headed for the emergency ward at the hospital. Di and Peter jumped into her car and followed.

In the car, Peter put his hand on Di's shoulder.

"He's going to be alright, Di. I've got a good feeling about this. I'm sure he'll be okay."

Di looked at Peter sideways then back at the road. She seemed afraid to speak.

"Push out that positive energy now, don't give up. He needs you to have faith and believe he'll be well. He's got everything going for him, you know. He keeps fit and isn't overweight. He's a strong man."

Di finally found her voice, and said, "Why do you say that? He's had a heart attack, for God's sake. He's the last person I would have expected to have one."

"Well, Di, I was a surf life saver for twenty years, and after a while I developed a sense of what would happen. Truly, I'm not wrong. Keep thinking positive and don't let him down now."

Tears ran silently down Di's face as she nodded. "I agree, he will be okay, he will."

They drove the rest of the way in silence and when they parked the car. Di resisted the urge to run. She walked purposefully toward the door.

Chapter Twenty-One

Tom Heart arranged a meeting with Charlie Savka and Gwen. He had not gone to his office; instead, he had asked them to come to his home.

Before they arrived, Tom shaved his father's stubble and replaced his pyjamas with clean, comfortable day clothes. He sat him at the table. "How are you feeling now, Dad? Can I get you anything?"

"No, mate, as a matter of fact I feel better than I have in ages. I was wondering yesterday if maybe that last lot of chemo may be working. They didn't give me much hope, you know, but something's changed, and I'm taking less medication than before as well. They said I could increase it when the pain got worse, but for some reason, I'm taking less. What do you think is going on?"

Tom smiled and squatted down next to his father's chair. With one hand on his shoulder, he nodded.

"That's the best thing you've said for a long time. You wouldn't be the first person that had a miracle, or at least a remission. I love you, Dad. I don't want you going anywhere for a long time. Stay here with me, I need you."

Tom dropped his head on to his father's shoulder. They had never been able to express personal feelings to one another, in the past.

Tony stroked his son's head, "I'm still here, and got no plans to go anywhere."

"Good," Tom said.

The doorbell interrupted their intimate moment. Tom stood and went to the front door, where he found Charlie standing on the doorstep. Gwen came up behind. They sat down at the table.

Tony had a grin from ear to ear.

Tom opened his laptop.

"Let's get this show on the road," said Charlie, as he smiled at Tony.

Gwen watched them all, a little mystified. She sensed the three men had a secret. She was itching to know what it was, but was smart enough not to ask.

"The plan today," Tom said, "is to agree on a course of action in relation to the missing ten million dollars, and to establish the facts about the identity of Brenda Simpson, alias Freya Holman. To begin, we will just go over the circumstances which have led us to this point."

Charlie nodded to Gwen, and she took up her story from how she first met Freya.

Tom tapped away on his laptop.

******

Peter and Di paced around the hospital waiting room after Di had answered questions and given Jim's medical history. Neither could sit, and there was nothing to say so they just kept walking around. Twenty minutes later, the resident doctor came to the room and waved them in. They followed him to a bay full of machinery and equipment. For a moment, Di thought they were going to tell her he was dead, but as soon as she looked at him, she saw he was conscious. He tried to smile.

"I bet that gave you all a scare," said a tall, mature man in a white coat. He put his hand out to Peter and Di. "I'm Doctor Kirby," he said. "I'm sorry it has all taken so long, but Jim here had a fight on his hands."

Di moved next to Jim, as best she could. He was surrounded with tubes and electrical equipment, all flashing lights and making little noises. She held his hand.

"Hello, Darling," she whispered.

She could not stop the tears that flowed freely down her cheeks as he tried to squeeze her hand. Her hands trembled as she held on to him, and she tried to hear what the doctor was saying.

He told Di that a cardiac bypass would be required, meaning Jim had some blocked blood vessels but surgery would fix that. He had a blood pressure problem and drugs would fix that. The doctor stressed that Jim would have to make some lifestyle changes and they would talk about that. Less stress, that was going to be the key and a few dietary changes as well. He could then look forward to a long, healthy life. Simple!

Di nodded, knowingly. She spoke the words in her head. *It was time for them to retire.* She knew Jim was not the type of person to take anything lightly, and these last few years at Keeala Resort had been extremely stressful for Jim, because he felt a great sense of responsibility whenever anything went wrong. He was a perfectionist and that made so many things hard for him.

The doctor scheduled Jim for tests, and later a move to the coronary care facility, so Di and Peter said their goodbyes and promised to return in a few hours.

Jim watched them as they walked away and he wondered how this could have happened to him. He had felt terrified when the pain struck him at the office and then he woke in the ambulance and later in the hospital. He was sure he was dying and now, watching Di walk away, he felt so alone and afraid that the pain would return. Jim looked up to see the intravenous tubing running into his arm. He felt oxygen in his nose and there were electrical leads attached to his chest. He could not move, and for a moment, fear paralysed him. He felt trapped, completely powerless. He closed his eyes and began to tell himself it was all okay. He was not ready to die yet. He had too much to do. *Calm down, old boy,* he said to himself, and he did.

******

Brenda Simpson was unable to relax. She could not believe she was off the hook and she still expected Gwen to ring her, or worse still, to turn up at any time. She had hidden her gun and ammunition but checked on them regularly, in case she forgot where they were, *or maybe they might get up and run away,* she said to herself sarcastically. The idea of having a gun in the house was unsettling and it worried her.

The day after Gwen rang her, Brenda went to her regular yoga class at the clubhouse. She wanted to re-establish her old routine, and hoped it would help her to settle down and put Gwen Clarke in the past. She met up with friends after the class and enjoyed her lunch.

"Enjoy the yoga?" said Harold Smith, to the woman he knew as Freya.

"Yes, I find it really puts my mind and body in a good place. How about you, Harold?"

"Exactly the same. It's as if I'm in another world for forty-five minutes. Hey, did you hear about the manager having a heart attack?"

"No. Is he okay?"

"We think so, but he had a pretty bad turn, I believe. You just never know when your time's up, do you? Last year, when we had that bus trip, we all thought we were goners, didn't we?"

"That's true," answered Freya, now reminded of the ill-fated bus trip that saw Harold's partner in a coma, and two others dead.

She took her leave of Harold and wandered off, caught up in her own thoughts. She had no close friends and spent a lot of time alone. In many ways, she was doing time in the same way Brett was. They were both just waiting for the time to be over and they could go back to living again.

******

"Don't worry about cooking dinner for me tonight, love. I've got work to do at the office and I might be late home." Vinnie shouted, as he tied his shoelaces and then made his way to the door, hoping he sounded casual.

"So what's going on? I was planning delicious zucchini burgers and artichokes."

"Well, take a night off, or why don't you have dinner at the club house? Do you good to take a break."

Charlene appeared in the doorway as Vinnie got into his car. She was disappointed. She planned to start cooking soon and maybe even make a dessert. She waved to him as he reversed out the driveway and turned, but then she ran out to the car and signalled him to wind down the window.

"It's okay, Vin," she said, "I'll cook it tomorrow night – give you something to look forward too."

"Oh, good," he said, as he wound the window back up and fought the urge to plant his foot down on the accelerator in frustration. As he made his way to the drug house, he tried to get his mind off artichoke and zucchini burgers.

"Where's Jason?" were Vinnie's first words, when he entered by the back door. He had gone straight to the lab and found Nat happily employed measuring and reading his recipe book.

"Oh hi, Vin, Jason's gone out."

"Out where?"

"Business," he said, "somethin' 'bout makin' new contacts."

Vinnie was already walking around looking for Grant. He found him in the kitchen, sitting on the floor and leaning back against the wall. Vinnie could see he was stoned and stood staring; trying to decide whether there was any point in attempting to get information from him.

"You bloody idiot, what use are you, usin' more than you earn. You plannin' to follow your friend Luke? That's where you're headed, you fuckwit."

They looked at one another and Grant had a smile from ear to ear. He could not maintain eye contact and his head rolled around on his shoulders. He said nothing, and Vinnie walked away in disgust. He went to Jason's bedroom, and poked around, looking for anything of interest. At least it smelled a little better than when Luke slept there. It was almost clean, Vinnie thought to himself. He wondered what Jason was planning, since he appeared he had settled in and had not left yet. He was going through the bedroom drawers when he heard Jason call out from the kitchen.

"Nat, come and get a look at this," Jason had said, in an exaggeratedly loud voice. He had seen Vinnie's car and knew he was in the house.

"Hi, Vin," said Jason, as Vinnie appeared. "Looks like we won't be getting much work from Grant today. I haven't seen him this bad for a long time."

"What do you expect? You haven't been here supervisin', have you? So where were you?"

Jason hesitated before he said, "Out making a couple of new customers."

"Oh, yeah. What have you got?"

"Actually, I came away empty handed. Someone directed me to his mate but when I got to his place he was already fixed up."

"Had any other new punters?"

"No, I haven't. Been a bit slow lately."

Vinnie nodded. He shoved his hands deep into his pockets. "Have you got yesterday's takings? I might do some bookkeeping while I'm here. Where's the bible?"

Jason reached up to the top shelf in the almost bare pantry. He handed the book to his boss and commenced making himself a cup of tea. Vinnie wandered off to the lounge and sat down to examine Jason's figures.

Jason ignored Grant and went to see how Nat was getting on.

"Couple a questions for yer, mate," Nat said, and the two went over the procedure again.

Nat tried hard, but his memory was poor and he was very dependent on the instruction book.

Jason thought about his idea of blowing up the house and getting away with the takings. He realised it would be a matter of changing some of the instructions in the book. Nat would not know the difference. He wished he had not become so attached to Nat, but he also knew his friend was on a downward spiral. They would all end up like Luke, except for Vinnie of course; he would just continue to get rich at the expense of these pathetic individuals.

"So have you thought any more about moving on?" asked Vinnie, when Jason sat down next to him.

"I'm not sure what to do. For the time being I'll hang on here, but in the future I'd like to continue my education. As I said before, I don't plan to end up like my father."

"Yeah, I understand." Vinnie began to wonder if he might hang on to the boy long enough to get someone else to take over. "I won't make it hard for you Jase. When you decide what you're going to do, just give me some notice so I can replace you."

Vinnie knew that was not going to be simple. Finding someone he could trust to run the show and not cheat him, and who could stay straight enough to perform the overseeing and bookwork, also the deliveries and pickups, was a big ask. A non-user was what he wanted, someone like his friend who did the job before Luke and Jason. Unfortunately, he was now doing eight years behind bars and would not be interested in setting himself up for another long stretch, if he ever did come out.

Vinnie had to acknowledge he was on to a good thing with Jason and he decided to try to keep him. "You know, I've been thinking about increasing your cut, mate. Now that you're doing two jobs, you're worth more. I believe in paying a bloke what he's worth – a fair day's pay for a fair day's work. What do you say?"

"What did you have in mind?

"A percentage, say twenty percent of our takings."

"Say thirty."

"Oh, no mate. I was being extremely generous here. Don't try to push your luck."

"Okay, make it twenty."

"That's better. Remember who's running this business. I've put a lot of effort into setting up this whole show and it's taken me years, as you well know."

Jason nodded. "So, beginning today, twenty percent?"

"Beginning today," Vinnie agreed. "Now, I've got some calls to make, so bugger off and start earning your money." He picked up the phone, but held it by his side. He called to Jason, "I want you to come up with some idea about what you're planning to do with Grant. He's your responsibility now, and I don't want this situation to continue. Just let me know what you decide before you take any action."

"Yeah, right Vinnie."

Jason stood in the hallway with his back to Vinnie and thought, *there's only one action that's any good for the lot of you. Soon, mate, soon.*

Nat returned to the kitchen to find that Grant had slid to the floor. Nat fetched a pillow and placed it under Grant's head. Grant started to snore. Nat looked at the prone body of his helper and realised he needed to continue without any help from his friend. *Might need a snort meself,* he figured.

Chapter Twenty-Two

They all agreed. Gwen had explained how she had come to identify Freya Holman as Brenda Simpson. She then explained how she had confronted her with the truth, then Charlie and Tony went on to tell Tom and Gwen all about the circumstances surrounding the embezzlement

Since Charlie had the most knowledge, and was anxious to take the lead role in approaching the insurance company, the decision was unanimous. They agreed on how they would split the reward and were all aware that they would have to wait until the money was recovered, before they would see any of it.

For Gwen it was okay now that she had her money back from Ron. She could afford to wait. She thought about Ron as she drove back to the shabby, little rental unit they now shared. She knew she was not finished with him yet. *Actually, I am finished with you now, you rotten, little sod. So don't get too comfortable, darling husband, you're soon going to see how it feels to be left, high and dry.* She mouthed the words to the vacant car seat next to her.

When Gwen got home, the place was empty. She tried to guess where Ron could be. She took a walk down to the pub on the corner of the block. *So there you are, with a couple of losers just like yourself,* she thought, as she watched him from the other side of the bar. He appeared to be very happy as he talked with two other men who had the look of the homeless. Ron was obviously shouting the drinks.

Gwen shook her head and went home. She called the real estate agent, to say she was moving out. Next, she rang a local removalist. "I need to move urgently," she said. "I'll make it worth your while if you can fit me in tomorrow." The deal done, she began to pack her personal things.

Ron arrived home two hours later. He did not notice anything amiss, but rolled into bed, still in his clothes and without any dinner.

Gwen settled in front of her computer to look for a new home. She listened with disgust as Ron snored away in the background.

******

"I'm off for a walk, love," said Ron, as he made his way to the front door about eleven the next morning.

"See you later," Gwen answered, as the door slammed.

Twenty minutes later, the removal truck drove up in the driveway.

"Perfect timing, boys," she said, as the two burly men came up the stairs. A nice tip encouraged the men to work quickly, and they were out of there by twelve forty-five.

"Reckon this one's doing a midnight flit," said one of the men, as they slammed the big truck doors. "Let's get outta here."

Gwen left one old chair behind. It sat in the middle of the empty room with a note attached. It read, *'Don't try to find me. I never want to see you again. I will be in touch via my solicitor about the divorce.'*

Ron staggered home around four that afternoon. At first, he thought he had the wrong house – then he saw the note. He had to read it several times before he managed to digest the words. He scrunched the paper in his hand, then lurched to the bedroom. Finding it empty, he slid to the floor and was asleep before his head hit the carpet.

******

Frank Pekalski smiled when he looked at Joy's profile. He was admiring her strong features and soft hair, when she turned under his gaze and asked, innocently, "What are you smiling at?"

"You. I haven't enjoyed myself as much in a very long time. Actually, I didn't realise how boring I had become until I began to talk. Almost all the people I met tonight are new to me, and I really don't know why I've acted like such a recluse. They were all so welcoming and sincere that I'm really looking forward to next week."

"Well, you don't need to wait that long. There's heaps of things you can join in on, before then."

"What do you do?"

"Yoga, writers group, bowls, tennis."

"That much? You must be busy all the time."

"True, and I'm never bored. Why don't you come to karaoke tomorrow evening?"

"You're going?"

"I am. It starts at seven."

"In that case, I'll be there."

They both stopped outside Joy's house and they turned to face one another.

"Thank you for introducing me to the land of the living again, Joy."

"My absolute pleasure, Frank. See you tomorrow night," she said, and turned to walk up the path to her door.

Frank heard her put the key in the lock. Frank marvelled at how light-hearted he felt. He had a spring in his step as he started for his own home. He had only walked a few paces, when a car came around the corner towards him. It's headlights were on high beam, and Frank was dazzled and stunned by the headlight beams that hit him. The car stopped dead with a squeal of brakes, and Frank made eye contact with the driver. Each knew who the other was. Frank stepped to the side and the car slowly moved away.

"Keep smiling mate, while you can," said Frank, to the back of the classic car as it slid out of sight.

Vinnie began to scratch; first his hands, then his head, then his legs. Cops always had that effect on him. He became agitated and tapped his foot. The encounter was just something else to keep him awake tonight.

******

The sound of the bedside phone shattered her sleep.

"Di Watersen," she said, as she switched on the light and juggled the handpiece.

"Mrs. Watersen, this is the coronary care ward at the hospital. We are concerned about your husband's condition, and think you might like to come in."

Di had held her breath as soon as she realised who was calling.

"What's happening?"

"Your husband has had another bad turn and his condition is not improving."

"Is the doctor there?"

"He's on his way now, and will be here in a few minutes. I suggest you may want to be here in case he has another turn."

"I'll be there very soon."

She hung up and raced around the room, switched on lights and grabbed clothes. Di was dressed and on her way out, when she remembered she couldn't leave the place without a manager. She went back to the phone in the kitchen and rang Ellen. Fortunately, she was home and agreed to come over.

"Let me know how things are going as soon as you can, please," said Ellen.

Di's mind was in a whirl. For the first time, she began to think of her life without Jim. No part of her was ready to accept that he may actually leave her.

"No, no!"

She banged on the steering wheel as she drove along the almost empty road at three am. Later, she would realise she could not remember driving to the hospital or taking the stairs, two at a time, rather than wait for the lift.

"How is he?" were her first words to the nurse at the station.

"Wait, please."

The nurse hurried off to Jim's bedside. Medical staff surrounded the bed. Di watched from the nurse's station, and took in all the attention Jim was getting.

In the course of her career, she had spent years working in this area. The gravity of the situation was not lost on her. Finally, the doctor walked over to her.

"He's holding his own now, Mrs. Watersen," he said. "You can sit with him. Come over."

They walked to Jim's bedside and Di's hands were cold when she reached out for Jim's. She knew no one could really predict how things would go from here, so she did not ask any questions. She sat on the chair beside the bed, and closed her eyes and prayed.

The morning dawned and Jim remained unconscious. Other patients came and went from the coronary care unit, while Di remained frozen to the chair, holding Jim's hand. Just before two o'clock that afternoon, he regained consciousness. He turned his head to the side and looked at his wife. She slept quietly next to his bed, sitting bolt upright.

He squeezed her hand and she immediately opened her eyes.

"Oh, Jim, you're back!"

"I'm back."

"I thought I'd lost you, my darling."

"You won't get rid of me that easily," he whispered.

The nurse came to Jim's bedside. She attended to his observations and then contacted the doctor.

"He'll be here soon," she said to Di, in her reassuring voice.

That had been the turning point in Jim's recovery. For no obvious reason, he recovered from his setback and improved hourly, until even the staff had to agree that it was amazing.

It was a long day for Di. She felt drained, but much happier as she drove home that evening. She heard the energetic voices of the karaoke group, and she smiled to herself as she parked the car.

"Life goes blissfully on," were her words to Ellen, who met her at the front door. Whether she meant Jim, or the singing voices in the clubhouse, neither knew. They hugged and Di gave Ellen a full report on Jim's improvement.

"What you need is a nice meal and a long bath, then into bed. That's my prescription for you."

Ellen turned, and Di followed her into the kitchen, where there was a place set at the table. Ellen served her tired friend a plate of chicken in sauce, and a tall glass of wine.

"Now, bath, bed, and sleep – as soon as you've finished," she ordered. "Ring me if there are any changes, but I have a feeling they will be good ones."

Ellen went back to her own home.

Di finished her meal, and put the dish and Splayd in the sink. She tipped the last of the glass of wine into her mouth, rinsed the glass, and put it in the drainer. She made her way slowly up the stairs.

"God, what a day," she said.

Chapter Twenty-Three

Twenty *percent isn't much, all things considered.* Jason did not care, now that he had started to create a new plan. *The mean bastard could have doubled that, and it still wouldn't be enough.* He looked in at Grant, still sleeping in his room, where he and Nat had carried him. Jason had no idea what he could do with Grant. He had not been able to help his father, so why, he reasoned, would he be able to help anyone else. He had slowly realised he could not blow up the house either. He knew he could not consciously inflict injury on anyone.

So, where to now? he thought. Money was still the only barrier, and Jason knew that if he stole from Vinnie, he would track him down. He could leave the country, but even then, Vinnie would probably use his extensive contacts to find him. *I've got to get another job. It's the only way, and another place to live, away from Vinnie and everythin' he represents. That is my only choice.* As he discarded first one idea, and then another, Jason had to accept that there was no easy way to make his transition to freedom. He walked into the lab to find Nat.

"How's it goin', Nat? Gettin' the hang of bein' the chemist, are you?"

"Yeah, mate, but sometimes I forget things, or I forget to look at the book. I sure would like it if you were still workin' wiv me. Know what I mean?"

"Yes, mate, I do, but no-can-do anymore. I'm goin' to make sure you get a raise from Vin as well. You're worth more money, so stick to your guns, and don't accept less."

"Okay, I will."

"Grant doesn't look too good to me, mate. What do you think?" Jason asked Nat.

"Yeah, he's fucked. Goin' to join Luke, if ya ask me."

"What would you do with him?"

"Give him another big dose and help him on his way."

"Will you?"

"Will I what?"

"Give him another big dose and help him on his way."

"What, now?"

"Yes, right now - while he's sleepin' peacefully."

"But he's me mate, Jase."

"All the more reason to help him."

"Can't you do it?"

"I wouldn't know how."

"I could show ya."

"No. He would understand if you did it. You're his friend, Nat."

"We could take him to the hospital and leave him there, like Luke, but if he didn't die, he'd have to come back here, wouldn't he?"

Nat could see Jason nodding.

"Well, okay, I'll do it," Nat said.

He turned and went into the lab. There were some things he did know, better than anyone else in the organisation. He walked over to a small bag at the end of the bench. It had been his shower bag, but now it contained syringes, needles, spoons, and small bags of white powder, along with other drug paraphernalia. He prepared and drew up a dose of his own personal mix.

"This'll make ya happy on the way out, mate, I promise ya."

Jason watched Nat flick the syringe, and then followed him to Grant's bedroom.

"You awake, mate?"

Nat spoke quietly to his old friend, as he placed his equipment on the side of the bed. Grant did not move and both men noticed his shallow breathing and clammy skin. They stood and stared, Nat began to tap his foot.

"I can't do this."

He turned away and walked over to the window.

"No, you're right, and I don't want you to either. Get rid of that stuff."

Jason pointed to the bag on the bed and left the room. A minute later Nat followed Jason outside and they stood together quietly.

"I can't believe what I almost just did."

"I'm sorry, Nat, I shouldn't have asked you. We're going to have to let Grant make his own deal with God, and fuckin' Vinnie can get stuffed."

"What now?"

"Nothing," said Jason. "Let's have a cup of coffee, and get back to work."

Grant was semi-conscious in his room and had no idea how close he had just come to the end of his life. So many times in the past, he had overdosed himself, as now, and had hovered between life and death, only to come back even less of a person each time he survived. Still, he wanted to live. He wanted to live as he did in his dreams, not how he did in reality. He sometimes thought back to how his journey with drugs had started, and what it was in his life that he could not face without them.

He remembered his kindly uncle. Uncle Lester was the adopted brother of Grant's father. He had come from a dysfunctional and unhappy home, and had been the first person to take Grant camping. Grant's father was a busy man and was more than happy to let his son go off on adventures with his brother, but from the first occasion, those episodes had introduced Grant to a world of adult behaviour that he did not like, and could not understand. To compound Grant's confusion, Lester swore Grant to secrecy. He was an innocent child – too innocent to disobey.

By the time Grant was able to understand how he had been used, his uncle had moved on and Grant was damaged goods for the rest of his life. The only way he could live with the past was through a fog of drugs, and the blissful relief of unconsciousness.

Grant emerged slowly from the haze. His eyes fluttered, as his level of consciousness became lighter. He felt the bed beneath him. He sighed and tried to move, but did not have the energy. He drifted back to sleep.

Jason and Nat worked on in the laboratory, creating a product to sell to hundreds of other victims who would watch their lives spiral downwards in a cloud of destruction.

******

While it was business as usual at the drug house, as Pekalski called it, his life was anything but. He had returned from the karaoke evening with Joy. They sat on his lounge, almost exhausted from the energy they had expended They had sung their lungs out. Never had he had such a good time, just singing. They sat and held hands, and prompted one another as they continued to recall songs they had not heard for years.

"Oh, that's enough for me," laughed Joy, and she sat back, swinging her legs and looking around the room.

"What, you mean I'm the winner? I've only just begun. Where's that song book?"

"I do think the neighbours might have had enough by now, Frank."

"Do you think so?"

"I do. We should call it a night." Frank held on to her hand as they stood and faced one another. Neither had had a relationship since they had lost their life partner, so they were both awkward, for a moment. They both looked down at the floor until Frank put his finger under Joy's chin and lifted her eyes to his. She was almost as tall as he was, and he didn't have to bend far to kiss her gently on the lips. They both smiled and then tried it again. Life took on new meaning from that moment, and they each felt as though they were stepping out of one life and into another.

******

Love was in the air, elsewhere, that night, as Ellen and Matt chatted long distance between Adelaide and Brisbane. Hardly a day went by when they did not speak by phone or Skype.

"Do you think Jim will be back to work when he's well again?" Matt asked.

"I have my doubts. When I hear Di talk about a long holiday, it sounds as if she wants Jim to have a stress-free life. I have no idea what their financial situation would be, but Jim is a very practical and financially astute person, so I suspect they could afford to retire. He must be close to sixty."

"So we would need new managers?" Matthew mused.

"What are you thinking?"

"Same as you, maybe. What if you and I applied for the position? We're well qualified and the residents know us."

"True, true. But the position is really for a married couple," Ellen said quietly.

"That could be arranged," Matthew said hesitantly.

Silence followed, then, "Matthew, that sounds almost like a proposal to me."

"Certainly not to anyone else, my love. Will you marry me?"

A smile spread across Ellen's face as she said, "Yes, Mr Weatherlee, I will."

"So are you saying yes?"

"Yes, I am saying yes."

"I want to hug you."

"Me too."

"I could book a flight tonight and be there tomorrow. What's more, I would have a perfectly valid reason for racing off – to help Di while Jim is sick."

"But darling, what if they don't want to retire and there is no job for us?"

"Just bide our time, I guess."

The next morning, Ellen picked Matthew up from the airport and they went to see Jim in hospital. They thought he looked comfortable and they did not mention their new plans. Just that Matt would help until Jim got back on his feet.

"I'm glad you're here, mate. I don't want Di to be the next one to have a heart attack, trying to manage everything herself."

"Relax, Jim. This is what my job is all about and I'm happy to step in. By the way, we have some news of our own. Are you ready?"

"I have a feeling I know what that news might be," Jim said, grinning and nodding.

Chapter Twenty-Four

Charlie Savka did not waste any time making contact with the insurance company associated with Brett and Brenda Simpson.

"That is quite an amazing story, Mr. Savka. If you don't mind, I'll call in the director and we'll go through it again." The young clerk left the room, and returned a few minutes later with the insurance company's director, close behind.

"So, Mr. Savka, you say you have some information regarding an embezzlement from five years ago. Would you like to tell me your story please?"

The director ordered coffee, and the three men sat together as Charlie went over his story once again. He had not tired of repeating the story, rather he enjoyed it more with every telling.

He explained he had a client who knew not only the identity of Brenda Simpson, but also her whereabouts. He also showed them the letter that the client copied. The director conceded that the author of the letter did sound like Brett Simpson. The director took a deep breath when he handed the letter back to Charlie. He said, "I don't suppose your client can ascertain where the money is being held?"

"No. We thought we'd hand what we knew over to you, and we expect to see the reward when the money is uncovered."

"Do you now? Unfortunately, nothing is that simple, Mr. Savka. If it were, we would have uncovered that money long before this. We have already spent a great deal of money ourselves, trying to track down those millions. To the police, this is a very cold case."

"I'm one of the people you employed to track that money five years ago. I wasn't paid out then, but you can be sure I will be this time." Charlie leaned toward the director and a small light of recognition flashed in the eyes of the other man.

"I see. If you decide to give me this person's present alias and address, I assure you if that money is recovered then you will have your reward."

"Good, so what happens next?"

"Leave that to us. We'll let you know as soon as we have something worthwhile to pass on."

"I have another copy of this letter and intend to inform the media about my situation if I'm not kept in the loop. There's no way I'm working for nothing, again."

"Of course not, Mr. Savka. I can imagine we may need to contact you and your client again, before we can recommence our investigation. I'll need contact numbers and names, and I'd like to talk to your client tomorrow, if that can be arranged."

"No. You can speak to me. Any information you want, speak to me."

The director frowned and took a deep breath.

"That could make the situation quite difficult for us, but for now, we will proceed as you wish. Today, I have to consult with other members of this organisation and I'll be in touch tomorrow." He stood to indicate the meeting was over. Charlie shook hands with the two men and left with a smile of satisfaction.

He rang both Tom and Gwen later that day and brought them up to date.

******

Tom rang Gwen to see if she was satisfied with the progress, so far.

"And how is your husband getting on now that he has settled in at home again?" he asked.

"You may well ask. I really don't know. If you're looking for him, you could probably catch him at the pub on the corner near where he lives."

"*He* lives?"

"Exactly! I've got my money and he's got his. We'll have a divorce as soon as it can be arranged. I'm very pleased to have my independence back and I look forward to not sharing any of the reward money with the old sod."

Tom almost laughed. He had to agree with Gwen that there was little to like about Ron Clarke and that he had created his own situation.

"Well, I'm sure you know what's best for yourself Gwen. We'll be in touch as this Simpson case unfolds, anyway."

He signed off and mused at the outcome of the Clarke saga. He looked forward to telling his father how it had all unfolded, that evening.

Tom was amazed at how much his father's appetite had improved and he now waited for his son to come home each day and cook a meal. Tom knew it could all change at any moment. Cancer was an insidious disease that could return when you least expected it, but for now he was going to enjoy whatever time he had with his father, and make it as happy as he could for him. As he drove home later that day, he thought about how much change his relationship with his father had gone through; so many highs and lows, from almost separation, to now an accord and acceptance of each other.

******

After Charlie had left the meeting at the insurance company, the director and gone immediately to make contact with the other members of the administration. Five years previously, they had expected to uncover the whereabouts of the $10,000,000 and see Brett Simpson behind bars for a long time. However, the money had disappeared, without a trace. They had used means, both legal and illegal, to trace that stolen loot but the man had been too good for them. They were able to prove in a court of law that he was the only person who could have stolen the money, but they had lost the trail and had never been able to recover it. They also knew that he had to have had an accomplice, obviously his wife, but she too had eluded them. She had disappeared without a trace.

The company had spent a great deal, trying to track down the stolen money; this was the first lead they had received in the past five years.

"So, we don't even know if Brenda is residing locally?" asked a senior manager.

"No, but I think this client is as anxious as we are to uncover where the money is hidden," said the director to whom Charlie had spoken.

"No one is as anxious as we are," corrected one of the members of the board. "And it's not just the money. Our reputation has never recovered since that affair. We need closure on all of this and I personally am prepared to do whatever is necessary to get that money back. I also want to see that woman behind bars. Nothing else will satisfy me." The others nodded their agreement and tapped the table in support.

"As yet," the director said, "we don't have access to the client this bloke is representing, but that could change. I don't like the idea of working through someone who already has an axe to grind."

There was general agreement that the director who called the meeting would continue to deal with Charlie, as long as things were progressing. The faces around the table would prefer to stay anonymous, as long as they needed to pursue the money, probably through illegal computer hacking. They all knew the process; first find the woman, get access to her computer files and then track down the hidden millions. There was always the possibility, they conceded within their group, that it was not in an institution, but sitting in a container in a hole under a tree. This, in their judgment, was unlikely.

******

When Charlie left the insurance company, he went directly to Tom's office.

"I believe they'll do just about anything to see an end to this matter, Tom. I had the sense that it was not forgotten at all, and that they would prefer to deal directly with Gwen. They'll want to cut us out, and I'm not going to let that happen. Gwen can afford to let us represent her, and she has no idea how to do a deal. They would rip her off for sure, so please, no mention to her about the details; give her the impression it's all very complicated. Know what I mean?"

"Sure, sure," Tom agreed. "I'll leave all that to you and keep my mouth shut."

"You know, mate, this business you've got here was a pretty profitable concern when Tony was at the helm."

"You mean it isn't now?"

"No, no, not at all. I mean your dad and I worked together a lot, and we were a good team. I have a feeling maybe you and I could duplicate that success – if you're interested."

"As a matter of fact, the thought had crossed my mind, Chuck."

Charlie laughed out loud. "He used to call me Chuck, as well. Did you know?"

"I did, it suits you."

"See what I mean. I think we are in tune."

"Let's talk it over with Tony tonight. Come home and have dinner with us. Dad would love to see you."

"You're on, mate."

Driving home that evening, Tom had the feeling things were looking up. His dad was improving, they looked like coming into some money soon, and now he may have a new business partner. *That's about all I need for now, thanks God. Mind you, a girlfriend wouldn't go amiss.* He started to conjure up some images, as the cars on the motorway flew by.

******

"The insurance company has had their legal team draw up this document for our approval," Charlie said, as he handed the envelope to Tom, who sat down on his office chair while he read it.

"So it sounds alright to me, what's your opinion?"

"I think I'll ask to have a few small changes made, like the clause where they say our information is subject to a time limit. They are saying, if they don't locate the money within a certain time frame, in this case six months, we forfeit the reward. I won't have a bar of that, and I don't really believe it will take that long. Hell, they could find it and then just sit on it until we lose out."

"The rest is okay. They agree to work with me, and not demand to interview Gwen. They said they'll do a bit of checking of their own. By that I'm pretty sure they mean hacking, and if unsuccessful they will go to the fraud squad with all they have."

Tony was delighted Charlie had agreed to work in collaboration with Tom. He could see they would make a good team and he knew how much his son needed someone to guide him. In their business, so much depended on the individual's insight, even intuition, but it all needed to be backed up with knowledge, and there was nothing that could replace the years of experience Charlie had. Tony trusted him, and he knew his old friend would head Tom in the right direction.

The insurance company was ready to begin its investigation as soon as Charlie revealed the identity and location of Brenda Simpson. He did this when the contract was signed.

Chapter Twenty-Five

Matthew Weatherlee had to decide where he was going to live, temporarily. Ellen wanted him to move in with her. Matthew's mother presumed he would be living at home with her. His job demanded he live on site at the resort, so he moved into the spare room at Di and Jim's and was happy to be near his friends.

Now that Myra, his mum, had met Ellen, they were all able to start to feel like a family. That had been something missing from their lives. Di invited Ellen and Myra to dinner, after Matt settled in and she too was feeling happier to have people around her. With Jim still in hospital, and Di going back and forth each day, a lot of the resort work was being neglected.

"I do have the time to help out," said Ellen to Matt, when she offered to relieve him of some of his paperwork.

"But you have your own two jobs – sales here, and life-counselling when you finish here in the evening."

"But I can cut back on that for the time being. I will when we get married anyway, so let me help you where I can, please."

"All right, but I'll be watching you to be sure you aren't overdoing it." He hugged her and thought how he must have done something good in his life to be so lucky.

As well as Matt and Ellen jumping in to relieve Di, Harold and Robert had been to the office and the residence several times to volunteer their services and see how Di was faring.

"What about the gardeners? Surely they need some overseeing at a time like this," Robert insisted.

"Actually, they work extremely independently, and I rely on them to come to me if they have any problems," said Di. "The catering staff, however, always have concerns. For some reason, that profession seems to attract emotional and unreliable people. If you would care to follow up on how they're going, it would be a great weight off my mind."

Robert smiled. He could see now that his talents were required and what better way than by his stepping in and bringing some organisation to the kitchen.

"I can do that. No trouble at all, my dear. Set your mind at rest, I will be over there in the morning and we will soon see how a properly run kitchen should look."

Those words came back to Di when she walked past the kitchen the next morning, on her way to the office.

"Well, if you know so damn much about it, what the hell do you need me for?" screamed the cook, into Roberts red face.

They stared one another down for a few moments, before Robert put his hands up for a truce.

"We both need to calm down," he said. He walked away and picked up the clipboard with the menu. "Now looking at this, I can see that certain things have to be prepared early and others almost at the last minute. It's called prioritising, and it's necessary for preparing a well organised meal, especially when you are cooking for hundreds of people at a time."

"So tell me something I don't already know." The cook stood with her feet apart and her hands on her hips, staring at Robert. "I have been the chef here for nearly six months, and that's longer than anyone else, so I hear."

"You are a cook, not a chef, and I assure you that record is not great. I don't understand why you are simply not grateful for my help. I do have vast experience in the food and catering industry and all you can do is complain."

The cook sucked her bottom lip in and visibly sighed. She turned then and slammed a saucepan down on to the stove. Robert could see she was not going to back down and he began to wonder what other tack he could take.

"So you tell me then, how can you get through all this work today with your helper away. I'm offering my services – and you aren't even grateful."

"No, you're not! You want to take over. I'm in charge here and I've been here long enough to know how to run things. If you really wanted to help, you would just ask me what you can do. Someone has to peel the vegies and wash up, why not start there?"

"Madam, I would have to be blind not to see that some things need to take precedence over cutting up vegies. I could have the sauces prepared early and the desserts could be chilling in the fridge. The vegies will go brown, sitting around waiting to go in the oven. If you can't see that, then you're not even a cook."

"That does it!" The woman pulled off her apron and threw it on the bench.

Robert grabbed it away from the stovetop before it caught alight.

She turned and marched to the door, "So you do it, mister smart-arse chef."

The screen door slammed and Robert stood alone, surrounded by fresh food and cooking utensils. He looked around and then he smiled.

"So let the fun begin," he said, then turned to pick up the phone. "Harold, I need you here immediately – in the kitchen." There was a pause. "No, she has quit. Bring a couple of aprons."

Robert began to make a cup of coffee for himself.

When Harold arrived, he looked worried and was more so when he heard what Robert had planned for the two of them. He shook his head and sipped his coffee, his only consoling thought was the knowledge that his partner worked better under pressure than anyone he had ever met. He steeled himself and stood up, tying his apron in place.

"Where do you want me to begin?" asked Harold.

******

The morning after a night of karaoke with his new friend Joy, Detective Pekalski found it hard to keep focused on his job. He was due at a meeting with two officers of the drug squad at nine thirty and he drifted into the office on a cloud.

"You're looking well, mate," said the senior officer.

"Feeling good too," Pekalski replied. "Got anything new from your end?"

"We're thinking we might raid that drug house pretty soon. Unless you've got something to add to the file, we don't expect to gain anything by waiting longer. We've tailed that young bloke for several weeks now, but nothing's changed. He's got a couple of new clients but his supplier still visits on Tuesdays and we've got a tail on him now, so he's of more interest to us than the guys in the house. The supplier of the basic ingredients will take us in the direction of the importer, we hope. We think it will be someone we've already flagged. So when we decide we can get them all there at the same time. We'll set up a raid. You can be there if you want, depends on whether you want to blow your cover."

"Maybe, I'll give it some thought."

Pekalski was not sure he wanted his neighbours to see him in the media reports. He would rather remain discreetly in the background, especially now that he had met Joy. It was important to him not to scare her off, or embarrass her with her friends.

******

While Pekalski met with his work mates, his neighbour Vinnie was meeting with his. He had established a pattern of checking the books every Monday morning. This had been noted by the officer watching him.

Jason monitored Vinnie's movements as well. He was looking for the right moment to disappear, and he wanted to be sure he did not go away empty handed. He worked out that the best time would be after he had done his pickups and deliveries, but before Vinnie came to collect; that meant sometime on Sunday, because the cash box was always full on Sunday afternoon. Jason knew Vinnie came on Tuesdays as well, to meet with the supplier and pay him.Jason thought his best time would be Sunday night, after everyone went to sleep and Vinnie would be at home watching a movie. Now that Luke's uninvited friends no longer dropped around, it was usually only Jason, Grant, and Nat in the house. Artie had another home to go to.

"I see you have not managed to do anything with Grant," was Vinnie's opening statement to Jason, when the three sat down for a talk.

"There ain't nuthin' he can do with Grant, Vin." Nat spoke up for a change. He usually said very little and never argued with the boss.

"Course there is. He could give the mongrel a dose he wouldn't forget. Or I should say, wouldn't remember. We don't need him hanging on, contributing nothing. That's not how to run a business."

"But we ain't murderers, either," answered Nat. "If ya think it's so easy, why don't ya do it yaself? The only trouble is, we'd know, wouldn't we?"

Vinnie sat on the edge of his chair. He was outnumbered, and surprised to hear the insipid, little idiot, speak up for a change. Vinnie got up and walked around the room.

"So, do either of you have any suggestions?" he said.

"Yeah," said Jason. "Just leave him alone. He hasn't got long. Why should we get blood on our hands so you can tidy up the place?"

Vinnie clenched both fists; he realised he would never have put up with this in the past. He was getting soft. He thought it was probably because he was living with a woman, and not keeping in touch with his mates. Whatever it was, he was not prepared to do the dirty work himself.

"So, leave him alone, you think. Let him sniff up or inject all the profits. I don't suppose you'll pay for all the stuff he's using."

"He's not using that much now," said Jason. "His system is saturated, I reckon. Why don't you go and talk to him. Maybe he'll do what none of us can."

Vinnie was on his way out of the room before Jason finished talking. Nat and Jason followed him, and stood at the door while he asked Grant what he was up too.

"Not been too well lately, boss," was the answer from the bed. Grant's eyes were glazed and his body odour was almost overpowering.

"We've been talking about your situation and thought you might like a very big dose of medicine. What do you say?"

The three men stood and watched as tears flowed from Grant's eyes and he began to sob.

"I'm gonna get better fellers, honest; I just need a bit of time to get over this flu. It's been on me for days now, but I'll be up and about soon. Oh no, don't ask me to top meself, you couldn't do that."

He coughed and cried, and rolled around in the bed. He tried to sit up but fell back to the pillow, coughing and spitting streaks of blood.

Vinnie turned away and pushed past the two men in the doorway. He went back to the kitchen and Nat ran to get Grant a glass of water.

"Do you want me to call a doctor, mate," said Jason, as he moved closer to Grant. He felt his forehead and wondered if the man did have some other illness. "Maybe I should call an ambulance."

Grant reached for Jason's hand and tried to hold it.

"No, don't, please. Let me just lie 'ere and sleep a bit longer. I know I'm gonna be okay in a few days. Please, mate, give us a chance."

Jason patted Grant's hand. "All right, stop worryin' – and don't think about Vinnie either. I'll make sure he doesn't interfere. Have a drink of water now, and then get some rest. I'll wake you later when we cook somethin'. You look like you haven't eaten for days."

"I'm not 'ungry Jase – just want to sleep."

His hand slipped from Jason's grasp and he began to breathe more deeply. Jason covered him and closed the door.

They all sat quietly at the kitchen table.

"See what I mean," Jason said. "We can't do anythin' for Grant now. I don't think he'd be any better off at the hospital either. We just have to let the situation take its course."

Vinnie looked at Jason and wondered how the kid had become so wise in the last ten minutes. He knew the boy was right though. It was the most sensible course of action – stand back and do nothing and let it all unfold.

"Get the book and the cash box, Jason, I'll check the figures."

Chapter Twenty-Six

Di and Matt were late for dinner when they sat down at the clubhouse dining table.

It had been an extremely busy day for everyone and Di was so appreciative when Robert told her that the kitchen was all under control. He had not told her that the assistant was off sick and the cook had walked out. All he said was that it was running smoothly and he wanted her and Matt to eat with them when they finished in the office.

"This is wonderful, Robert. I had no idea the cook was capable of this type of cuisine. You must have the knack of getting the best from people. You should be congratulated, and you also Harold. I hear you helped out as well."

Matt was already eating his dessert and nodding his head in agreement.

"Actually he did a little more than just help out," Robert began to explain. "We're going to have to advertise for a new cook."

"What? A new cook? We've only just broken in this one," Di said. As she jumped up from the table and headed for the kitchen to get a glass of water. She pushed the kitchen door open, and then stepped back as though punched. She let it swing closed. On her second attempt she held it open a little longer, and then let it swing closed. Finally, she walked forward and into the kitchen.

She gasped, "Oh my god."

She took a few steps forward the looked around at the biggest mess she could have ever imagined. Her eyes were wide and she held her breath. She felt a hand land on her shoulder.

"Bit of a mess, isn't it?" said Robert.

"You could say that," she murmured, and nodded. The hands turned her away from the kitchen and back to the table.

"I know it looks bad now, but don't you give it another thought," said Robert. "We'll have that cleaned up in no time. Harold and I are very fast and very efficient. Just leave it to us and it'll be spick and span by the time we go to bed tonight."

At the table, Harold explained the situation to Matthew, and declined his offer to help clean up.

"No, we work well together and we made the mess, so we'll clean it up. I do hope it won't be too long before we get another cook though. Robert is a grand-plan person, from way back. He just doesn't always manage to clean up as he goes along. A small character flaw, that's all."

Matthew went and looked at the kitchen. He returned to the table, leaned over to Harold, and whispered, "I'll see the ad goes in, first thing in the morning. You're a very brave man."

Harold tried to grin but somehow it ended up looking more like a smirk.

******

"I suppose it's to be expected, but I've noticed quite a change in Di's attitude to the resort lately." Ellen was speaking quietly to Matthew while they sat on the upstairs balcony of the manager's residence.

"How do you mean?"

"She seems to be withdrawing and not showing much interest. She's at the hospital every day, and that I can understand, but it's more than that. Now that you and I have stepped in, she never asks about how things are going or about the residents."

"I think you're right, her concern for Jim takes priority over everything else, and there's not much to be done about it really. I'll have a talk to her tonight when she returns from the hospital."

"I like it here. I think we could be very happy, starting life in a situation where we work together. On the other hand, it could be a recipe for disaster, but I think we get on well and respect one another, and that's important if we are to spend so much time together."

Matthew thought for a minute then asked, "Do you feel okay about doing this type of work and not continuing with your life coaching?"

"I won't let that go. I've put too much into it, so I'll just keep my hand in, if that's possible. Maybe one day a week? Who knows, perhaps we may wish to move on from here one day, and then I'd be glad I still have a career."

"We are presuming, of course, that Di and Jim will retire and we'll get their position. Maybe Andrew Sleighmen has other ideas about who should take over," said Matt.

"Maybe. I think perhaps we should delay wedding plans until we know what they're doing, and also whether we will have this job."

Matthew agreed. "To change the subject," he said, "I can't help wondering about Harold and Robert. They're both so well intentioned, but I think we may still have had our cook if Robert hadn't been so – what's the word – helpful? I've advertised for a new cook but it's always hard to get the right person for a place like this. Perhaps you could give me a hand with the interviews, when they start."

"I'd be delighted," Ellen said. "See how well we work together. We make a great team."

She leaned over and gave her fiancé a kiss on the forehead.

They both heard Di's car pull into the driveway. They stood and waved to her from the balcony.

"I'll be right up," she said, as she waved back.

A couple of minutes later Di joined them on the balcony. She had poured herself a glass of wine as she passed the fridge.

"So, how's your day been?" asked Ellen.

"Well, I'm starting to relax. Jim really is getting better. He is, as you know, in rehab now and doing a little exercise and therapy. I can see him improving every day, and he's actually enjoying it. Now he's telling me to get home and go to the gym, as well. Don't you just hate it when someone gets enthusiastic about their epiphany and is not happy unless everyone else joins them?"

"I know what you mean," Matthew said, with a smile. "Do you have any idea when he'll be home?"

"Soon – we hope in a few days. His doctor is very happy with him and said if he keeps to his new regime and diet, he'll be strong enough for the bypass surgery within the next few weeks. He will have to cut down on what he drinks as well. I've long had a suspicion that he is sometimes a cupboard drinker. Anytime the stress rises, he calms himself down with a slug. He didn't think I noticed, but I did. He'll have to stop that now."

"So I guess that means more time off. Do you know how long?" Matt queried.

Di took a big breath then slowly let it out.

"Well, this is something Jim and I have been talking about today." She paused as if trying to find the right words. "We've decided to retire. We are aware of what a strain it is on you two, doing your jobs as well as ours. Also, we know Jim can't expose himself to more stress, even when he's fit again. It's his personality; he will always be a worrier and we are both getting a bit too old for the problems this place represents. Really, I think it should be a lot easier, but we seem to have attracted nothing but one serious problem after another in the time we've been here. I think we're jinxed."

Matt went to interrupt; Di put her hand up. "Just let me finish. The long and the short of it is that we have decided to end our working career. We have enough super so that we can manage if we are frugal. We can thank Jim for that, but we both think it's time to throw in the towel, so to speak." Di looked from one to the other for a response.

"Well, we're not surprised," said Ellen. "We've been talking here tonight about what you might do. It seems like the right decision to us and we also have considered applying for the job, after you leave."

"Oh, surely you would be the perfect choice – the obvious choice. As a matter of fact, I will recommend you when I send off my email to head office tomorrow."

Ellen reached out for Di's hand. "Thank you Di, we would appreciate that and we would apply as soon as you resign. So what would you do with yourselves, once you leave here?"

"We do have a little house, down the coast. It's rented out now, but we could arrange to have it back in three months. So we would take a holiday first, then return to do some long overdue renovations and start a new phase of our lives."

They all sat and let it sink in. They all knew this was a significant moment. It was a beginning for Ellen and Matt, and an ending for Di and Jim.

"I wish Jim was here," said Di, as Matt slipped away to grab the bottle of wine from the fridge and two glasses. He returned and topped Di's glass then handed one to Ellen.

He raised his glass. "To new beginnings for all of us," he said.

"To new beginnings," chorused Ellen and Di.

They drank and then sat, each with their own thoughts, until Di said, "I'm going to miss all my friends here, and you two, of course."

"We expect to see you regularly. Who knows, we may even sell you a house here one day," Ellen said.

That was all it took to open the floodgates. Di broke down and started to cry. She pulled a handkerchief from her sleeve and blew her nose.

"Silly me, this should be a happy occasion. Oh, I wish Jim was here. Oh dear, I should just be happy he's still with us and able to have a retirement. I'm sorry."

Matt and Ellen both moved together to comfort Di and they all fell together on the chair. They untangled and Ellen announced she was going downstairs to get dinner. This gave Matthew and Di a chance to talk about the details of the handover and how best for them all to get what they wanted.

Dinner was late, but they all felt they had achieved a lot that evening, Di especially, because she benefited from Matt's involvement and she wanted to have all the details tidied up before Jim came home. Just moving out was going to be stressful enough, without all the resort business to attend to. Now they had clarified the situation, they could put plans into action.

Chapter Twenty-Seven

Vinnie took some time looking over the book after his conversation with Grant and the boys. He was in no hurry to get back to Charlene's dinner. She was trying a new dish every night now, and was really enjoying being creative.

Vinnie decided he could not handle another one of her extravaganzas and ordered a pizza takeaway. He sat in the lounge, munching on his pizza and re-checking Jason's figures.

"I'm off now, Vin," Jason called, as he went to the front door and grabbed the car keys off the table. "Will you be here when I get back?"

"And what time will that be?"

"About two hours – got my deliveries late because we have a new customer and I can only catch him after six."

"Yeah, well I'll see how I'm going. I'll probably wait and collect the takings, but if I don't, I'll catch up tomorrow. You got your phone on you?"

"I have, Vin. See you, Nat," Jason said, as he walked past the lab.

Nat was absorbed in his collection of bubbling cauldrons and test tubes and did not hear. Later, as he sat at the bench in the lab, Nat tried to make sense of some of the abbreviations Jason had written in the recipe book. He came out of the lab to check with Jason.

"Where's Jase, Vin?" he asked, when he saw Vinnie sitting alone.

"Gone on his delivery run. Why?"

"I asked him to go over some of the instructions in his work book. He must've forgotten. What time will he be back?"

"Said he'd be a couple of hours. Should be back soon."

"Oh, well, doesn't matter, I'll still be here when he gets back. I'll catch him then."

Nat returned to his cooking in the lab.

Vinnie was stretched out on the lounge, watching television, when he felt the first vibrations. A small explosion followed. Vinnie jumped up and ran to the door of the lab.

Nat was in the middle of the room. He held a wooden spoon in one hand and a bucket in the other. There was black smoke rising from the bucket. Nat looked stunned.

"Shit, nuthin' like that never happened to me before," he said, as he looked up at Vinnie. "I've been tryin' to figure out this recipe Jase give me. Anyhow, I think I've got it nailed now, but just come and take a look at this, just to be sure."

"No, mate, I'm going home. I'll leave the cooking to you experts, but maybe you'd better leave the rest till Jason comes back. He shouldn't be long. Tell him I'll see him tomorrow."

Vinnie strode off out of the house; the takings could wait another day.

Nat went back to the bench, and smiled when he finally deciphered Jason's notes. He continued with the mixing of the ingredients.

Vinnie heard the explosion, three blocks away.

******

The street was a disaster scene when the fire truck arrived. The house was well alight and no one could get near it. They started to hose down the neighbouring houses and tried to prevent the spread of the flames. Several sirens could be heard approaching and the street was fast filling with spectators. A secondary explosion occurred just as the first police car drove up and three officers spilled from the vehicle. It was obvious that clearing the vicinity was their first priority and they shouted to the crowd to back up. Despite the best efforts of the firemen, the houses on either side caught alight. People were running in all directions and kids were screaming. Police were setting up a roadblock, and more emergency vehicles, including an ambulance, arrived.

This was the scene that confronted Vinnie when he drove in the end of the street. He got out of his car and watched in stunned silence. He pulled his phone from his pocket and rang Jason. There was no answer. Vinnie began to shake when he thought how close he had come to being a charred mess in the middle of all that. He pulled his car to the kerb and sat watching the action unfold.

From the other end of the street, Jason crouched in the darkness. He stared in shock as his home and friends disappeared in a flaming pyre before his eyes. Only when his phone rang, and he saw it was Vinnie, did he realise that this was the opportunity he was waiting for. If Vinnie thought he had died in the fire, he would not be looking for him, and Jason had more than five thousand dollars in his pocket. It was enough to get away with, and added to what he had been saving, was enough to start again in another state. He felt the wad of money in his pocket, then stood and walked back to his car.

Despite this positive outcome, Jason experienced a great sense of guilt as he drove away, dry eyed. His mind was a jumble of thoughts; he even wondered for a moment if Nat had managed to get out, but his good sense told him it was not possible. Then he remembered he had not gone over the instructions with Nat, as Nat had asked him to do earlier. He knew if he had, this explosion might not have happened.

Vinnie stayed at a distance and watched from his car until the fire trucks started to pack up, almost two hours later. During that time, he thought about Jason, Grant, and Nat; also the fact that he had just lost the major source of his income. It was a rented house, but the equipment had all been his. Fortunately, Luke had rented the house in his name, so it could not be traced back to Vinnie. Jason had taken over the rent payments until the lease was up for renewal. Now, Vinnie would have to find another way to make money. It occurred to him that he may have to work.

These, and other worries, crowded his mind while he drove home. He had no idea Jason was making his exit out of town, and on his way to New South Wales. Vinnie pulled into his garage and was almost knocked over by Charlene, as she threw herself at him.

"My god you're here. I saw it on television, just now. What happened, were you at the fire?"

Vinnie peeled her hands from round his neck and walked into the house.

"Yes, I heard the explosion as I was driving away. I was lucky not to have been killed." He flopped on to the lounge and Charlene sat on the floor next to him. "Get me a drink will you, love."

She jumped up, left the room, and returned a couple of minutes later with half a glass of whisky on ice.

Vinnie sat and sipped in silence.

"So was anyone hurt?" asked Charlene. She was unable to remain silent another second. "What about your friends who lived at that house, are they okay?"

"When I left, Grant and Nat were there. Jason was doing a run but he was due back anytime. I rang him when I went back to watch the fire, but there was no answer."

"So where are they now?" Her eyes were wide as the truth slowly dawned.

"As far as I know they all died in the fire." Vinnie sighed deeply, almost choking on the words.

"Oh, my God." Charlene covered her face with her hands as the enormity of the situation sank in. "I can't believe it, those poor, young men. They had nothing, and now they're dead." She moved to a chair and sat back, staring.

"Now listen, we have to talk very seriously about this right now. Are you listening to me Charlene?"

She nodded.

"We are not to discuss this with anyone. I mean, you'll probably hear other people talking about it in the next few days, but, whatever happens, you cannot let on we knew anything about the house or the people in it. Do you understand what I'm saying?"

She again nodded.

"It could mean a lot of trouble for us if the police find out what we were doing in that house. They may even blame me for the deaths of those boys."

Charlene looked up at Vinnie now and he could see she did understand. "So, what about your business? How will you earn money now?" she asked.

"I have no idea. I might be able to go and see a few old friends, but it's been a long time and they most likely won't want to know me. I've been running my own business for so long now, I haven't needed to bother with that lot, and it's not something I want to do."

"What about me? I could get a job."

"Doing what?"

"The club – where I used to dance. My old boss always said he would have me back anytime."

"You may not have noticed, sweetheart, but that was three years ago, and you've blown out a bit since then. Just because I prefer my women chubby, doesn't mean he wants a fat pole dancer."

"I'm not chubby – and I'm certainly not fat." Charlene stood and ran her hands over her belly. She lifted her dress and looked at her thighs.

"See what I mean?" Vinnie smirked. "What's your next best idea?"

"Well, I could go see the supermarket. Checkout chick was one of my first jobs ever and I'm a lot slimmer than some of the girls I see working there. Only trouble is, my legs get so tired these days. I wonder what else I could do?"

"You'd better give that some thought, love. I have to check out some possibilities of my own. We can pull our belts in but we've still got to eat."

Vinnie got up and walked out to the tiny back garden. He looked down at his hands and noticed he was trembling, he could see he was not as tough as he thought he was. He had not had to worry about earning an honest living for years. Mostly, it had been how much he could earn, not whether he was going to eat or starve. What worried him more than anything though, was his fear of being connected to this situation. People were dead, questions would be asked.

******

Jason Ethridge was in shock as he drove south along the motorway, out of Queensland and into New South Wales. All he could think about was the flames leaping from the house and the unheard cries of Nat and Grant. He told himself that it was the best outcome for Grant, and he wondered if he would have actually felt the fire. Jason hoped that Nat would have been killed instantly by the explosion and had would not have suffered the agonising pain death by fire. He kept telling himself, *it's all over now, and that's all that matters, it's all over now.*

He brought his thoughts back to driving as he saw the exit sign to Kingscliff, and made a decision to swerve off the highway. He had not been there for many years and it was a place of good memories for him. He remembered Luke had taken him for a holiday there when he was about thirteen, and they had camped near the beach. He smiled as he thought how much fun Luke had been in those days. *Whatever happened to you, Dad?* He pulled up under some trees on the beachfront and sat. He let the memories drift by for a while and then he put his seat back and went to sleep.

******

It was extremely difficult for forensic police to examine the charred and crumbling structure, which was all that was left of the drug house. They attempted to ascertain whether there were any bodies to retrieve, but the authorities had to consider the safety of the examiner. It was twenty-four hours before the investigators removed the skeletal remains of two people from the scene. The drug squad was on board and they made sure the media received no information about what evidence they found after the explosion.

Vinnie had already assumed Jason had died in the fire, and while that solved certain problems for him, an even more important one remained – his income, or lack of it, as it was now. Two days after the explosion and fire, he was considering that very subject when a forceful knock on his front door demanded his attention. Vinnie rose from the lounge chair and walked to the door.

"Mr. Vincent Markwell?"

Shit, thought Vinnie, *the cops. They didn't take long to put two and two together, the bastards.*

"Yeah, that's me. What do you want?"

"We would like you to come down to the police station to answer a few questions, Mr. Markwell," said the older of the two detectives.

"What about?" Vinnie was immediately on edge.

"A house fire that occurred two days ago, not far from here. Come along please."

"Now hang on, just a minute. What makes you think I know anything about it?"

The younger detective touched Vinnie on the elbow.

"Hang on," he said. He called over his shoulder to Charlene.

She appeared in her apron and gasped, surprise all over her face, when she saw the two men standing either side of Vinnie.

"What's happening?"

"We are taking Mr. Markwell to the station for questioning, madam."

They disappeared into a waiting car and Charlene looked on, mouth agape.

******

The detectives questioned Vinnie for several hours. He had waited for his lawyer before he said a word, but he now knew that the house been under surveillance for some time before the fire. He had been followed to several known drug users' houses, and there were photographs of him supposedly making a deal. They also knew where he got his supplies from and what went on at the drug house. Some of it would be hard to prove, Vinnie thought. He knew the next step would be appearing in court, and then he may be bound over if the prosecution could get their evidence together.

He was very depressed and worried when Charlene picked him up outside the station just after five pm. Vinnie explained the events of the last few hours to Charlene, as she drove him home. "They won't get me for the deaths of those three, though," he said. "No evidence – the most I can be charged with is dealing, possibly manufacturing, but that's unlikely."

"How come?"

"The house was rented in Luke's name. Jason took over the payments when his old man died. There's no connection to me, on paper."

"Yeah, well I admire your confidence, Vinnie."

"Watch where you're going will you, you stupid bitch. Haven't I got enough to worry about without you driving me into a pole?"

Charlene looked straight ahead and kept silent.

Chapter Twenty-Eight

The insurance company had bought in the best computer hackers in the business. They traced Brenda Simpson's activity for two weeks, but were still unable to find the account where she had planted the stolen money.

"So do you think it's time we called in the fraud squad?" asked the director, at a meeting of the company's key personnel.

"Not yet, mate. I got a few ideas I haven't tried and I don't want to quit before I've tried everything," said the company's Chief Financial Officer. He turned his attention back to his laptop.

The director paced around the room, concerned by how much time all this was taking them. He had to answer to Charlie Savka every time Charlie rang up for an update.

"It's all giving me the shits," he said to the other others present at the meeting. "I'm beginning to think this is all a waste of time. We should just let the cops take it from here."

The majority ruled and decided to give the hackers another week.

The hackers were two young men who made a good living renting their skills out to the highest bidder. They had put in long hours chasing leads in the case of Brett and Brenda Simpson. They found they were up against a very worthy adversary and had to admire how well Brett had covered his tracks. According to their agreement with the insurance company, they would be paid when they found the missing money. 'No find money – no get paid', was how the director had put it to them, so they worked long into the night and became more frustrated at the end of each day.

It was late on Friday evening, two weeks after their chase had begun, that they had their first real glimmer of light. They had been able to discover that Brett Simpson was unknown to any of the major financial institutions. They could tell that he had broken up the ten million dollars into smaller sums, a method known as smurfing, or structuring, and he was able to move a large sum of money from its source in an accounting firm, to several banks, and from there to a bank in Russia. One of the hackers traced the name of an investor who had bought a controlling interest in a small bank in a jurisdiction with weak money laundering controls, in this case, Russia. This had occurred five years ago, which was not long before Brett Simpson went to jail.

The hacker sat and looked at a list of names on his screen. He guessed Simpson must have created a false identity, or even more likely, multiple identities, months before the embezzlement took place. The hacker stared at the names and finally settled his gaze on one – Igor Kazakov. This person had become known to the Russian bank when it was in financial difficulty and anxious for an injection of funds. Kazakov, probably alias Simpson, was now the major shareholder in the bank.

The director of the insurance company was delighted.

"Wow, good work boys. How the hell did you do it? Just when I was about to give up on you. This is great news." He could hardly wait to inform the other members of the board.

"What now?" one member asked when they were together for a meeting.

"Get it back the same way. A different route of course, but now all the money is in one spot, we can slip in there and remove it. Naturally, the bank will discover the loss but they can only deal with Brenda and she won't have a clue about how to get it back. The money is ours, boys. We've certainly waited long enough."

The insurance director offered the two hackers a bonus to keep working and keep quite. The insurance company had no desire to involve the fraud squad in their illegal hacking activities, even if it was to reclaim what was rightfully theirs. By the end of the next day, the entire ten million had been removed from the Russian bank. It returned, via a circuitous route across the internet, to the insurance company. Having to keep quite would do nothing for their reputation, but the return of the money would do everything for their financial bottom line. For the time being, the money would be hidden in the balance sheets of several subsidiary companies and dummy legal entities. It would eventually be drip-fed back into the main financial instruments of the company.

"I have some good news for you, Mr. Savka," the director said to Charlie. "Naturally all this is in confidence, and your being paid your ten percent is entirely dependent on your silence – and that of your associates. I'm sure you will remember the confidentiality clause in our agreement?"

Charlie had a grin from ear to ear. "Naturally," he said, and listened to hear the words he had been waiting for. There would be celebrations with Gwen, Tom, and Tony tonight.

******

When Jason Ethridge woke in the early hours of Monday morning, he found he had a stiff neck and a numb shoulder after having slept all night in the front seat of his car. The first rays of sunshine came in shafts through his windscreen. He sat up, rubbed his neck, and then got out of the car and stretched his arms and legs. Jason looked through the line of trees along the beach. Early morning walkers and joggers pounded the beat in the sand. He walked over to a tap in the park and scooped water on to his face and into his mouth.

"Good morning," said a walker, as he passed Jason on his way back to the footpath. Jason nodded and looked along Marine Parade toward the shops. He headed back to the car and drove down to a cafe that was in the process of opening. His mind remained in neutral as he sipped coffee and ate toast, not yet ready to engage in serious thought.

Half an hour later, he headed back to the sand dunes where he sat and watched the peaceful morning open into a new day. He locked his hands together under his thighs and dug his heels into the sand. Now, it was time to make some serious plans. He wondered where to start. He thought first about who, if anyone, might be looking for him. Sadly, he could think of no one and he then began to think that in this case it was a good thing. If no one was looking for him, he was free to go anywhere and start the life about which he had so often fantasised. With so many choices, how could he possibly decide? Especially if he wanted to appear dead to the likes of Vinnie Markwell.

There was something about Kingscliff that made him feel at home. He did not feel threatened and he did not feel like an alien. He wondered if there was any work going that he could do. His thought processes moved up a notch and he strolled back to the car, where he scratched around on the floor for the note he had written to himself some months previously. *It's here, I know it's here.* He pulled a piece of paper from under the passenger seat, "Yes!"

1. Get out of that place.

2. Get my own place.

3. Get money.

4. Find out about uni.

"Well, what do you know. I've got myself out of that place and I've got money. All I've got to do now is get a job and a place to live. Fuckin' easy. Then I can see about going to Uni."

Jason laughed when he realised he was talking to himself. He sat smiling to himself. He had been alone for much of his life but had longed for a family. He had a feeling now that all that had gone on before was preparing him for this moment. He was ready to start his own life. He was free.

He was free, but very busy that day. He booked a motel room in Kingscliff, and then went the few minutes north to Tweed Heads to buy new clothes. He had a good feeling when he walked out of the store with undies, shoes, several sets of shorts, pants and shirts. He bought himself a jacket as well. He felt like a new man. *Altogether I've spent less than five hundred dollars,* Jason thought, as he did the mental arithmetic and justified the expenditure to himself. He returned to the motel, where he showered and changed into some of the new gear. He then went job hunting. By five-thirty, he had had two interviews and one promise for the next day. The interviews had been at two fast food outlets, and the one scheduled for Tuesday was at a beachside cafe – a waiter position. *I'll have a job tomorrow, that's for bloody sure*, he said to himself as he gnawed on the fried chicken pack that was his dinner.

The next day he accepted a position at the same fried chicken outlet and answered a "Room to Rent" offer on the noticeboard. It would be perfect – only a couple of kilometres from work and close to the beach. *A modest, but satisfactory beginning*, Jason thought.

******

The drug house, burnt to the ground, would have what remained demolished. The forensic police investigators had spent more time than usual, trying to pinpoint the cause of the explosion. They were not sure of the chemical cause, but they did know it was caused by some miscalculation of chemical combinations. They had been unable to identify the two bodies and this had left a few unanswered questions. The drug squad could speculate on who those bodies were, but they had no proof.

Detective Inspector Pekalski had suggested to his boss that he interview Vinnie Markwell at his home at the resort, off the record – sort of. Pekalski had the impression he could get Markwell off guard at a time when he would be vulnerable. They were well aware of Markwell's involvement and wanted to see him go down with the rest of the network.

Pekalski knew his neighbour would be on his guard when he went to his house to speak to him.

"Yeah? How can I help you?" It was a frosty opening statement.

"Hi, Vinnie. May I call you Vinnie?"

"Just get to the point, mate."

Frank explained to Vinnie that it was an informal discussion and he was trying to discover if one of the bodies recovered from the drug house could have been that of Jason Ethridge.

Vinnie was completely uncooperative. "I don't even know why you think I knew anyone who lived there," he said, after Pekalski explained how he could help him. "I've already told you, I don't know anything, about people or drugs." He slammed the door in Pekalski's face and turned to Charlene, who had stood back and listened to the conversation.

"Surely you must know who was in the house when it burned down?" she asked.

Vinnie's face went red. He looked ready to explode.

"Get out of my way – and shut your face. Just remember, we know nothing. No one can be charged for knowing nothing." He marched past her and threw himself on to his armchair. "Never admit to anything – that's the golden rule to success in business and in life – never admit to anything!" he shouted to the room.

Charlene was beginning to tire of Vinnie's tantrums. For a while, she believed they could have a happy life, now that they had a decent home and new friends, but Vinnie was not a man who was easy to live with. He had no idea of how to compromise or change his habits. She felt she had changed a lot since their move. When she compared her life with that of others around her, she could see she was entitled to respect herself and that she was as important as Vinnie, or any man, for that matter. Some little voice inside her said she should wait, though; not be hasty, do nothing for the moment, wait for the outcome of the investigation of the fire before making any changes.

Two weeks after the fire, they were living on Charlene's wages. She had a new position as assistant at the local movie theatre. She collected tickets, worked behind the confectionary counter and changed posters in the entrance lobby. She loved it, and the odd shifts didn't worry her at all. She got to see and talk to lots of people and even saw snatches of all the best movies.

Vinnie still didn't have a job. He never thought he would be kept by a woman, especially under these conditions. His greatest worry however, was being kept by the state. Not having cash to lay his hands on meant that he could no longer afford the attorney he had been able to employ in the past. He was due to answer charges in court before the end of the month and he had no real defence organised. He tried to do a deal with his attorney, but the man was adamant – no money, no counsel. He had used the last of his available cash for his bail. The man had dropped him and did not want to represent him. Vinnie would have to apply for legal aid. His chances were not looking good.

It was this, and other pressing issues, that crowded Vinnie's mind as he drove along the service road by the motorway, travelling south from Brisbane. Suddenly, he realised he was being crowded by another vehicle on his right, forcing him onto the roadside. He was forced to a stop. Two men jumped out of the other car and ran around to his door. He did not have the presence of mind to lock the car, and they opened his door and dragged him out on to the road. They marched him round the other side of their car, which was facing into some bushes. The road was a neglected stretch of what used to be the old highway. It was deserted at 11am.

Vinnie felt his whole body shaking when the men threw him against their car and he recognised two of them as old mates he used to know – back in the days when he was in a bikie gang, nearly fifteen years ago. It was like a dream, or a nightmare, to see those faces.

"So, we meet again, Vinnie. The boss tells us you've been gettin' lazy in yer old age."

Vinnie had trouble finding his voice, "I was on my way to see him now, boys. We've got business to discuss. Didn't he tell you I was on my way over today?"

"The thing is, mate, he don't want to see you unless you got the cash you owe him. He don't want you wastin' his time, beggin' for time he can't give ya. He says you're goin' to jail soon and he wants you to settle up before then."

"It all went in the fire, he knows that," Vinnie said in a small voice, as he looked at the ground and cringed.

He waited for the first punch to land. He did not have to wait more than three seconds before a punch landed hard into his stomach. As he bent over, a sickening upper cut snapped his head back. He crumpled to the ground and spat blood and two teeth onto the dirt. He tried to roll away, but hands grasped him by the collar and lifted him up. He blinked, and saw a fist coming full force at his jaw. He fell to the ground. He heard a dull thud. There it was again – every couple of seconds – like a drum beat. Then, the pain registered, as he felt the heavy boots kicking his ribs. He tried to protect his chest with his hands but felt a sharp pain in one of his fingers as the boot connected with his hand. He rolled into a ball and gasped for air, trying to keep his face away from the heavy boots. They gave one last kick and then walked away. Vinnie lay in agonised silence. He heard their car drive off. He lay, wounded and bleeding.

He did not move for some minutes, then slowly tested his fingers. He opened and closed them, all except two, which hurt like hell and refused to move. Blood oozed from his torn skin. He felt his face and grimaced as he touched his cheek. He stuck his tongue between his swollen lips and realised his two top central incisors were now missing. He reached into his back pocket, withdrew his mobile phone and called Charlene.

"Juth come and pick me up plethes. I've had an athcident and I can't drive," he said weakly, He spat blood to the ground, pressed his sleeve to his mouth, listened, and continued. "No, I don't need an ambulanthe; ring no one, juth come yourthelf, now."

He told her where he was and staggered back to the car He dropped into the front seat and waited.

Chapter Twenty-Nine

Jim returned from the hospital at the same time Charlene brought Vinnie back to the resort in her car.

"Who's that up front?" Jim asked Di, as they lined up behind Charlene at the security gates.

"Oh, that troublemaking Markwell. The one Frank has been watching."

"Oh, yes. Anything been happening on that front while I've been away?" Jim looked interested.

"Well, I know Frank has been to have a few words with him. I'm not sure what about, but I think Mr. Markwell is a disaster waiting to happen."

"My dear, it won't worry us now that we're leaving, will it?" Before Di could answer, Jim reached over and squeezed her shoulder. Di shook her head then turned into their driveway; soon to be someone else's driveway.

"And what news on the new managers, have we heard anything yet?" asked Jim.

"Now that you're home, we can cover for Matt and Ellen while they go to Adelaide on Friday for a meeting with Andrew Sleighmen They'll be away all weekend because if they get the job it might be their last decent break for a while."

"And what do you think their chances are?"

"If my recommendation has anything to do with it, they will definitely get it. You can read the e-mail I sent off to head office; I think they'll be perfect in the job."

They walked together into their home and Jim looked around to see if anything had changed.

"Everything looks good, the gardens are spot on, I see. How's the paperwork in the office?"

"Not a thing to do. Everyone has made sure you couldn't find anything out of place to worry about. As I told you before, if we get the go ahead from Andrew we can start packing up and I've given notice to that couple renting our place on the coast. We need to go and take a look at the condition it's in. I know we need to do a lot of work, but we can stay away on holiday while it reaches a stage where it's okay to move into. We can do the last bits of decoration after we move back in."

"Sounds like you got everything covered."

Jim contemplated the end of his working life. He felt a fluttering in his stomach as he thought of never having to work again. He planned to play golf, but that aside, he had no idea how he would fill his days.

Di had already suggested she would like to become a volunteer nursing home visitor – sitting with older people, listening to their stories and sometimes watching them cry.

It was not Jim's idea of how to pass the time; perhaps some other voluntary work. Maybe he could be useful at the primary school, not far from their house. He wondered if he might become involved in woodworking, something he enjoyed but never had time for. He also wondered if perhaps he could have done the renovations to their old house. He laughed when he thought about how much trouble that could stir up between he and Di.

She looked at him and asked, "What's so funny?"

"I was just wondering if perhaps I should be doing the renovations on the house."

"You've got to be joking. You've never done that sort of work before. No love, let's leave it to the experts. We want to get in this year, not next."

"Sure," Jim answered, knowing it was a stupid idea.

******

Charlene helped Vinnie out of the car. She almost ran into Harold and Robert, who were walking their dog, Gypsy.

"Sorry about that," she said.

They both looked at Vinnie, being almost carried by Charlene.

"Oh my God, what happened to you?" asked Robert, with genuine concern.

Before Charlene could answer, Vinnie mumbled, "Car athcident," and he turned to go into the house.

"Here, let us give you a hand. You can't manage him all by yourself."

The two men took over and Charlene stepped aside, leading the way into the front door.

"Here will do, thankth, fellerth."

"You should get a doctor to look at those cuts on your face, mate," said Robert.

"Yeah, I will, thankth again." He gave a perfunctory wave and Robert and Harold took their leave.

Vinnie went through the door Charlene held open, and headed for his armchair. He lowered himself down, very slowly.

"Jeeze, that was no car accident," said Robert, as soon as they were out of earshot.

"Course not. He's been beaten up. Did you see how swollen his face was? His clothes were filthy, and torn. No, that was no car accident, Rob. He's got some very unpleasant friends, I'd say."

They walked on, and wondered what sort of man gets beaten up in that way and doesn't go to the police.

"He's got something to hide, I reckon. I'm going to mention it to Frank Pekalski if he's at dinner tonight. He should go along and have a chat with him."

Robert agreed.

They ran into the detective at the door to the clubhouse, later that evening.

"How's it going, boys, written any good books lately?"

Some of the residents had commented on how happy the detective had seemed of late. He was chatty and smiling, nothing like the withdrawn person he was when he first moved in.

"We were hoping to run into you this evening, actually. Can we have a word?"

"What, now?"

They both nodded and he stepped back outside the door, just as Joy arrived, smiling and heading straight for her new friend, Frank.

"Be with you in a minute, Joy. I just want to have a word with the boys, here."

They stepped aside and Harold quickly told the detective about the condition Vinnie Markwell was in that afternoon.

"Right, I appreciate you telling me. I'll check into it tomorrow. I have a vague idea what it may be about and I'm really glad you let me know. Let's go to dinner, shall we."

They walked back and joined Joy.

"I notice nothing is as important as his date with Joy, these days," commented Robert sotto voce.

"Yes, I've noticed that too. Love is in the air, methinks."

They joined the crowd for dinner – the same small groups gathering for pre dinner drinks and still discussing politics, and sex, and religion.

When Jim entered the dining room there was a big cheer and applause. Some residents whistled and several women reached up to give him a kiss and congratulate him on his recovery. Di stood back, smiling as Jim absorbed the attention.

It seemed he had been missed, and he realised he had mixed feelings about his impending retirement. He thought of how many friends he had made at Keeala Resort and he was wondering how he was going to feel when it was just the two of them, without all the different faces and all with their own stories to tell. He felt quite sad.

"Good to see you back, Jim. Are you feeling ready to get back into harness again?"

Jim looked up from the dining table to see the sisters, Penny and Lottie. They smiled down at him, "We missed seeing your happy face around the place."

"Thank you. I can't say how much I missed all of you as well. I don't know how I'll be ..." He stopped mid-sentence as he remembered he and Di had agreed not to mention their impending retirement until they could announce their replacements at the same time, " ... when I walk back into that office," he finished smoothly.

"Well, we have to say Matthew has been great. Not as good as you, of course, but we all missed him after he left, and it's great to have him back again. We'd like to keep you all."

They were joined by more well-wishers, and Jim became aware of how loved and accepted he felt. *I couldn't ask for more than that, as I move into my retirement*, he thought as he looked around. It was a happy, relaxed crowd of people who ate, and talked, and drank their fill in the clubhouse that night.

******

In Vinnie Markwell's house, Charlene leaned over her lover, cleansing his wounds again as she pleaded with him to tell her why this terrible thing had happened to him.

"For Godth thake, woman, leave it alone. I told you, it wath a case of mithtaken identity."

"In that case, you should go to the cops."

"Leave it. Get me thome more of those pain killerth and turn on the televithion."

Charlene shook her head and thought once again how little she knew about the people with whom Vinnie was involved. Exasperated and worried, she went to fill a glass of water to give him with his pills.

"I don't want water," he said, and brushed her hand aside. "Get me thome whithky. I'm in pain here, can't you thee."

"Sorry, Vin, we haven't got any. We only had enough money for food this week, and there's bills waiting next to your computer. I had no idea how short we were until I used my card at the supermarket yesterday and found there wasn't enough in our account. I had to go and put stuff back. I honestly have never been so embarrassed. That hasn't ever happened to me in my life before." Charlene walked out of the room.

Vinnie swallowed the mild analgesic Charlene had given him and waited for improvement in the pain in his face and ribs. His jaw ached abominably, and the two teeth he had lost felt as though they had left behind their roots.

Vinnie tried to watch the television, but gave up after an hour or so. He made his way to the bedroom and crawled under the cover. His life was crumbling around him, and he was not even able to escape into the refuge of sleep. Worst of all, he had no alcohol. He realised about midnight, that he would have to see a dentist first thing in the morning, and if his ribs and jaw were fractured, maybe a doctor too. He rolled around the bed moaning until Charlene could take no more.

"You can't go on like this, Vin, I want to take you to the hospital." Charlene stood next to the bed, with tears in her eyes as she stroked his head.

"You're right, I've had it. Leth get drethed and go, now."

On the way to the hospital, they concocted a story they would tell the hospital staff. They planned to say Vinnie got into an argument with his brother at a family gathering. They would say that it was not unusual for the brothers to brawl, and the other man has gone away just as bad, and no, they would not be informing the police; family loyalty and all that. Neither was astute enough to be aware that this sort of incident would automatically be reported by the hospital to the police.

"I'm afraid you look have some nasty injuries, Mr. Markwell," said the examining doctor. "Looks like a possible fractured mandible – that's your jaw – and I suspect some broken ribs. We will need to admit you and do further investigation to confirm the extent of your injuries."

Vinnie cursed and winced at the same time. He wondered what else could happen to him before he went to court. He knew now that he would have no chance of approaching any of his old friends for financial help. He would have had to make any such approach in person, and he could think of no other way to access money. *I could sell the house. That would raise enough cash to pay the greedy bastard, but what if it didn't sell straight away? Maybe I could sign it over to him. It's worth finding out about.* Vinnie mulled over every possibility he could think of to raise enough money to pay for his representation in court.

Being held at Her Majesty's pleasure was beginning to look better than trying to survive in his present circumstances. He resigned himself to the inevitable.

Chapter Thirty

Tom, Tony, Charlie, and Gwen sat at a round table in a Chinese restaurant in Brisbane. They drank sparkling burgundy as they waited for the first of the banquet dishes to arrive at the table.

"Here's to two hundred and fifty thousand dollars each," Tom announced, and they all raised their glasses for the third time.

They were celebrating the receipt of the reward money, split four ways, as agreed.

Tony had double the reason to celebrate. His doctor, a couple of days earlier, had given him the news that his last two rounds of tests had confirmed he was in remission.

"And here's to life," Tom said.

"Hear, hear!" responded the others.

Tom glanced sideways at Gwen, seated next to him.

He said, "And here's to the best looking woman in the room," as he raised his glass again and smiled at her.

Gwen blushed, something she had not done for years. For a second she wondered where Ron was tonight, and then she swept the thought from her mind and looked at Tony. *I've seen worse,* she thought, and *at least he's intelligent.*

They celebrated and talked of what they would do with their money. Gwen said, "I'm thinking of buying a little house in an over fifties resort; maybe Keeala Resort. I'll have enough now with what Ron returned, plus this two-fifty grand. Then I'll be set for life and I might even get someone in to do the cleaning," she laughed. "Maybe Brenda Simpson?" She almost fell out of the chair laughing at the thought.

"Well, we three are going to set up a new office and only take the cases that interest us. We can pick and choose and even take long weekends whenever we feel like it. I may even play bowls," said Charlie. "We really are all set now."

******

It was not a time of celebration for Brenda Simpson.

Someone from the Russian bank contacted her, and in broken English, said, "If you have not transferred the money yourself, then your account has been hacked into and every cent removed. No other account was affected - yours has been specifically targeted."

Brenda was speechless. She could not understand how anyone could have accessed her information. She wondered if

Gwen could somehow have found the bank details when she had been cleaning the unit. That seemed unlikely, Brenda thought, given that she had separated all parts of those details and had them well hidden. She went to check in her hiding places and found them intact. Who else could possibly know? She did not know where Gwen lived, and even if she did she was not going to admit to stealing ten million dollars. How could she possibly tell Brett that they had no money, not a cent? Her household account was intact, and she did own the house she lived in, but Brett had big plans and he had well and truly paid for them. She cringed at the thought of telling Brett that all their money was gone. It was the only thing kept him going, in that hellhole of a prison. She decided not to rush to give him bad news; maybe something would happen before his release occurred. Brenda just could not accept it was all gone. It did not seem possible.

We could both end up on the old age pension, she thought. No, oh no. She shook her head.

****

Charlene decided it was time to consider her options. Never before had she really contemplated leaving Vinnie. She was by nature, a loyal person, but she was beginning to realise how he was dragging her down with him. She knew now that she wanted to live a full, happy life, and with Vinnie's incarceration looking increasingly a possibility, she needed to evaluate her position.

When Vinnie suggested selling the house, without any thought as to where she was going to live, she realised it was time to start looking out for herself.

Ellen Brooks was in the sales office when Charlene walked in. "Good morning, Charlene, what may I do for you?"

"As a matter of fact, I could use some advice if you don't mind."

Charlene sounded very businesslike and Ellen was surprised at the change in her demeanour from the silly, frivolous attitude she had come to expect from Charlene.

"Certainly, anything I can help you with, it would be my pleasure," she said. She smiled and pointed to the chair in front of the desk.

Charlene seated herself. She looked down at her hands as if gathering her thoughts. "Well, it's like this, Miss Brooks."

"Oh, please call me Ellen."

"Yes. Well, Ellen, Vinnie and I are having a few problems, and at the moment he's in hospital. He's ahhh ... not well."

Ellen nodded but did not interrupt for fear of spoiling the other woman's train of thought. She looked at her, encouraging Charlene to continue.

"He has been talking of selling our house, to raise some money he needs urgently. What I need to know is, can he sell it without my permission?"

"If I remember correctly, you're joint owners in the property. I'll just take a look at the details here." Ellen tapped on her computer keyboard, scrolled down a list and brought up the information on the screen. "Yes, it is joint ownership, and you would need to be in agreement to put the house on the market."

"What if he wanted to sign it over to someone else? Could he do that?"

"No, the same story. You are a joint owner and he would require your agreement and signature to change the ownership. And of course, in a resort like this, the person would have to be suitable, that is over fifty."

Charlene sat nodding as she digested the information.

"Good, good," she said. "So there is no way he can make me sell, if I don't want to?"

"No."

After a long pause, Charlene stood and said, "Thanks, Ellen. Knowing my rights helps me a lot. Thanks again."

"I must say you do look a bit worried, Charlene. Look, don't go round carrying the weight of the world on your shoulders. If there's any way you think I can help you, at any time, please consider me a friend who is more than willing to help. As I'm sure you know, sharing a problem can lighten it sometimes."

Charlene smiled, and said, "You're a kind person, Ellen. I'll remember that."

She walked out and back to her home. She went to the kitchen, brewed a coffee, and sat at the kitchen table. She assessed her situation and concluded that her wage alone would barely support her. She simply did not earn enough to support Vinnie as well. He would have to get some kind of employment, and soon. That is, if he did not go to jail.

******

It would have been very hard to dampen Ellen's mood, no matter what might have come her way. Matthew had flown back from Adelaide the previous night, with the news that Andrew Sleighmen had endorsed their application for the position of managers of Keeala Resort. Sleighmen, Matthew had told her, had said he had his eye on someone who could fill Matthew's position of area manager, and Ellen could employ a new sales person.

Ellen and Matthew could hardly wait to share their good news with Di and Jim. They rang the doorbell at the manager's residence at an early hour.

"Oh, that's wonderful news," said Di. She gave them both a hug. Jim was not so effusive. He shook their hands, but still harboured reservations about his retirement. They all went to sit on the balcony and discuss plans over coffee.

"We also thought we would like to announce our engagement and set a date for the wedding, here," Matthew said.

Before he could continue, Ellen jumped up and said, "And we could be married by a celebrant in the garden here, and have the reception here also, with all the residents."

"That's an awful lot of guests," said Jim.

"It doesn't have to be formal, just some long tables in the garden, with drinks and nibbles. Some decorations and music, oh, it would be beautiful. What do you think?"

"It sounds absolutely lovely, Ellen. How soon do you plan all this taking place?" Di asked.

"It would have to be soon, like before you two go, maybe in the next two weeks."

"Hmmm, that is soon, but not impossible, if we all pitch in. The celebrant would be your first concern and then there's just the catering to organise. I'll make sure we don't ask Robert to help in the kitchen though." They all had a quite laugh at that observation.

"The celebrant has already agreed. I have a friend and he says he'll fit us in. We just have to come up with a date by tomorrow."

"Oh, tomorrow," said Di. "Yes, well I suppose that's possible." She looked at Jim.

He nodded resignedly, then stood up and walked to the balcony rail. Silence fell suddenly as they all realised Jim was not able to feel their joy. He turned and saw all eyes were on him. He sighed deeply.

"It comes to us all, I guess. I just haven't had time to digest it yet. Please continue. I'm in full agreement, so far. What day do you think?"

"Two weeks from last Saturday. I could do up a flyer and a letterbox drop. I don't have many friends close by, but I could e-mail them and Matt's as well. I don't want a conventional wedding dress, I'm sure I could buy something, readymade."

"Ever the practical one," smiled Matthew. "The simpler the better, as far as I'm concerned."

"What about a honeymoon?" asked Di.

"At a later date. We're happy to let things settle before we hand over to relief managers. Just being together will be as much as we could wish for," said Matthew.

"You both sound so happy. We wish you all the things you hope for yourself." Di stood and hugged them both again. She shared their happiness and could feel the love between them. Di recalled she and Jim had been just the same way a few years ago.

"So what do you want me to do first?"

"I have a list," Ellen grinned, and pulled a face as she drew out a clipboard that had lots of notes attached.

"You have been busy," said Jim, making an effort to join in.

They huddled together to go over Ellen's carefully constructed plans.

"All we need is for the weather to hold and the rest will be easy," said Ellen.

Chapter Thirty-One

Detective Frank Pekalski went to Vinnie's house, the day after he heard that Robert and Harold had seen the man looking as though he had been bashed.

Charlene answered the door and told the detective Vinnie was in hospital.

"Oh, I'm sorry to hear Mr. Markwell is in hospital. Can you tell me what happened to him?"

"Ummm ... well ... he was in a car accident actually. But he'll be okay, now that he's in hospital." Charlene was unprepared for questions.

"So perhaps I should see him there. Which hospital, which ward?"

"Oh, I don't think he's up to visitors, just yet, but I'll tell him you called. I'm sure he'll be pleased."

"Mrs. Markwell, I have to tell you, it would not be a social call. If he has been in a motor vehicle accident, then chances are it should have been reported, unless of course there was no other party involved and no damage to property."

"Yes, that was it. I think he ran off the road and into some bushes – just lost his attention for a moment and boom, straight into the bush."

"I see. And what sort of injuries did he sustain?"

"His ribs, and he must have hit the steering wheel because he also broke his jaw. He was wearing his seat belt, of course, but he still got a bit of whiplash. You must see it all the time, Detective."

"Call me Frank, after all, we are neighbours, aren't we. May I come in?"

Flustered, Charlene stepped back to allow the man to pass. He headed for the lounge and seated himself.

"This place is very nice, Mrs. Markwell. You certainly know something about interior decoration."

"Thank you. I love it here. But you know I'm not really Mrs. Markwell. Vinnie and I were never married, not that it matters to us, but some people think it's important, don't they?"

"True. Fortunately now-a-days, we can all please ourselves about such matters," Pekalski agreed. "Now, how are you managing here, by yourself? I'm sure I've seen you going out at odd hours, and hear you have a new job."

"Word gets around here fast, doesn't it?" Charlene wrung her hands and looked uncomfortable. "Yes, I do have a job now. With Vinnie out of work, we still have to eat and neither of us is entitled to any sort of a pension."

"So how did Vinnie lose his job, Charlene?" Pekalski asked quietly

"Well, the house burnt down, of course." Her hand flew to her mouth, her eyes widened, and she muffled a gasp.

"Would you like to tell me how that happened? I'm sure you had nothing to do with it."

Charlene began to cry, and shook her head. "No, I don't know how it happened or what Vinnie did there. Please don't ask me anything else. I really don't know."

"It's okay, I can see you're upset. I'll call and see Vinnie in hospital later today."

"Oh please don't tell him you've been speaking to me."

"Of course not. Don't worry, I won't say a word. I'll be off now. Please let me know if you have a problem I can help you with."

"Thank you." She closed the door behind him then went back to her armchair and sat with her face in her hands.

******

The following day, in the hospital, Vinnie suggested to Charlene again that he was going to sell their house. He said he had made contact, by phone, with the sales person from the resort, he had a lot of thinking to do, and he really was not in the mood for entertaining her.

It was becoming painfully obvious to Charlene that she was more of a convenience in his life than someone he loved. She could see he had no intention to consult her.

******

Detective Pekalski was experienced enough to recognise the fragility of Charlene's loyalty. He saw her coming home from work the next day, as he was conveniently in his garden watering the plants when she pulled up. He waved to her and then walked over.

"How's Vinnie today?"

"I think he's improving, I thought you were going to see him yourself."

"Ran out of time. Maybe I'll catch him tomorrow. Do you know how long he's expected to be in?" Pekalski already knew all the answers to his questions, but needed a reason to engage Charlene as a sympathetic neighbour.

"No, I don't." She hurried off in the direction of her front door.

Pekalski followed.

"You seem upset, Charlene. I'm sure you'd feel better if you could talk about it. Why don't you come over to my place? I was about to open a bottle of wine. Would you join me on the patio?" She followed him without speaking. He helped her to a chair on the small outdoor area at the front of his house. He went to get a bottle and two glasses.

They sat in silence and sipped at the wine. Pekalski had played this silent game many times. He knew the first one to speak would lose the contest of wills.

It took all of three minutes before Charlene burst out, "All right, I'll tell you." She took a gulp of wine and looked directly at Pekalski. "He's a drug runner. He's been in the drug business ever since I've known him – maybe twenty years, maybe more."

Pekalski nodded, looked down slowly at his glass of wine, then raised his eyes and stared directly into Charlene's eyes.

"And do you know if he was involved in the destruction of the drug house and the death of the two men?" he asked.

"Oh, ah, I really don't think so. Do the police think he was?" Charlene looked afraid.

"We're still investigating the deaths of the two young men. Did you know them?"

"Yes, oh, well not well, not well at all, but I had met them. They were all drug addicts who lived there. Except for Jason, that is – Luke's son. I don't think he was. Did he die too?"

"We're still trying to identify the bodies. We would really like any information about those men. They would have family somewhere and I'm sure they would want to know what happened."

Charlene began to sob and Pekalski patted her shoulder. "Any light you can shed on what happened to those men would be helpful," he said, "and not just to us, if you get my drift."

Charlene straightened up and took a big gulp of her wine. She looked at the detective and asked, "Would I be charged with an offence because I knew about this and didn't report it? Vinnie said that I could go to jail, just knowing about a crime and not reporting it."

"This is true, but if you help us, we'll help you. Seriously, Charlene, you can be protected from prosecution if you give evidence in an offence like this. You could not know this, but we have had that house under surveillance since Vinnie and his mates moved in. We do have a file on the men involved, but having evidence to present to court is another matter. I suspect you have been witness to enough unlawful activities to give us what we need to put Mr. Markwell away. I don't know how he treats you, but I know he has been directly responsible for the deaths of those two men. Will you please help us to prove it?"

Charlene nodded.

Pekalski could see that she was ready. Whatever had happened between Charlene and Vinnie recently, Pekalski could see she had made her decision.

******

Pekalski drove Charlene in to make her statement. The previous night he had spoken to his boss, who had agreed to give Charlene the protection she required, in exchange for her cooperation. It had been a harrowing experience for her, dredging up all the information she had stored away on Vinnie. She surprised herself when she was able to recall incidents and names, places and dates; all valuable information for the prosecutor. Charlene had a lot more to tell Pekalski than he had expected, and he had been all morning getting it sorted out.

As Pekalski drove Charlene home from the station, she asked, "What will happen to me if Vinnie gets discharged from hospital before his case is heard?"

"Don't worry about that, Charlene. With this evidence, we'll be picking him up from the hospital and taking him to the lock up until he goes to court. We already have a guard posted outside his room. You won't have to speak to him again."

"This may sound strange, you know, but for some reason I'm not worried. I never thought I'd have the guts to grass him. He always made it clear that no one ever leaves the business, but the bastard's wrong. I'm going to fit him up for good. How long do you reckon he'll get?"

"I'll make some enquiries for you, but one thing's for sure – you'll have the next ten years in peace. Frankly, with all the other stuff you've given us, I suspect it will be much longer."

Pekalski was satisfied with the morning's work, particularly with the way Charlene had opened up. When he dropped her at her door, he was genuinely appreciative of her assistance.

"You have done a great service to the community, Charlene, and you do yourself credit. I know it could not have been easy for you this morning, and we all appreciate your help. Now remember, don't worry, we've got it all under control, but if you're the least bit concerned, ring me. Okay?"

As she got out of the car, she smiled at Pekalski and gave him the thumbs-up gesture.

******

More than one person made Pekalski happy that day. He was looking forward to inviting Joy out to dinner in the city, and then on to a new show that was opening. While he tried to keep his mind on the job, his thoughts constantly escaped to images of the woman who had so recently captured his imagination. He was amazed at what now represented his idea of a good woman. The list in his head was growing hourly.

Joy looked good; she was intelligent, perceptive and diplomatic. She was kind, sensitive, but also outspoken and unafraid to express her opinions. He was unable to find fault, either in her appearance, or in her expression. They had discovered a similarity in their views about most of the important issues of life. They did not agree on politics and only vaguely on religion, but both actually enjoyed disagreeing and debating those issues. At some point in their lives, they had both discovered that tolerance was the key to happiness.

All that said, Pekalski could not believe that any relationship could be that easy or that good. He rang her from his mobile while he drove back to the station and was disappointed when the answering machine took the call.

Joy listened to the message. She was tempted to grab the phone, but she held back.

The previous day, her friend Val had commented to her that she had noticed the detective in the company of the floozy, Charlene.

"I reckon she could cause some trouble around here, flirting with other people's husbands," Val had said.

"But he isn't anyone's husband," Joy contradicted.

"True, but she has a husband. I know the type – next thing you know they'll be having wife swapping parties."

"You can't be serious. Surely the detective is free to talk to anyone he wants to."

"Talk, yes, but she's been seen going out with him in his car. Sounds like a date to me. Not only that, but she was seen sitting on his patio with him, drinking wine."

Joy sighed. She wondered if she could have misjudged Frank so badly. Could he really be the type to go out with someone else's wife? She thought perhaps she needed to back off a bit; maybe they were rushing their relationship.

Chapter Thirty-Two

The manager's office was a hive of activity, with Ellen and Matthew attending to the many details necessary for them to be married in a little more than a week.

Jim had been banished to his garage to pack up, getting everything ready to move into storage.

Di buzzed back and forth, dealing with the new cook and making decisions about the reception.

Jim looked up suddenly when he heard a knock on his garage wall.

"How's it going, mate?" It was Harold.

"G'day, Harold, come in. Have you ever seen such a mess?"

Harold walked into the gloomy light and saw the chaos.

"Sure, that's what our kitchen looks like every night after Rob finishes creating one of his cordon bleu delights. Are you allowed time off for a cup of coffee?"

"Too bad if I'm not. Let's have one anyhow." They walked together into the clubhouse and over to the coffee machine. "What brings you down here today?" said Jim.

"Well, I'm still having trouble accepting the fact that you're leaving. I don't mean I don't think it's the right thing to do, for you. It's just that you've become so much a part of this place; no one can imagine it without you and Diane."

Jim smiled and hung his head in thought. He was not a great one for accepting compliments and that was indeed a compliment to him.

"Well, thank you, Harold, that's very nice of you to say so, but, as I keep saying, it comes to us all. It's a bit like death and taxes, we can't avoid the inevitable. I will say I wasn't quite ready for retirement, mentally, that is, but like everyone else, I will get used to it – maybe even enjoy it after a while. I think perhaps I've spent too much time working in my life, and I can't imagine doing anything else. But look at you Harold, you seem perfectly content, to me. Are you?"

"Yes, I am Jim. You will find something you're interested in and it will fill your days to the point where, one day, you'll wonder how you ever had time to work. You won't be alone in feeling strange for a while, but it won't last, I promise. By the way, you've become the talk of the town after your retirement announcement at dinner the other night. At least we're all compensated by the prospect of having Matt and Ellen replace you. They're well liked around here, and both good at their jobs. I think they'll be a big hit."

"So do I."

Di came dashing past with her arms full of white ribbons. She turned and came back to where the men were sitting. "You know, I have plenty of jobs for people with time on their hands," she said.

They both stood and shook their heads.

"Sorry, we've got work to do," Jim said, as they disappeared

Di watched them go. She had never seen either of them move so fast.

******

Joy Rayne had come to value her independence. After her husband died, she thought she'd never get used to living alone. But she had, and now she enjoyed it, most of the time. When she met Frank Pekalski, the attraction was overwhelming and she immediately recognised it for what it was. She was in love. *How can someone, my age, possibly feel like this,* she asked herself. At that moment, she saw his car go past the end of her street, heading for his home. She thought of what Val had said about Frank earlier that day. She decided the only way to find out was to ask him. *Why muck around in doubt, when I can just find out.* She pulled her door closed behind her and strolled up the street.

Frank stood in his driveway, with his back to her. He was talking to someone and seemed quite animated.

"Hi, Frank!" she said.

He turned and she saw Charlene step to the side, to look at who was interrupting them. Charlene scowled.

Joy stood still.

"Oh, sorry. I didn't realise." She turned and hurried back the way she had come.

Frank ran after her and said, "Wait up, Joy, I've been trying to catch up with you all day."

"Really? Well maybe you should finish your conversation with the young lady there." She took off and rushed over to a small group of women who were talking on the footpath. She immediately joined in the conversation with her friends.

Frank stood in the middle of the roadway, mouth agape. He did not know what just happened but he was sure it was not good.

The women walked away from him, still engrossed in conversation.

Charlene walked up to Frank and stood next to him.

Joy turned and saw the two of them walk off together.

Val, who had been in the group of women, took Joy's elbow and moved away a couple of paces. She tossed her head in the direction of the two withdrawing figures.

"See what I told you? My experience with men is that you can't trust any of the bastards."

Joy's phone was ringing when she opened her door. She looked at it then walked over and picked it up.

"Hi, it's me, Frank. Joy you looked upset just now. Is there a problem?"

"Have you been dating Charlene Markwell while her husband's been in hospital?"

"No. Has someone said I have?"

"Yes."

"Who?"

"Why? Are you going to arrest them?"

"No. Do you want me to?"

"No."

"Can I come round there, right now?"

"Yes, the door is open."

Frank closed Joy's door behind him in less than two minutes later. They both sat down in the lounge and looked at one another. Suddenly Joy started to giggle.

"What's so funny?" he said, as a smile started to break out on his lips.

"I'm an idiot. I believe you, you know. I was told you were having a fling with Charlene and was going to ask you about it, when I found you, just now, in conversation with the person in question. But I know you've got better taste than that. And you aren't the deceptive type. Why would I listen to gossip?"

"I see." Frank nodded as he began to look at the situation as others may have. "And so you were coming to ask me, were you?"

"I was."

"Well, I like that. It's good to know that you were going to be direct and not just presume the worst of me. Actually, my association with Mrs. Markwell is purely professional. I'm not at liberty to say any more, but it is work, pure and simple – police work," he said. He stood and took Joy's hands in his, as he helped her to stand. He looked her in the eyes and said, "All that aside, does all this mean that I almost just lost the love of my life?"

Joy's mouth opened. She closed it again, smiled, and said, "No way, boyo. Now I have you in my life, nothing is going to come between us."

"Nothing?"

"Nothing. What, are you deaf or something?"

"I must be. Could you say that again?"

"No, if you missed it the first time, that's just tough. I love you, you stupid man," she mumbled.

"You what?"

"Love you, you dummy."

"Not as much as I love you. Will you marry me?" he mumbled back.

"Yes!"

"Calm down, I think I get the message."

They fell together, laughed, and hugged. Neither could remember ever being so happy.

Later that evening, Joy and Frank walked down to see Jim and Di at the manager's residence. They had rung in advance saying they had important news and they wanted to share it with them.

The ex-managers did not take long to guess what that news might be and had a chilled bottle of sparkling white wine ready for the visit.

"Come in you two," Jim said. "And what's the joke? You look like you have both just won the lottery."

"We have," answered Frank. "We're getting married. So what do you think about that?"

"Congratulations," Di and Jim said together, "that's wonderful."

"It is isn't it? We decided tonight and thought we would do it here, real soon. How about that?"

"Well, the first thing that comes to my mind is a double wedding."

"Of course, Matt and Ellen are getting married in a couple of weeks, aren't they? I wonder how they would feel about a double ceremony."

"Let's ask them." Jim picked up the phone and handed it to Joy when Ellen answered. They heard her squeal down the line, "We'd love it."

"And as they say, the rest is history," Jim said to Frank, as they listened to the one sided conversation. "Sounds to me like you're getting married – soon."

Frank squeezed Joy's hand then put it to his lips and kissed it. "That's what it sounds like to me," he repeated.

"Now, this changes things a little bit," said Di. "We were about to do a letterbox drop with everyone's invitation. So now we can say, the double wedding, etc."

"Oh, maybe not," said Joy. "Perhaps we could make it a surprise. Not tell anyone until we all arrived together."

"Yes, I like that," said Frank. "More exciting if we all just turn up, together."

"Actually, I like that idea too," said Di. Her mind raced to all the changes she would have to make with the reception.

They sipped their wine, and started to discuss what needed to be done in the following days.

Frank could not wipe the grin from his face as he listened to everyone talk. He thought it must surely be someone else they were discussing. *How could my life have turned around so completely*, he wondered.

Chapter Thirty-Three

Vinnie Markwell was unprepared when the detective informed him that his status had changed, and that there were new charges laid and his bail revoked.

Still in hospital, he had spent much of his time on the phone, chasing money for his defence. Only the previous evening, he had received a positive response from the last source he had expected. His brother, Marc, had agreed to pay for Vinnie's counsel. Although his brother probably owed him more than one favour, Vinnie had not expected him to come to his rescue.

"Okay, I guess I owe you one anyway," he said, when Vinnie rang him.

Marc was doing well in his trucking business and could afford to help his brother, for a change. At about the time the police were standing in Vinnie's hospital room, Marc contacted a new lawyer and gave him an outline of Vinnie's situation. At the time, Marc had no idea about the new evidence that would be presented as a result of five new witnesses coming forward. Charlene had suggested all of those witnesses. She had given the police the names of four of Vinnie's old clients, people who could identify Vinnie as the person they had dealt with. They would attest to the fact that Vinnie had been involved in the manufacture, selling, transporting and trafficking illegal drugs as an organised business.

Charlene would also swear that Vinnie was present in the drug laboratory on the day it exploded. She would also confirm that he knew the person manufacturing the drugs was an addict and not either physically or mentally stable. She had another list of illegal activities, not directly associated with illegal drugs, but of interest to the police and related to his character. His previous convictions would also be taken into consideration when he went to court.

On Monday morning, the detective from the drug squad introduced himself to Vinnie and explained that he would have a guard outside his room until he was ready for discharge. That, he was informed by the doctor, could be within the next couple of days.

"New evidence, Mr. Markwell," he said, as he handed Vinnie the sheet of paper outlying the extra charges and again informed Vinnie of his rights. "I suggest you have your counsel make contact with the prosecutor."

Vinnie sat in the chair next to his bed, in stunned silence. He read the new charges and saw that they began with manslaughter and continued with a list of crimes he thought the police could never have known about – *Unless Charlene and several other 'old friends', have dobbed me in*, he thought.

He hung his head as he screwed up the paper and let it fall to the ground.

The next day he met his new lawyer.

"I will be your legal representative in the criminal court. Your case is set down for two weeks from tomorrow. You are to be transferred to the lock-up later today. We can talk again there."

He spent about half an hour with Vinnie, walking around the room the whole time. He was not perturbed by the charges and he could not tell Vinnie when he had last won a case.

"It's not surprising really, since I usually represent cases that have a poor chance of winning. I believe everyone has a right to be represented and I am there for the underdog. That's you, on this occasion, Mr. Markwell, and I will see to it that you get a fair go. You can rely on me."

Vinnie saw immediately why Marc had chosen this particular person. After the meeting, he felt like cutting his own throat.

There were no better offers coming his way, and that night when Vinnie was settling into his new cell, he finally gave way to despair. If Charlene had actually told half of what she knew about his activities, he was gone, for sure. Before he finally fell asleep, he started to recall some of the abuse that had been inflicted on him when he went to prison, last time. Being forewarned was no comfort.

******

Charlene took her mail from the box and turned over the wedding invitation in her hand.

"Nice for some people," she said out loud. As she walked back to her house, she ran into Ellen. She congratulated her on her appointment as manager, and also on her upcoming marriage.

"Thank you. I hope you and Mr. Markwell will join us on our special day."

"I may, but Vinnie definitely won't. He's in jail and will most likely be there for a few years. The longer the better, I say." Charlene looked at Ellen, who stood transfixed, struggling to comprehend what she was hearing. "Oh, you might as well know, soon everyone will anyway," Charlene said.

Ellen reached out, put her arm around the other woman's shoulders, and said, "I'm so sorry, please remember my offer of help. You must be having a hard time going through this all alone."

"It had to come to this one day. I just wish I knew he was never coming out. Sooner or later, he will get out and then I had better be long gone."

They walked together to Charlene's house. Lost for words, Ellen waved her good bye and went to the manager's office, where she shared the news with Jim and Di.

"I'm not surprised at all," said Jim. "Frank has had a particular interest in the man since he arrived. I wonder if Charlene will think about selling out."

"I advised her last week that two signatures were required for a sale. I have no idea how one does that if one's partner is in jail."

******

Jim had a lot of time to reminisce while he packed. First, he cleared up the garage, then started on his office. He left the house until last. He thought about the fire he had responded to, not too long after he and Di had taken over. He remembered the old lady, Jessie Thornton, who had been murdered, and how long it had taken for the murderer to be found. There was the horror bus trip when some people died in a road accident. His mind flashed to the abduction of two of the residents and the ongoing dispute between two other couples. Never in his career had so much negative activity happened under his watch. He speculated about the location of the resort and economic climate at the time, but nothing suggested why there had been so much criminal activity. He hoped it might change, now that new managers were taking over. He thought he would not wish that much trouble on anyone.

He felt his pulse elevate as he re-hashed so many details from the past. He put his fingers to his wrist and counted his pulse. He realised he was getting himself quite upset with all the focus on their past troubles. Suddenly, he remembered some advice given to him by a nurse in the hospital. 'Focus on the positives, Mr. Watersen and let the rest go,' she had said. 'Whenever you think of something that's upsetting you, change the subject. Put on a different playlist in your head. He did. He started to count all the new friends he had made and thought about the many celebrations in which he and Di had taken part. There were the weddings and birthdays, the dances and the karaoke. There was all the time he had been able to spend with the love of his life, as they worked together. That was something they could never have enjoyed if he had had any other sort of job.

Slowly, slowly, Jim began to smile as he thought about what was in store for them in the next phase of their lives. They would travel around the country in a motorhome for several months, and then come back to their investment home on the Gold Coast. Jim was actually looking forward to making it into a home he and Di would be proud of. The time he would now have to get to know his grandchildren was something else he had never really thought about. He started to imagine himself joining a gym, and swimming in the ocean each morning. By the time he taped together the packing boxes for the bedroom, his mood had lifted. He had a smile ready for his wife when she came rushing into the room to see how he was going.

"So, I see you're going ahead in leaps and bounds in here," said Di, as she looked into the wardrobe. "And doing a good job as well. I never would have taken you for such an organised packer, but now I'm pleasantly surprised."

"Yeah, well you can lay off the soft soap and come and do your stuff, anytime you like."

"I do have to do mine, of course. You couldn't possibly know what I want left separate for our holiday. Speaking of which, have you left a box with clothes you will need for our trip?"

Jim pointed to a large heavy plastic carry bag, straining at the seams.

"What do you call that?" he asked.

Di nodded her approval, although she wondered how he could need so much.

"Dinner's ready now anyway, and after that we're getting together with the others to discuss the last minute issues for the wedding. You'll have to spend the last few days with Ellen and Matthew in the office, but I guess you've got that covered, hey?"

"I have."

They held hands as they went to dinner.

******

Vinnie's trial came up only two days before the wedding.

Pekalski had offered Charlene witness protection, in the form of secret accommodation and even a guard, but she had declined. This was something she had to live with. She could not hide for the rest of her life. It was the start of a new life for her now, and she felt up to it.

She arrived at the courthouse. She was ushered to a seat with the other witnesses. She sat with her hands in her lap and said to herself, 'So let the fun begin.' The prosecutor presented his case and the jury listened with great interest. The counsel for the defence presented a case based on the fact that everything was hearsay, and it could not be proven. The witnesses stuck to their stories. The fact that many were unknown to the others but all told a similar story, painted a picture for the court that was clear. When Charlene gave her testimony, it was clear and concise. She had a good memory for dates and details and was a most credible witness.

The next day, the jury found Vinnie guilty. He was held over for sentencing.

"Can you believe, they got him on everything," Harold said to Jim when he came back from a day in the public gallery. "He was found guilty on the two charges of manslaughter, and many counts of dealing, trafficking and manufacturing illicit drugs. The list just went on. I really think the judge is going to throw the book at him when he hands down the sentence. Vinnie's history goes so far back it looks as though he has never had any other occupation aside from drug dealing. I sure wouldn't want to be him. This particular judge has a reputation for coming down hard on drug crimes. I reckon we won't see our friend for a long time – which is as it should be."

It was time for the old and new management to give their full attention to the wedding the next day, Saturday.

Chapter Thirty-Four

The sun was slow to rise on the morning of the wedding, or so thought Frank Pekalski as he sat on his tiny patio at 6am. The clouds parted and the soft summer sun rose gently into the sky, bringing with it all the happiness he felt radiating from his heart. The smile had been on his lips since he awoke and he had a sense of serenity he had never known before.

The previous night, as he tried to sleep, he had considered the possibility of retirement for the first time. He planned to discuss it with Joy when they were away on their honeymoon. He was living among mostly retired residents at the resort and could see they all seemed to thrive on it. However, he wasn't sure; he had always expected to work into his sixties, mainly because he couldn't imagine anything else. Now, with Joy, the possibilities were endless. Frank picked up his towel and headed for the pool to release some of his energy.

Joy too was in a euphoric state. She walked around the dress she had chosen. It hung on the front of her wardrobe. It was soft, lime-green chiffon with a green lace shoulder wrap. She had lime-green and white flowers for her hair. She was satisfied with the outfit and walked out to the kitchen for a cup of tea. Her sister, who had come to stay for the wedding, emerged from the guest bedroom.

"What time is it?" asked her sister.

"Close to seven. I just couldn't sleep any longer. How did you sleep?"

"Good, thanks. A bit excited – I'm really looking forward to today."

"Me too," said Joy.

She had a smug feeling as she made her tea and thought about Frank. She wondered if he was up yet; how he had slept. Then she began to think about their holiday, starting tonight with an overnight at the hotel in Surfers Paradise. After that, it was off to New Zealand, where neither of them had been before. A life together, stretching out ahead of them – it was so unbelievable and so perfect.

Ellen and Matthew were already talking on the phone, each in their own rooms. Matt was in the manager's residence and Ellen in her own little unit, outside the resort. Neither of them knew what to talk about so they just chatted about the weather and the plans until finally they agreed to hang up and meet on the lawn, next to the lake, in a few hours.

Di and Jim were also up, eating breakfast and discussing the big event. Everything was done and ready to go.

"I'll put up the balloons as soon as I've finished here," said Jim. "Are you doing the ribbons?"

"Yes, then I'll set out the table for the celebrant and then I'll be in the kitchen, probably until ten o clock. Then, my dear, I expect to meet you back here and we can dress and be at the lake by a little before eleven. How does that sound?"

"Perfectly timed as usual," said Jim, as he grinned and got up from the table.

******

When Jim arrived at the lake, Tom, the old gardener, was showing Lachlan where to put the chairs.

"Great day for it, boss. How does all this look?" asked Lachlan.

"I think we'll need all the chairs we have today, unless some people don't mind standing. Give us the lot anyway," said Tom.

They worked together, and by 10am, everything was in place. There were balloons and ribbons on the backs of the chairs, fanning out around the oval of the big end of the lake. The music was set up and the celebrant's table looked lovely under the palm trees. The gardens were perfection.

"Couldn't ask for better than this, eh," said Tom, as he and Lachlan slipped away to dress. There were birds in the trees and a soft breeze to temper the soon to be hot sun. The buffet tables were also set out on the lawn under a cluster of trees.

One of the first guests to arrive was Myra Weatherlee. She sat and looked around with pride as she waited for her son to make his appearance.

By eleven, a swarm of people had gathered on the lawns. The sounds of Mozart filled the air. Everyone surged forward when Matthew took up his position near the celebrant's table He waved to Myra.

Jim spoke into the microphone and welcomed everyone then announced that he had a surprise.

"A little extra treat for everyone. We are happy to announce that this will be the wedding of Ellen and Matthew, and they will be joined by Joy Rayne and Frank Pekalski."

He turned as Frank stood next to Matt and waved to everyone. The sound of clapping and cheering resounded around the lake.

"I see you are a romantic bunch, but there's more," Jim said. Silence fell as Jim pointed to the two impeccably dressed gentlemen approaching the dais.

"Harold Smith and Robert Wieland will today, exchange vows and declare their lifelong commitment to one another."

More cheering and clapping followed, as the two men walked up to stand behind the two bridegrooms. The wedding march sounded and the crowd parted as Joy and Ellen walked together with their hands around a bouquet each and their eyes on their loved ones.

The celebrant waited until the noise subsided. Harold and Robert stood back while the brides and grooms lined up in the picturesque setting. Everyone laughed as an errant dog ran across the small space of grass between the guests and the wedding party. He was shooed on, and then a grandchild called out to Joy, "Love you, Granny," which was followed by a whole group of guests imitating with, "Love you Granny."

The ceremony began and was over in fifteen minutes. Then, Robert and Harold stepped forward and exchanged their vows. The music rang out with bells and the air was alive with streamers and balloons.

A new era for Keeala Resort had just begun.

The End

Author Kumari and husband John live in an Over 50's resort in Queensland.

In their past careers, John was a business manager and Kumari, a registered nurse.

After their marriage in 1992, they combined their skills to manage retirement resorts in N.S.W. and Queensland. They used to joke that the many interesting characters and unusual situations they encountered would one day provide a wealth of material for a book.

When Kumari became wheelchair bound following foot surgery in 2010, she realised the period of physical inactivity presented her with a golden opportunity. She decided to weave her memories of those management years into a fictionalised story. The result was not one novel, but a series.

The series follow the trials and tribulations of the residents, employees and diverse characters of Keeala Resort. Kumari also introduces social comment about ageing issues and some of her characters draw her readers into a dialogue about the social and practical questions encountered in people's mature years.

Sixteen grandchildren fill in the spaces when she is not writing.

www.ingramcontent.com/pod-product-compliance
Lightning Source LLC
Chambersburg PA
CBHW070216030726
47505CB00006B/1701